MARK B SAYERS

LOOKING FOR SOMEWHERE

©2024 Mark B. Sayers

First Edition Published 2024 by London Orchid Books Limited

The right of Mark B. Sayers to be identified as the author of this work has been asserted by him in accordance with the Copyright, Designs and Patents Act 1988.

No part of this book may be reproduced or transmitted by any means, except as permitted by UK copyright law or the author.

For licensing requests, please contact info@marksayersbooks.com

ISBN 978-1-7384738-0-9 eBook
ISBN 978-1-7384738-1-6 Paperback

Mark Sayers

www.marksayersbooks.com

Cover photo Marta Branco pexels.com

MARK B. SAYERS

LOOKING FOR SOMEWHERE

Zenka,
Thank you!
Mark

PROLOGUE

12th April

Dear Mr Chambers

Further to our earlier discussion, please accept this as my formal letter of resignation. I know that you are dedicated to Heating and Plumbing in a way that I will never find. I have spent the last three years working with dedication, but this isn't the life I dreamed of.

I understand that under the terms of my contract my last working day shall be the 12th May.

Thank you for your support and I wish the company the greatest success.

Yours sincerely

Adam Cook

LOOKING FOR SOMEWHERE

Chapter 1
Time to go

The mist hung above the brook as the blinds rose and the greyness of the day seeped into the room. It clashed with the brightness of his yellow socks as he tried to bring a smile into the day. Heading downstairs to open the door and let the cat out, to chase the shadows of last night's visit from the fox. Sometimes there would be a rabbit taking the new growth from the flowerbeds; the race to safety would begin, but the rabbit always won. Weetabix into the bowl, milk, put the kettle on and so far, so normal.

He started playing a podcast wondering if you could get the same podcasts abroad. He checked his social media. Laughing at the contrast between videos of people fighting for no apparent reason and people showing overwhelming acts of kindness that would always bring at least a tear to his eye. Wishing that there was more of the happy stuff in the world. He didn't know why he cried so much these days, he wished he didn't, but it was happening more, that new song was the latest thing, the way she half sang those words. I can't just think those thoughts again he decided, I've got lots to do. So much to do. Time to go.

His shoes were on and his coat was waiting on the end of the banister when he heard the car pulling up. Stepping outside, carrying the coat he thought he might not need, and closing the door. One last look at the doorbell. Wondering if the image it captured would be seen by anyone - or even if someone would bother to look for it. He strode over to the car with an overwhelming sense of self-belief.

That belief disappeared though the second he settled into the passenger seat of his friend's car, the smell of garages and grass cuttings, petrol and hamburgers filling his head. He looked up at the stained fabric above him, evidence that the car had made too many trips to the DIY store or the local dump. Despite the advancements in digital radio since his childhood the cars speakers still managed to make the singer appear to be in a different room to the band. His senses were taking in everything around him. He could feel every one of his senses absorbing each moment. This wasn't quite the departure he had seen in his dreams but, it was a necessary detour. One last wait at the roadworks and they were through the village. As they passed the vicarage at the edge of the forest, the rain came. Let it rain, let it wash the world away he thought. 'Are you ready A?' his friend asked. The tears came again.

It had been a wonderful week for most in the city; the sun had been shining and London always looked its best in the sunshine. Even the commuters on the tube had been smiling. There had been some great new music coming out and spring had definitely broken through, but today almost felt like winter again. Things looked brighter towards the city, the high-rise blocks looking like some giant pin cushion with tower blocks and offices stabbed into the London clay. Then the was a gap before the next collection of tower pins rose around the docklands. One Canada Square the original and still the tallest rising now above an increasing collection of towers. It still thrilled him to see the city, the way it kept changing, but remained the same. He had a very vague recollection of the days when that whole part of London was waiting for development. He still didn't believe that the tallest building in London had been St. Paul's until just ten years before his birth.

He looked out at the people in the other cars, wondering how they were feeling. What were they up to? Were they as miserable as he was, was everyone? No, they were smiling, and their smiles looked real. They weren't too busy to stop, have a drink, listen to their friends, have fun. He looked at his friend, did he really understand? He hadn't asked any questions, he never really did, perhaps that was why they were still friends. Anything important had been kept at a distance. Football, music, other people and places; they were all perfectly adequate conversations to have, why would you want to talk about feelings or emotions, hopes or dreams?

They reached the giant roundabout at Beckton where the A406 meets the A13 and he sighed. Looking to the sky he could already feel the relief. He still didn't know where he was going, he had collected a bundle of cash over the last few days and despite the fact that he had spent his whole life being organised and making sure that he would never be late, never doing anything embarrassing, always being the responsible one, today was the day that ended.

He knew he was going to the airport, City rather than Heathrow or Gatwick. He had a limited budget so rather than be disappointed with a dream of somewhere overly glamorous and exotic, he knew he had to be able to afford the flight. He still retained a certain amount of reality. The first flight that met his criteria and that he could buy a ticket for was the one he would take, wherever that might take him. He'd planned this much; the plane would need to be leaving no less than two hours after he arrived, he wanted time to book his flight, check in, and depending on the length of the flight, he wanted time to get some food at the airport, and he wanted to have a beer. Why not enjoy the whole experience?

As the car pulled up outside, he looked to his friend "Do you want to come?" as he expected, his friend smiled, said,

"Yes please, good luck mate" and turned away. They had shared so much over the years without really ever sharing anything. A quick look at his phone confirmed the time: 06:56 and perhaps more importantly 97% charge.

"Thanks." he said, reaching out for a handshake and then, without looking back, he spun around and strode confidently into the airport. He knew if he looked or paused, he would cry and, this trip was to stop that.

He wasn't going to stop until he found a space where he could see the departure boards. It wasn't long, City was such a convenient airport he almost laughed. 08:55 Belfast, one minute too early and well surely that wasn't far enough, 09:05 Dublin, 09:15 Malaga both with British Airways.

"Ok here we go, BA.com". He liked that it was British Airways, inheriting from his parents that old fashioned belief that certain brands could be trusted, and BA still had that kind of feel, he wanted things to be done properly. Agree to Cookies - of course, what kind of tinpot says no? What would happen if he did?

Search for a Flight, yes, from LCY to Dublin, Outbound. Today... no return. Not even the spinning wheel delayed the next page popping up. There was nothing left in economy, was it worth business? He was going to do things differently but, no, he couldn't justify that. "Spain it is then, LCY to Malaga", he spoke out loud then realised that he had and looked around concerned that he would look like the bloke you didn't want to see at the airport.

He knew it was Spain. He had no idea exactly where, near the coast, it must be. Isn't Madrid the only Spanish place that isn't on the coast? Outbound Today, no return... yes Economy I'm not going to be silly he told himself. He had no idea how long his money would last. Three more clicks and he was on his way, heading up the escalator to passport control with a feeling that he hadn't felt for years. Last check, wallet, passport, phone. All present and correct.

The security was so simple and now he was airside, first stop WH Smiths. He had a quick look at the travel section, he didn't want the Lonely Planet guide, he wasn't going to be lonely anywhere anymore. He did want to know where Malaga was on the map. He would look it up later on his phone, but he still liked the idea of looking through pages, and he had a need to learn Spanish. Again, all that kind of stuff could be done on his phone. He was quite happy with an online translator but, nothing could beat a proper dictionary. They only had the concise English/Spanish version but that's ok. Travelling light was the best way. He had started looking through the pages even before he had thought about food.

How long was the flight? In his excitement he hadn't even thought about that, would they serve food onboard? He never understood people's complaints about airline meals, you are being fed a proper meal, hot food with picnic cutlery, above the height of Everest why are you not happy about that? He had once eaten at one of those fancy restaurants in London where the price seemed to be as high as it was purely because the restaurant was at the top of the building. No one would have paid those prices at ground level, surely. But that time he was trying to impress so he pretended not to notice the price and instead focused on trying to spot all of the buildings that he could recognise.

However much he enjoyed the sight of the roofs of London, the bright sunshine above the clouds made any airline meal delicious. He had always chosen the window seat when he could, intending to learn the names of the various types of cloud and what they meant. Cumulus, Nimbus, Cirrus. He recognised the names and he had, on a number of occasions, looked at the corresponding photographs of examples. Remembering them however had been beyond him so far. He had always wanted to be an expert in something, but his brain didn't work in that way - he knew lots about everything. He did ok at quizzes and people he met thought he was clever, but he knew that his knowledge was general. If he ever met a true expert, it would not be long before he felt out of his depth. Today though he was an expert on the unknown.

He approached the bar and looked along the pumps, seven thirty in the morning. Yes it would probably be the earliest time he'd ever had a drink, even on that stag do they had waited until eleven. Not recognising any of the names hanging over the bar annoyed him, he wasn't after a craft experience, he wanted a drink not hints of citrus or caramel in a pint glass. Although the principle of this journey was to take risks, break the norm and push the boundaries, he ordered a craft lager. Let's not choose something that I might not like this early into my new life was his justification. The bartender didn't even blink, a pint at that time in the morning, yes, in an airport everything was perfectly normal.

Chapter two
Within Ten Minutes

Tilly had arrived early as always, picked up her coffee and smiled at the barista as always. She didn't know if it made any difference, but it felt like she received quicker service than most of the customers and the bearded man always seemed genuinely pleased to see her. Little things like that made her feel better about herself.

Walking into the office the usual chat was being had around the room. Rugby was the office's sport of choice and she found it hilarious that they had never sought her input into what had happened during that weekend's games. Listening to them you would have thought that it was them who had spent hundreds of cold wet days watching their father play all over the country and for a few, all too short years playing at the very highest level earning 28 caps for France. The comments she heard were the type she had heard all of her life - "If only they hadn't kicked…" "I don't know why they didn't…" Monday's Experts her father had called them. None of them would be able to stand up out on the pitch with 15 opponents staring at them and a crowd baying for blood, but, the day after, with their mates they all know how to simply run straight past all of them and become the champions of the world.

She too had watched the game, sitting in her usual seat, alongside her father and his friends. She had always thought it would be nice to take her colleagues to a game one day, just to see their faces as she was welcomed at the door and to see their reaction when they bumped into one of the television commentators or pundits as they wandered the corridors or in the corporate hospitality zone. And to see their response as the 'star' greeted her with a hug or a kiss. People they would recognise from their Ultra HD TV's or their latest 'behind the scenes' podcasts. She would know all the stories already, know their opinions and, almost always, predict exactly what their opinions would be on anything that had happened during the match.

She didn't say much, listening instead, analysing all the options and weighing up the balances before forming her own opinion and she had done that since being a little girl. Her interest in the tactics and the nature of the game would delight the old professionals, who would supervise her whilst her father was playing. The wise old heads were always keen to share their knowledge and experience, telling her who to watch or why things were good or bad. And she was always keen to learn.

She had often been pestered, when she was younger, by players in the bar after the game. Her intellect had usually scared them away. She was now a little older, but she would still see some of the players looking at her as she walked in. She liked the fact they looked although, her trust in men was limited.

She had found her success in business. Her desire for facts and data led her through university and beyond. She didn't like the limelight, her dislike of incompetence meant that she had to take control. It really did seem that most of the world's population were happy with idiots and did not care that most people who spoke knew very little about the subjects they claimed to be experts in. That is why they were still babbling on about how much better the game would have been if only they had...

Tilly adjusted her chair, somehow the cleaners never

returned it to the perfect spot, she woke up her screen and, as she always did, logged onto the news pages before checking her emails. She had scanned the news app on the tube, but she waited until arriving in the office to read the details. There was a small story about a girl she had been at school with who had become famous and had a bad bit of plastic surgery, and a story of a politician that she had met a couple of times. She had no interest in reading any more than the headline, she was sure the accusations would be true, she read on regardless. She could tell some stories about him. Her experience with him still made her laugh, if only because she had been strong enough to keep him away.

As she read more, that gentle feeling of memory was replaced with a greater sense of sadness. She was reminded of a different time. Bumping into the supposedly great and good of Paris with her group of friends always around her. She felt the loss for her youth. She wondered if Matilda's mum was still alive, didn't she have a brother? Alex? She had memories of her whole class, Alice, Lucy, Grace and Isabelle. All those names came flooding back, a previous world.

The phone rang, that was enough to shock her out of her memories, who phoned these days? Not zoom, not an email, an actual phone call.

'Hello,' was that professional enough? Should she say her name, her job title, she remembered when there had been a script for answering the phone,

"Eagle Strategy Consultants, Good Morning, Tilly speaking how may I help you?" (everything had been easier in the old days when everything had to be done properly) and now here she was, owner of the business and still unsure of how to answer the phone.

"Hi Tilly, Sorry to call you at work, have you heard anything from Jada?"

Within ten minutes she was inside a cab. She had collected her notebook and the bag she kept at the office in case a change of clothes was ever required and was on the phone to her PA.

"Please, I'll tell you more later, but right now I just need you to clear my diary for today. I know I've got the call with Brian at 3 and I'll do that. The rest can be bumped. And see what you can do about tomorrow just in case, I'll let you know as soon as I can."

She caught a glimpse of the face of a cyclist at her window and almost looked back in recognition. Right now, everyone she saw seemed familiar; this taxi driver must have taken her somewhere before, the traffic warden who was watching as she jumped into the cab. Everyone seemed to be watching her, making a note of what she was doing building the portfolio of evidence that would be used against her later, she was sure.

Tilly checked her watch as she stepped out of the taxi at the airport, she didn't like flying, instead she had forced herself to get used to it. She didn't like the idea of anyone thinking that she didn't belong in first class. She knew that she travelled enough and earned enough not to need the savings at the duty free, but she still couldn't resist the opportunity to wander the aisles smelling any new scents available. She preferred a bottle she had found in an almost secret shop down Caledonian Road alongside the flower market. She wasn't so snobbish that she wouldn't wear a brand that advertised on television although she would always make it her own by the time it had merged with the lotion she always ensured coated her skin. Her sense of smell was one of the first that told her parents that she was different, identifying every little ingredient in her food or a drink, distinguishing between flowers and trees, not just in the garden, but throughout the forest by the age of six. Each of them identified by their unique smell or their touch. Her friends would say that the trees all smelt the same. She knew that her brain processed things in a different way to her classmates.

As she approached the duty free the atmosphere changed in her eyes, she could almost see the aromas. To save time she headed to the men's section only. People would presume that she was shopping for her husband or her boyfriend, she was happy for them to think that, there were too many thoughts in her mind to focus on relationships right now.

The first display called out to her, almost every scent linking with a memory of her past. Her ex-husband, the scent of denim and fear, the next, memories of her father, they no longer made his scent, but this one was not too dissimilar. A smile of recognition crossed her face as she inhaled those molecules, at the same time memories hit her of the orange trees on the walk to the church where her family tomb sat. That thought was enough to take her away from the shop. She knew her route, dodging the tourists, aiming straight to the area closest to the gates. Choosing her seat looking out across the runway watching both the planes and the rowers, out early on the dock beyond the runway, always going backwards.

Chapter three
Breakfast On The Balcony

Shyamal had also been at a game the day before. He wasn't too fussed about basketball, any event held in the arena would be a good enough reason to go. He loved the arena. One of his first memories after arriving in the country had been being taken to see an ice hockey game there. He remembered the chill from the ice as he first entered the huge cavern-like structure. Of course they had been amongst the first in the building, his father believed in value for money and seeing the stewards taking their places, then directing people who didn't know their alphabet to the right rows and those who didn't understand numbers to their seat. All this was entertainment even before the first players came out to warm up. The young Shyamal had been hooked even before he heard the sound of the skates on the ice.

They were up in the cheaper seats high at the back of the stands and yet, even up there he could hear the cutting of ice by the blades on the skates. The sounds took him temporarily back to his uncle's house at Christmas, swiping the carving knives back and forth against each other before slicing their meat for dinner. The excitement grew as more players joined the ice until the whole rink appeared to be covered in a swarm of hockey players, all firing their pucks at full speed towards the poor keeper in a perfectly synchronised routine. By the time the Zamboni appeared to clean the ice for the game to start he knew his dad had made the best decision ever to come to this country. When the lights went down for the pregame lightshow and the teams came onto the ice, he wanted that moment to last forever.

That was only nine years ago, He had grown up living on the streets of Dhaka. As the youngest of seven brothers Shyamal had been sent out to work with every other child in their area until, one day, his father had found the church. He had been making a delivery in a part of the city not far from where they lived. If his father had received the education that Shyamal had, thanks to this incident, he may have been able to read the sign that said 'Only Christians May Enter', his father had heard those sounds. He still willingly describes them to anyone who questions his faith as "The sounds of the Lord Almighty".

The building looked cool and clean, and the door was open. Shyamal's father had a curiosity which led him through that door to find the church seemingly empty except for the luxurious sound of the organ. He had stood in the centre of the church, feeling the music in his bones, until he was spotted by the organist who stopped playing and came to speak to the now enraptured father. His father still claims that it was God who had been creating that music and the man that appeared from behind the decorated screen was surely an angel. The links between that church in Dhaka and a parish in East London had resulted in Shyamal and his whole family moving to England with a chance for Shyamal and the rest of his brothers to go to school.

His executive box at the arena, his penthouse looking out on the park and everything that he could ever have wanted all existed thanks to that education and the love of music that Shyamal shared with his father.

Shyamal took his breakfast onto the balcony enjoying the sounds of the city waking beneath him. The ground was slightly damp under his feet and drops of dew still sat on the metal rails that prevented him falling to the street below. He leant against the rail, not minding the way his shirt sleeves mopped the water away as he watched the people in the park. The cyclists late for work, dog walkers being paid to walk rich people's dogs that they were too important to walk themselves and the eager tourists, heading off to take selfies next to more of the wonderful sights this great city has to share.

His friends moaned about the weather, but London is meant to be grey. Look at the architecture, Buckingham Palace, the Bank of England, St Pauls, they were all meant to be grey and, it made it that much more special when God gave a blue sky to stand behind them. When the sun glinted off the gold on the Victoria memorial or the flames at the top of the monument on Pudding Lane in the City.

London had plenty of colour, not too much, there was a class to it, a pleasant surprise when you saw it. It was not overwhelming like the primary colours of New York or Tokyo, filled with colour without class like a young man hurtling around town in an outrageously bright Lamborghini or Ferrari.

It amazed him why people would choose to deface their cars in that way. He was all for people showing their creativity, that only worked if you had creativity of your own. Paying someone in a garage in a side street of Enfield to make your car unique by doing the same as everyone else did was not an exhibition of your creativity. He checked his watch, took one last deep breath before heading inside. He placed his bowl in the sink and diligently turned the tap on to prevent the cereal cementing itself to the bowl. He wasn't going to wash it up, but he wasn't quite a teenager.

Yellow socks today, he didn't wear many colours except for his socks and his handkerchief which had to be bright. Comfy shoes and, after grabbing his jacket and keys, he was ready to go. He had to wait a few seconds for the lift, which was unusual. It probably just meant that Jason was getting a delivery. Everyone knew that

Jason ran a crafty little business on the side from the front desk. He probably earned more from that business than as a concierge from the management company here Shyamal had assessed. Certainly, judging by the holidays Jason took his children on. Shyamal knew that Jason would do anything to help his children and that was all Shyamal needed to know. If waiting for the lift or using the stairs occasionally meant that those kids got a better holiday then so be it.

Sure enough, when he reached the basement, bay three had at least six large cardboard boxes in it and a smiling Jason stood alongside, always looking like a child on his birthday,

"Hey Shy, How was the game?" Jason said. Shyamal knew other residents in the block hated the way he and Jason spoke,

"He's an employee not a friend" Number 6 had told him,

"He's a human not a dog" was Shyamal's response. That had pleased him so much knowing how much Number 6 doted on those stupid little fur-balls. He had been introduced to Number 6 when he had first moved in. It was clear from day one that 6 had disliked both Jason and most other people, so Shyamal had never made the effort to remember their name. Why would he mind if letting Jason use the lift really annoyed 6?

He had the choice of cars, today though, as the sun was shining, he jumped on the bike and cycled out onto the street. He wasn't surprised when the taxi sped up to pass him despite the fact that they were going to have to stop in another 20 yards.

Chapter four
Just Travelling

The flight had left on time and everything had gone exactly as expected. The cloud cover meant that he only got a short glimpse of the green fields as he waved goodbye to England. The clouds had cleared soon after they had crossed into France and had continued to be clear giving wonderful views across the Bay of Biscay and the mountains as they reached the north of Spain.

He had been expecting to be overwhelmed by the temperature as he stepped off of the plane, but it didn't feel uncomfortable. He hadn't been certain what to wear when he got dressed this morning. Not knowing where he was going, the simple rule of layers meant that simply by taking off his hoodie he was ready for the Spanish sun. Ambling down the stairs he tried to take everything in.

As he hit the tarmac, he could almost feel the heat through the soles of his shoes. His Londoner's instinct to rush was difficult to override and the bustle of the people around him was tricky to resist. Despite the rush of the crowd, that bustle was soon stopped by the family, who really could have waited for others to pass before trying to work out who was going to carry each bag and which child each adult was going to supervise. How many children actually do ever get lost in airports? he wondered. They were all going to be forced into the same corridor. To the same place. How far off track could a child get? He shared a look with the women who had sat in the row behind him which brought a nice smile. She looked a little nervous, albeit there was something in it that instantly told him that she was someone he could talk to, of course, if he could be brave enough.

He wondered if he should slow down and allow her to pass, but then he'd just be following her and that could be creepy. Deciding instead to hope that the queue would end up in one of those zigzag patterns and he would be able to think of something witty to say to make himself sound fun and intelligent, interesting, not weird. He had never felt confident enough in the past to try. As the crowd started to collect in front of him, he slowed down and she came to stand alongside him. He was a little taller than her and although he guessed that the gathering was the start of the queue for passport control, he was not entirely sure. He dared to glimpse sideways and noticed that she was looking at him.

"Brexit hey?" She said with the raising of an eyebrow.

"Guess so" he replied, before immediately realising that that wasn't the suave intelligent impression that he wanted to portray. "Quick, say something else" he demanded of his brain. "Do you come here often?" He instantly blurted, then blushed. He hadn't intended to say something quite as cheesy, to his relief, she smiled.

"No, I'm just passing through." As she finished her sentence there was a little giggle that really caused a reaction inside his brain.

"What about you? Where are you heading?" She seemed genuinely interested. In all of his time planning his escape he had never once thought about how to answer that question,

"Um I don't quite know, to be honest I didn't know I was coming to…" He had to check where he was before he gave his answer. "I'm just travelling." He was quite pleased with that last answer. People could fill in the blanks for themselves.

"So where do you go once you pass through security? You aren't carrying much luggage?" He could detect an accent although he wasn't able to place it.

"I guess I'm heading for the bus station, and I'll see where they are going." He had thought on the flight about which direction he could take. If he went west, he could only ever end up in Portugal. He had thought perhaps he'd reach Gibraltar and hop across to Africa. Adam wasn't sure that he was experienced enough a traveller for that so, it was either inland towards Madrid or, northwest along the coast, maybe up to Barcelona.

He'd been playing 'Holiday in Spain' by Counting Crows for a lot of the journey and that line about flying to Barcelona had brought a tear to his eye every time. To be fair it always had, now, now he was genuinely taking a plane to well, not Barcelona but close enough. "Somewhere nice I hope" he almost whispered.

"Have you ever thought about Valencia?" she said.

"Valencia?" He knew there was a football team. Other than that, he had no knowledge of the city. "I don't know, is that where you are heading?"

"Yes. Well, near enough, I'm meeting an old school friend. Odd story. I'm not sure I know the whole story yet, it's a bit of a rush so… I got the flight here and I'm going to hire a car and drive up there. I could do with a navigator."

The whole conversation had shocked him, and now, now

she was asking him to drive with her. How far was Valencia? He had no idea, it couldn't be far he thought. The aim of this whole experience was to take a few chances and see what happened. So why not see where this road leads he decided.

They headed over to the car hire desks and whilst she was speaking to the assistant in perfect Spanish, he loaded up the maps on his phone. Five hours thirty-eight minutes? How big is Spain? Surely there was a closer airport than this? So many questions were whizzing through his head when she called out "Do you fancy the sports car?" nodding towards the advertising poster showing a flashy convertible with an excessively happy looking family whizzing down to the beach. He just looked back at her in shock as she turned and instantly spoke again to the girl. A few forms were filled in and payment was made before she almost waltzed back towards him,

"OK we're off, I'm sorry I didn't get the sports car. I didn't want to get sunburned whilst I drove and I'm not sure it's the right kind of car for where I'm headed."

He really wouldn't have minded what they were travelling in, he was sure that it was nicer than the bus and he also was sure that he could learn something from her. She obviously had a confidence that he lacked, she spoke the language and, she obviously had a bit of money. On arriving at the car park kiosk where she was to collect the keys, a large white Mercedes was sitting waiting for them.

"I'm sorry I didn't name you as a driver. I trust you, but I'm not sure I know quite enough about you yet. I don't even know your name!" She giggled again. He was more than happy to just throw his bag into the back and jump into the passenger seat.

"There are two routes to Valencia, one a bit more inland, one a bit more coastal. There is currently just ten minutes difference in time so, which do you fancy?" He asked.

"Let's take the coastal route, it will be better if we see the sea." She pressed the ignition button and a map immediately appeared on the screen. Of course a hire car would have satnav he thought to himself. Why would she need a navigator?

"Can you type in 'Calle Puerto Santo, Sendero" and, almost reading his mind she said "I know I could just use the satnav, but the roads here still confuse me so I could really do with someone just to help me out a bit. It's a long drive too and people look at me strangely if I'm talking to myself. Whatever the car tells us, we can take that coastal route." The explanation made sense and he had no reason to doubt her motives. He felt his luck was turning already as his journey was off to the greatest of starts.

Chapter five
New Music

It was just past nine when Shy entered the office. He had bumped into an old acquaintance literally just outside his office and they had chatted for probably twenty minutes. His life was constantly being interrupted by uncles, cousins and various others. He echoed his Father's values. Everyone had to be met politely and he had to ask how the family were. He would report his meetings to his father later but somehow, his father would already know the gossip. In this part of East London, the community knew everything, and news spread quickly.

He connected his phone to the speakers in the office and his sounds filled the space. He stood for a moment just bathing in the beat, the bright colours of the room contrasting with the dull brick wall which was all that could be seen through the windows. New visitors to his office would often ask him why he worked here, but this was where it started. Where he felt that connection. He knew that the quality of lunch options might be a little better in other parts of town, he had though, decided that he didn't want people working for him that had to have the latest food fashion to keep them hydrated and nourished. He needed people with energy. People who were willing to get their hands dirty and who weren't afraid of popping into Stepney Fried Chicken. Besides the area was becoming more fashionable. He suspected that the property value must have at least doubled since he bought the place just a few years back.

With the music on, you didn't hear the sirens as much and the sound of the air ambulance coming into land at the hospital just down the road made him feel like he was operating in a war zone, which was exactly how he liked things. He picked up the ball from Jo's desk and threw it at the hoop, of course it missed but, if he had been an athlete, he wouldn't be here now. He opened his laptop and the three giant screens around him woke up with an explosion of colour.

The first six pop ups were exactly as he'd expected, New York had gone to bed happy, Mumbai had woken up with a few moans but nothing he wouldn't be able to solve once they had had their lunch. He checked his watch, noticed his heart rate was a little higher than he would have liked so decided to leave his responses until after he had had his shower.

By the time he stepped out of the shower room, the office was filling up. He was still towelling his hair dry as he arrived at his desk, and before he had sat down, he heard Jo, she was still new to the team but her enthusiasm and professionalism impressed him.

"Hey boss, I've got some new music for you when you are ready, great new band I saw last night, and they would certainly be interested."

"Morning Jo, please let me tune in first, add it to the playlist." Dealing with the music was always his favourite part of any project, there were always new bands in London waiting for someone like him to show an interest. Thankfully there were also always enthusiastic people like Jo. Those who really didn't realise that they were working from 8am 'til 6pm each day in the office and then usually from 9pm to 2am out networking and discovering new bands - he always said bands or singers or guitarists. He wanted to call them what they were, four friends wanting to make music are a band. Shy didn't like to dress it up. Using terms like artists might fashionable and be what the narcissists did or those who wanted to take more of the 'artists' money because of delusions of grandeur. How long before football teams are no longer 'teams' but have become collections of sporting artists? Yes, Erling Harland was a brilliant goalscorer but, he's not an artist, he's a machine.

By the time he'd responded to Mumbai he had heard why Jo was excited. The crash of drums to kick things off was nothing new but it had the energy they always looked for. Yes, the Royal Philharmonic would always sell records because they had the best clarinetist and the best French Horner (he wondered what would you even call someone who played that instrument before just quickly choosing 'Pierre' as their name until he thought that he ought to find out the proper term later). He wasn't looking for the technically best players though, he wanted the energy. Looking for those who wanted to be the best at what they did, not those who performed songs written by a computer performed by a computer programmer. He grabbed a drink from the fridge and sat back. He'd give them three songs. He had heard too many bands present him with one good song, maybe even a great one before following it up with a whole load of formulaic trudge. He hoped that this band weren't like that.

Shy was convinced before they had even finished the second track.

"Jo, where did you see these guys?" he called across to where Jo was stood in the 'breakout zone'.

"I knew you'd like them" she called back with a smile, "I've already checked, they are clean, the guitarist books all their gigs, the drummer drives because he doesn't drink at all, a religious thing apparently and they are playing again tonight at a different venue." She had known as soon as they walked on stage the night before that they were exactly the kind of band she was looking for. She hoped that Shy would see the same potential that she had. There was a different air around them.

She was used to having no problems meeting a band after the gig. The offer to buy the whole band a drink was usually enough. She generally made it a rule that she wouldn't reveal where she worked until she had seen a band at least three times. This lot were different. Rather than heading straight to the bar after their set, this group were all helping to break down the kit, even the singer.

They looked more like a professional crew packing up after the Rolling Stones at Wembley, ready to take everything straight to the airport for the next leg of their tour than a group in a pub in North London. It also seemed like this band took just as much care over their kit as Keith Richards or Slash or Eric Clapton ever had. Actually, bad examples she thought but, she knew what she meant.

A word with Mick who ran the venue told her all she needed to know, Mick was a great bloke, a far bigger player in the London music scene than he would ever admit to and only he knew how much he was responsible for the success of Shyamal's business. According to Mick this was the first time they had played here and in a room this big. He had heard good things and certainly he felt that they were ready for it.

"Professionally speaking," Mick told her, they were so good that he knew that they didn't have a manager. She always laughed when venue owners criticised managers to her, they knew her role but somehow, she seemed to have escaped that tag.

She had spent most of the gig planning her approach. She had a few tried and tested techniques which could work.

The giddy fan girl approach. This worked only for the newest bands but at the right time it worked so, so easily;

The casual conversation with the right names dropped. Hints of the biggest names, maybe show them a photo;

The more aloof questioning. "Have you guys ever thought about…?";

The gentle ego build. "Hello, I happen to know a blogger / reporter / radio producer would you be interested in…;

The full ego. "Hello, I'm Jo from BashFull Records and…".

    As bands grew in their own self confidence so her approach needed to grow to match their egos. She really didn't know how to get things started with this bunch though. Maybe she should go big early, they were good, it would do them no harm to know that others thought so too. She knew that someone else must have seen them or, if not yet, with the gigs Mick told her about coming up, it would only be a few days before someone else is sniffing around. It was the guitarist that booked the gigs, so he was obviously the business head, but no singer doesn't want to be the focus so she needed to find a chance to grab them both.

    So, magazine writer, blogger, radio producer or record company rep, she had been all four despite only being twenty-one herself so she could easily play the part of each. It was up to her to decide which character would most interest this group. When she had first worked for Shy, she was sure that holding the card saying that she worked for 'BashFull Records' would have opened every door. It still amazed her just how many bands were more interested in the instant attraction of a YouTube blog or a radio play rather than the work of recording. It was clear that these guys were serious though, she decided it was full ultra professional record company representative that she needs to bring out tonight.

She approached the stage when both guitarist and singer reappeared and just politely asked if "The band" would like to come to her table for a quick chat before they left. Jo walked with natural confidence, adding as much swagger as she felt was appropriate, straight to the bar and bought a soft drink before heading back to her table. Frantically she grabbed her notebook and started scribbling. Everyone she knew just recorded voice memos or typed notes onto their phones nowadays. Jo was already thinking of her future, she knew that her phone would be out of date in five years' time let alone twenty-five. Having her notebook, she would have a perfect record of London's coolest bands before they were famous. That alone would be at least worthy of a place in some museum. If any of the bands got really big, this book could be her retirement fund. Well, that was her dream. She turned to a new page. She had already finished a couple of pages of notes on tonight's set. Recording their style, influences, how they looked, what they wore, and, as the gig had gone along, she had started to make a note of what they could do to improve, how they could sound on record and, more importantly, how she would market them.

She wouldn't let the band see those plans just yet so, leaving a blank page for her to finish those notes later, she wrote the band name in big block capitals, added today's date and she underlined it twice. She was aware that someone who didn't know might think she was writing a bit of primary school homework to put on the classroom wall, she believed that it made her look far more organised than she thought she was. Checking her watch, it was twenty-five minutes since they had finished their set and she had just decided that they weren't going to reappear. That would be OK. She already knew where they were playing tomorrow, she could easily just change the date on the page. She was checking her social media to see if anyone else was talking about the gig when the guitarist suddenly appeared in front of her and reached out his hand. She half stood, taking the offered hand and gestured to the seats at the table as she saw the rest of the band at his shoulder.

"I'm Paul, this is Leonard Moore, our Bassist, Jim on Drums and you've already heard from Jack the singer."

Jo shook hands with each of them as they all politely sat at the table. Now she really felt like the teacher, here were her class. All registered and ready to learn.

It had only felt like a few minutes that they had been chatting when Mick appeared and asked if she wanted to head to the bar upstairs where he said he'd keep the bar open for them or did he need to give her the keys to lock up. Almost as one the band apologised and said that they needed to get moving as they had another big gig tomorrow. The fact that they thought tomorrow's gig was big was wonderful news to her. They either hadn't heard how good they were, or not enough people had told them yet.

"I know where you are playing tomorrow, could I perhaps meet you guys before the gig? And, I've got someone I'd really like you to meet." They all looked to Paul.

"Sure" He responded showing those slightly crooked teeth that gave his smile just that little bit of extra interest,

"Leonard and Jack are both working tomorrow but we plan on being there by half past six to set up. We are usually set up in just thirty minutes. There is going to be another band on before us tomorrow that I wouldn't mind seeing, if we could meet at say seven. It then gives us an hour before they'll be on stage, would that be OK?"

Jo couldn't help letting her smile spread even wider,

"That all sounds perfect - I'll see you tomorrow."

Chapter six

What Are You Running From?

Tilly had driven for a couple of hours. They had been talking about various subjects, both of them hoping that certain questions weren't asked and because of that they had both avoided asking anything too personal,

"Are you hungry?" Tilly asked and, before he had answered she started indicating to leave the motorway. "Almost all the best food places will be close to the sea so if we just head this way and stop at the first that we find, is that OK?" She knew she hadn't given him any choice, but she also knew that he was unlikely to say no. He had shared some sweets a few miles back and she had enjoyed the way he unwrapped them carefully before handing them over. She had watched him ensure that he didn't touch the sweet whilst folding out the wrapper and presenting it as a perfectly prepared gift like the most exclusive canapé in the best restaurant in Paris. She was trying to remain focused on the road whilst watching him with one eye and had almost expected him to offer it all the way to her mouth. She quickly realised that that would have probably be far too intimate for someone like him. She suspected that he was someone who built a relationship very carefully.

It was only a few minutes before she saw a sign for a restaurant. On a drive like this her preference would normally have been for a quick burger or sandwich from a petrol station. Tilly knew this trip was going to be different and she didn't want this part of the journey to be over too quickly. She had no idea what was going to happen next. They both ordered quickly and then she looked at him properly for the first time.

He was perhaps a little older than she had first thought. Wiser, but, at the same time, he also looked like he was in need of some support. She knew that they would be at Sam's house by nightfall so this was her chance to listen to him before she would find out what Jada had been up to. Tilly usually had no problem being direct but something about the way he spoke had caused her to be more hesitant. While she was trying to decide how to start the conversation, he stepped in asking what had brought her to Spain today. She knew that she couldn't lie so she told him.

Matilda Oriana Felice Rinaldi - Tilly to her friends, had been born in Milan, her father had been a dentist to the rich and famous, an early adopter of a range of cosmetic techniques that are now common, back then, he was one of the very few with the skills and confidence to give anyone magazine perfect teeth. More famously, her aunt had held office in the government until a relatively minor scandal had occurred. The newspaper stories had caused enough of an effect on the family name that her father had relocated to Paris. Where they were welcomed by both the fashion and political elite.

When her father decided to retire, he had chosen Spain. She was 16 at the time and although her father had given her the option to stay in Paris, she felt that the benefits offered by the shops on the Champs-Élysées were not enough to outweigh the chance to sit outside by the pool. Her classmates from school were all still friends and they would all follow you on social media - liking the posts of your latest ski trip or the latest pair of shoes that you bought. She was sure that she could still call up at least half of them and within a few minutes she would be being told that they would tell the housekeeper that she was coming and she could stay at their flat in Paris or New York or Berlin or at their holiday home in Bermuda, Miami or Cape Town for as long as she liked. She knew it was all superficial, but it was all that she had known, until she had met Sam.

Tilly had had met Sam when she arrived in Spain. Her father had bought a picturesque site, with views of the mountains, in a conurbation just outside a small town about an hour outside Valencia, close to the mountains and the beach. It had everything that he could have wanted, he had bought a flat for her Grandparents in the town itself and another for them to live in whilst he had the house built to his design. Sam had been the one who had treated her as a human at her new school.

The area was popular with people who had come and built their holiday homes on the hills outside the town walls. The town itself had plenty of people who depended on the support of neighbours to keep food on the table and the dark streets of those neighbourhoods hid a number of illicit enterprises willing to hire those who needed to earn money. The arrival of a girl from Paris, dressed like she had just walked off of the catwalk, caused a huge amount of jealousy amongst the girls and the start of a war amongst the boys who all wanted to claim her as a trophy.

Sam had approached her at the first break, and they had been almost inseparable during those first two years in Spain. When discussions had started about university, Tilly had been offered a place at the Sorbonne. She still didn't know whether it was because of her ability or her contacts but she had rejected it. She knew that Sam's family could not afford for her to study for another three years. Tilly also knew that, academically, Sam was more worthy and more suited to further education. Together they worked to convince Sam's parents that if they got on the same course, they would be able to be housemates. Tilly's parents would cover all the accommodation costs and her allowance would easily cover enough for them both to live on. Sam hadn't wanted the charity and had promised to pay Tilly back in a solemn contract that they had both signed on a very emotional hot spring night.

Whilst they were at university, Sam had fallen madly in love with Jada. Tilly had known almost from that first day at school that they would never be going out looking for boys together, but Tilly didn't need that. She received more than enough attention from them. After University, Sam and Jada had lived in Valencia, Sam working at the university whilst Jada went straight into business.

"They are both my best friends and, if I'm being honest, they both know more about me than I think I know myself." For the first time since she had begun talking, she looked directly at him, seeing him looking at her, their eyes met and held for a nervous second. Throughout her story he had been quiet, attentive and clearly listening to every word.

She was thankful that he had given her time to tell her story as she wanted to tell it. She could see in his eyes that he had questions but the fact that he hadn't leapt in meant that she had just talked and in doing so she realised that she had told him more than anyone else had learned about her for a very long time. She hadn't needed to worry about what he thought, she would only have to see him for another couple of hours. They managed to keep the conversation fairly light during their meal and it was only after they had both finished eating that her thoughts went back to her current position. She truly didn't know what to say about why she was here.

As she stared out of the window looking for an answer, he reached for his glass and almost theatrically finished the last of his diet coke.

"Do you want to get moving again?" he asked.

How did he know that she had run out of things that she had been able to say? She called for the bill. On the drive so far, she had tried to teach him a few phrases in Spanish however, she wasn't yet ready to let him try to say them out loud to anyone else. He offered a "gracias" as the waiter placed the bill on the table but before he'd even finished the word Tilly had placed her card into the waiter's hand. He had blushed and offered to pay. Tilly was used to paying for everything. She didn't yet know his story and she was sure that he would always be a gentleman and pay but she was also confident that she was the richer of the two. Although that would be true of at least 99% of the population.

As they got back in the car, she decided it was time to be a bit more honest with him. "Look, I don't know much but, you should know, Jada has been kidnapped. I don't know who by or why. That is why I'm going to Sendero."

They drove in silence for the next twenty minutes. She decided that she had probably scared him but, to be fair, he had still managed to look far more relaxed than she felt she might have done in his shoes and, he certainly hadn't demanded to be let out of the car immediately. The silence was getting to her though, it was giving her time to think, and she didn't want that right now. Time for a change of subject.

"What are you running from?" she asked.

Knowing that he didn't know where he was going, she reckoned that unless he was one of those who would just travel to 'find himself' he must have been running away from something, or someone.

She felt him look at her, feeling like he was assessing her, asking himself if she would understand or should he tell her something simpler. Looking back at him for as long as she dared take her eyes off of the road for, she hoped that he would tell her the truth. She didn't know why she cared so much but she wanted him to be honest with her.

"Myself I guess" he offered and then he went quiet again.

It wasn't the answer she had expected, and it didn't answer her question. She looked at him again and could see him trying to process his thoughts. He had waited for her to tell her story so, she decided, she would try the same tactic. It had taken her a long time to learn how to slow down her speech to an English pace. English was her most recently learnt language and was the one that she had the least confidence in. French, Spanish and Italian she spoke fluently, and she was able to think in each of those languages; none of which were known for slow speech. She had noticed that a lot of Londoners could speak just as quickly at times, but she had found that most English speakers at least paused for thought sometimes.

She wondered if he was ready for another question when he started again, "I've done nothing for too long. I've lived in the same house on the same road in the same town. People come and go and I've just always been there, I've had enough of answering peoples questions. 'What day is the bin collection?' 'Can I take a parcel in?' Can I keep an eye on their cat whilst they are off doing something more exciting?'

"I saw a quote that said that you should be the star of the book of your life, and I realised that I wasn't. I've spent my days supporting other people and so now, I want to do something for me."

Tilly wondered if she should tell him that he had started his journey by doing something to help her. She thought that that would be a bit cruel. Besides she guessed she was helping him too. It went quiet for a little longer with both of them considering their journeys to this point and both thinking of what may lie ahead. Adam with excitement and a fair amount of fear and Tilly with trepidation and a hell of a lot of fear.

It was Alicante before he started to recognise any of the place names on the signposts, and then it was only Alicante and Benidorm. He had enjoyed reading all of the place names, remembering Douglas Adams' claim that 'the world is littered with spare words… doing nothing but loafing on signposts pointing at places.' He tried to imagine how they should be pronounced. For the first few, he had asked Tilly but even after she had slowly pronounced each name several times, he had still struggled to create the right sounds.

Despite enjoying geography at school, he didn't remember any mention of the physical geography of this part of Spain, and he certainly wasn't expecting the mountains. The sharpness of the cliffs softened by the appearance of small orchards of orange trees. He had been expecting to see beaches and a deep blue sea, he really hadn't been ready for the true rugged beauty he had seen.

He allowed his mind to wonder what was going to happen next, where was he going to spend the night? He had thought that he would probably end up in one of the resort towns where he presumed that he would have found a cheap hotel a few minutes out of town and that he could find some work in a bar for a few days (weeks, months?) before moving on. Now here he was heading for a place he'd never heard of which his very quick Google, whilst Tilly had visited the bathroom, had told him had been inhabited since the Palaeolithic era.

Without wishing to make any firm plans whether he was going to stay in that area or travel onwards tonight, he had discovered that there were a couple of hotels in the town around their destination. He hadn't had time to look to see if they had any spare rooms and supposed he should really give it some thought. The whole presumption that he had made when he left his home that morning was that wherever he was he'd be able to at least find somewhere that he could sleep. He had slept perfectly well in tents at festivals and so, if necessary, he'd just buy a tent somewhere and be fine. In one of his premonitory dreams, he'd imagined finding a happy farming family with a habitable outbuilding who would take him in. While working on the farm the daughter fell in love with him and they would live happily ever after. That was never going to be realistic though.

The screen on the satnav indicated that there was less than half an hour of the journey left. It was his last chance to ask her the question he'd been thinking since she had told him her reason for being there. Actually, there were lots of questions but he wasn't sure that she would know the answers and, he didn't feel like he knew her well enough to intrude. He had cued the question in his head many times and then been distracted and paused. Why not just ask? He took a big breath and…

"So, what do you think happened? With your friend?"

"I wish I knew. I really do." It was honest although the words themselves seemed so helpless. She knew that Jada's family were not exactly the ideal family but surely Sam would have kept her away from too much trouble. All she knew for sure was that Sam was scared, more scared than Tilly had heard anyone else ever be. Together Tilly and Sam had always been the leaders of their group, they decided when they were going home or when they were moving onto the next club. They were the ones people looked to when they needed a taxi or when they needed advice to carry on dancing with a boy or if they should leave him. Since that call from Sam, she knew that she needed to do something. She could feel the goosebumps growing and the hair standing on the back of her neck as she inwardly contemplated what could be going on.

Having Adam on the trip had helped her. She had passed her driving test at the first attempt, just two weeks after her 18th birthday and had regularly driven to visit her old friends from Paris at their holiday homes all along the Mediterranean coast. Driving alone through Spain hadn't been what had made her reach out to this stranger from the queue. She was scared by the thought of being alone.

On the plane she had been thinking the worst of what might be found. She had wished that she had someone to share her fears with. It wasn't fair on Adam. She felt that she had railroaded him into the trip and he had been a perfect passenger. She too was now thinking about what would happen when they arrived.

Sam was only expecting her. It had always been 'just Tilly'. When her friends had asked (and they regularly did) when she would meet someone and settle down he had always responded with the saying that she remembered her grandfather telling her after she had taken an early boyfriend to visit them, "Better alone than in bad company" she had known at the time that the boy was not a good choice and she had declared on that day that she would wait for the right one to arrive.

How would Sam respond to someone from the queue for passport control? Could she just tell her it's the way that British people met? In queues? The secret language where one raised eyebrow or a shoulder shrug was the equivalent of a ten-year marriage? Sam would probably believe that. Sam had been shocked by Tilly's decision to move to London. The weather, the food, the time that people in England had dinner. Then of course there was the way that the people were so, so, she struggled to think of the word before deciding that the word really was just British. So British.

Could she ask him to stay? Why would he trust her? She might just be getting him into a really dangerous situation, Tilly felt responsible for that. Would that be fair? He said he was looking for an adventure, something to create a story. He could say no. She had nothing to lose, deciding that the question had to be asked.

"What are you going to do tonight?" Before he had a chance to respond she carried on, "Sam has plenty of spare rooms, if you'd like to stay, you can have a look around town in the morning." She had used that tactic of asking a question whilst giving an instruction since she first learnt the technique from an ex. Ask a question so that they think that they have a choice before telling them what the answer is by making them think of the second decision they could make after they had chosen your answer. It takes someone to be really sharp to realise that they could give an alternative answer to the question and besides, whenever she'd used it on British people, they had been too polite to ask her to rewind a little.

Adam looked out of the window for a second, was this the question he knew he'd been hoping for even if he would never have admitted that and he certainly wouldn't have asked to stay the night. He didn't yet know Tilly let alone this Sam and he'd already heard that Tilly was seriously worried about her situation. He had enough problems of his own without getting involved in someone else's but equally she had already shown him such kindness. If he refused, then she would surely feel hurt? Who held the power here? Could he toss a coin?

"It's not really fair on Sam is it, opening her house up to

someone she doesn't know?" He knew how Tilly would respond, but he wanted to not appear greedy. It really wasn't fair, was it?

"Of course, she won't mind, it's an open house, she lets anyone stay, if you don't like it you can leave in the morning." Now she knew she had given him the idea of staying even longer. Knowing that neither she nor Sam were afraid of standing up for themselves Tilly had also thought that currently, surely having a man around at the moment might be useful. Equally, he seemed like he had a balanced head, they might need someone who wasn't as emotionally involved to help them think straight.

"Well, if you are sure then it really would be very kind. Honestly though, if Sam isn't happy you have got to let me know immediately and I'll head off somewhere else." They both agreed. Tilly knowing that Sam would also be happy to have someone else staying. She was always better with others around her, and Tilly knew that although it had only been this morning when she had first cast her eyes on Adam, she now felt like she had known him for years. More importantly, something inside was telling her that she needed him.

Chapter seven
Enjoy The Gig

Shyamal had sent one of the bright new office recruits to the restaurant on the corner, if they were going to a gig in the evening then the least he should do is buy the team dinner. If the band were good they could be working until late, and although he knew that the staff were being paid well above that which most people their age could expect to receive, he wanted all of his staff to feel valued. He had known what it was like to work for a shady boss who knew what to say in all their corporate chat but who would never dream of putting that into practice. He wanted his employees to believe that they were as much a part of the business as he was. They had to believe in their purpose and knowing that he only recruited people that he believed in, it was important that they felt recognised. Of course, people's lives might change and give them reason to leave, Shy though wanted to make sure that no one would ever leave the company because he had made them feel undervalued or that he asked too much of them. Everyone should want to work there, not feel it was a laborious task.

A resounding cheer rose as the masses of food appeared. It was only Shy and Jo that were going tonight, once a band were signed, he would take the whole team out. He felt guilty if he was eating whilst others were working. The kitchen always threw in some extras for them. He remembered how delighted the chef had been when Shy had asked if his biggest band could have their photos taken in the restaurant. They still had fans coming to eat there just for their own chance to recreate the scenes.

He was just finishing his drink when he heard Jo call,

"Are we ready then boss?"

"Two minutes" he replied, "Can you arrange a cab?" He went back to his desk and changed his shoes, picked up his keys, contemplated his jacket before deciding, no. He wouldn't walk home tonight. He left the office feeling good. He knew Jo would already have a cab waiting for him. Going to see a great new band in a venue he liked and going there with a beautiful girl. He knew he could never tell Jo that. He saw beauty in all of the people that worked for him but was far too professional to say anything that could be misconstrued. In years gone by his position enough would have meant he could say whatever he wanted to whoever he liked but, the world was better now. Even twenty years ago he probably wouldn't have had the chances he had now. He didn't want to risk all that he had for just one comment. He knew that he felt good as he stepped out of the office and straight into the cab, Jo jumped in and they set off.

He loved London taxis and although there were a whole load of other firms offering luxury cars on an app, he still loved the traditional 'London' scene. Waving your arm in the air as a cab appeared and then being transported by someone who actually knew where he wanted to go. In the cab he was always stuck halfway between the tourist's delight in spotting the famous sights and the knowing cockney's pride of spotting the things that had deeper meaning. The stories of the city that in his eyes every true Londoner should know but that sadly these days few did. He had been shocked just a few weeks earlier when one of his new starters hadn't even known what The Monument was for, and they had been born in the city. He had added a book on London to the Christmas list that he always kept on his phone for when he had an idea for a gift for anyone he knew. He wondered if he had told Jo that according to a United Nations definition, any area that has at least 20% trees is a forest and London has 21% and so was technically a forest. He guessed that he probably had so stayed quiet as they turned out of the tree lined square that had reminded him of that fact.

The traffic was better than usual, meaning that they arrived a few minutes early at the venue but, if Jo was right, that would only be seen as a good thing for this band. Jo bounded over to a tall chap who couldn't have been more than 19 but who looked like they had stepped straight out of Rock Star school.

"Shy, meet the singer, Jack, Jack this is Shy…" Jack responded exactly the way that she had wanted him to. He recognised Shy immediately, most people did, even those who aren't interested in music. He had become rather famous for being willing to speak up for the quality of English Rock bands. Believing that everyone should be encouraged to play music and perform, whatever genre they wanted to. However much those celebrity judging panels claimed they were looking to give opportunities for those with real talent, it couldn't possibly be a coincidence that all the winners fitted into a very small demographic. Those few outliers who had snuck through with original talent had either been sidelined into very niche areas, had had real difficulties 'adapting to their new life' and, then retired from celebrity or had needed a whole host of therapies. His campaign was doing well but as he said in his last magazine article, as long as the newspapers were looking for photos of celebrities on the beach, they were creating problems for not only those forced to live the celebrity life but also those who inevitably found themselves being influenced by it.

It didn't help that Jack was so attractive but, when seen with the rest of the band, Jo had really thought that it could help. They were effectively the perfect model band, she hated to judge anyone but here she had a walking set of stereotypical music fan types, there was the attractive whimsical poetical one, the nerdy one, the larger one and…

"Oh, here's Jim…"

"JIMI!" Shy shouted with excitement and laughed, they both almost ran at each other and embraced, Jo and Jack just looked awkwardly at each other.

"Jo, meet Jimi Chandra. His father and I are old friends!"

Jim beamed before explaining to the group, "He's one of my uncles," he turned to Jack, "I hadn't said anything because, well, you know…" They were all smiling and excitedly chatting as they headed inside to meet the rest of the band.

It took at least 20 minutes and the first drink for the band to get used to the idea that Jim had this link to the legend of Shy and, for Shy to realise that the little boy that he had often carried home from school on his back was now being introduced to him by his staff as part of the best new band in London. The conversation had flowed perfectly until Paul spoke up,

"I'm really sorry Jo, and Shy. We are onstage in 30 minutes; we really have to prepare."

"Of course," Shy responded, "Go on - enjoy the gig." As the band moved off, he just sat back, looked at Jo and laughed.

Jo had just returned from the bar when the stage lights went down. The venue really wasn't large enough for a big theatrical intro. Most bands just walked on to the small stage and plugged in whilst looking a bit awkward. They would start playing after someone had said OK and counted them in but, tonight, the lights had gone down.

The bar and the emergency lighting still meant that everyone could see the guitarist walk out but everyone was looking, anticipating something a bit different.

There were only about sixty people in the room, which was nowhere near capacity but it certainly wasn't bad for a Wednesday night. The spotlight lit up the very second Paul hit the first chord. No-one had noticed that Jim and Leonard had joined the stage until they crashed in to the rhythm and by the time Jack leapt into the centre of the stage, almost cracking his head on the low roof, everyone in the building was not only looking at the stage but at the very least, bobbing their heads up and down or tapping their feet. Shy was doing both whilst leaning back in his chair, the smile on his face just getting wider and wider. He turned to Jo. "You know I bought him his first drum kit? It was to wind his dad up!"

It was a long time since Shy had seen such an impressive set put together by an unsigned band. A little slower section part way through allowed Jack to really prove that he could sing, and Paul showed just how beautifully his guitar could sound but, throughout the rest of the gig it was just relentless, future hit after future hit.

None of the crowd had known any of the songs except for the covers of a track by The Jam and a cheeky race through a Blink 182 hit but that really didn't matter because every song sounded like they should know it. Not because it was formulaic but because they were so enthusiastically delivered, with such choruses that from the second minute in, you truly believed that you knew each song. During the third song, Shy was imagining them at the Hammersmith Odeon and by the sixth song they were headlining Glastonbury in his head.

By the end of the gig, everyone in the room was a fan and the biggest of those was Shy. You could see the pride that he had in

Jim from the very first beat and Jo was certain that she was on for a bonus. By the time the band returned to the table after the gig, they knew that they were going to sign with Bashfull records. It was the label that they had all spoken about at their monthly business meetings that Paul had insisted on since he'd put the band together.

Paul had known Jack since school days. Leonard had played in a band with that had made a record and done a six-day tour of Germany before breaking up. His experience meant that he was the only one who had been through the process. Jim was the newest member. When Jim had first seen them at a pub in East London, they were using a drum machine. Jim had approached them during the set and asked if he could play along.

When they had come off stage the first question the bandmates had for Jim was why had he not told them about knowing Shyamal Mohammed? His response was one that he had rehearsed many times. Knowing that one day it was inevitable that they would find out. The band knew what their targets were, he knew that it wouldn't be long before Uncle Shy heard and so he explained that he didn't want anything to happen before they were ready. It made sense to the others.

They had had perhaps the shortest band meeting ever straight after the gig before heading out to answer the questions they were sure that Shy would be asking them. As soon as the band had left the stage Jo had gone to the bar manager and asked what drinks had been provided for the band and ordered two of each so when the band arrived, they had drinks waiting for them. She made sure they knew that if they wanted anything different they could have it although they all seemed very grateful with what was waiting. The last band she had done that for had all made ridiculous requests for champagne or impossible cocktails and by the time they had finished ordering she had lost interest in the band who had broken up not long after.

The band were keen that they didn't get forced into anything too quickly. Shy swiftly reassured them that that wasn't his style. What he did have to offer was an idea that the band hadn't even thought about. One of his other acts was setting off on a tour of, as Shy put it, the teenagers' party places, Marbella, Malaga, Benidorm, a different kind of gig in Valencia and then a night in Barcelona. Five gigs in seven days to a completely new crowd but, before those gigs, he would give them time at a rehearsal facility in Spain where they could work on their songs or any new stuff with one of Shy's network of producers and tech guys. After the gigs, they could decide if they wanted to stay there and work some more, away from home and catch some sun and enjoy the opportunity or to come home.

The band had known with one look that there was no way that they were going to refuse that opportunity. Shy had given them fifteen minutes alone to discuss it. He knew that both Leonard and Jack had jobs to consider. He had also assessed in just the small time that they had spent talking, that they loved the band more than their jobs and so, given the opportunity, they would both run away with the band. Shy was conscious though of giving the band a free choice and to ensure that they didn't feel compelled to act hastily despite knowing that as soon as they said yes to him, their world would change dramatically. Shy and Jo had barely sat at the bar and ordered before Paul came over with their decision. They returned to the table and Shy instantly called Jorge in Spain to sort out the accommodation and the studio and Mac from the office to book their flights immediately. Within ten minutes they knew that they were flying out the next day.

Chapter eight
Houses Like This

Adam could feel himself tightening up as they approached Sam's house. He didn't much like visiting houses of people he knew let alone someone he had never met before. Did she even speak English? Tilly had ignored the satnav as they turned off of the motorway and driven down to the beach and past a small harbour before the road then turned and started climbing steeply. The houses grew in size, as did the cars parked outside as they reached the clifftops. The natural bay was hidden between two cliffs and as they rose it seemed like the builders had literally moved the hills aside to fit the properties in. The walls rose higher and the more it felt like the approach to some Bond villain's lair in the mountain. He could see the end of the street where the road literally ended with the bare rocks of the mountainside, a flimsy metal chain ostensibly to stop traffic driving onwards to the rocky outcrops and seemingly the sea below. Tilly pulled over to stop in front of a large steel door in the stone wall that edged the road on the right-hand side. The wall was more reminiscent of a Welsh castle than the image he had of a Mediterranean villa. She picked up her phone from the central console and quickly called her friend. Adam could hear the relief in Sam's voice. He didn't understand a word that was said, but the relief was clear. Within a second the vault-like door started to slide open as the machinery effortlessly allowed the door to disappear into the wall.

He hadn't been ready for the brightness of the sunshine appearing from behind the door. He could see the drive leading into a garden. The angle of the sun streaming through the gate meant that everything else was hidden. As Tilly started to move the car forwards again. She almost ran over the figure that appeared, sprinting towards the car. Sam was in tears as she reached through the open window and hugged Tilly tightly. Adam shuffled in his seat, he was sure that Tilly hadn't spoken enough to tell her that he was coming, and Sam obviously hadn't been expecting anyone else and yet here he was now awkwardly witnessing perhaps the biggest display of emotion that he had ever seen.

Adam looked at his watch after what seemed like forever, Sam's sobbing had become a little more controlled. Adam still had no idea how Tilly was responding. She was still completely hidden by Sam's tremendous head of hair, as she had run to the car, he had been reminded of those inflatable men outside a car sales yard. Although only about 5ft, tall her slim limbs flailing and the huge amount of brown curly hair very much gave him that image and he was struggling to remove it from his head. Eventually, Tilly managed to speak, "Sam, meet Adam, he helped me to get here from the airport, he knows a little bit about what you've told me, I hope it's OK?"

Sam broke away from the embrace and looked across at Adam with a combination of shock and embarrassment.

"Oh, I'm so sorry," she immediately said in perfect English, not only in pronunciation, but also in the very nature in which a British person would apologise.

"I didn't realise you were there, please come in. Tilly, drive straight up to the house you can leave the car just there." Sam leant back away from the car, she looked both ways along the road before turning towards the house.

Adam was sure this was a set from a film, he was sure that at least one of the buildings would be full of guns and explosives. To his left was a garage block, there were four doors, all closed, each section looked like it must be able to house two cars at least. Tilly drove towards the opposite end of the house. There were three floors that Adam could see, they were approaching another apparent cliff face with a huge section cut into the rock that Tilly was able to drive through. Above them was a perfectly formed circular building with huge glass windows. A terrace surrounded floors two and three with, he guessed, fantastic views out to sea. Before he could see much more, they were underground and his eyes adjusted to the muted lighting.

He had already lost count of the number of times he had said wow and as he looked across the collection of vehicles in the underground garage he kept repeating himself. Closest to the entrance were two giant Jet skis and a powerboat, then a deep blue Range Rover that was obviously equipped for every eventuality, snorkel exhaust, a cage for storage on the roof, tow bar and winch system. Then a white Range Rover with tinted windows, looking like it was fresh from the showroom and heading straight to Cheshire with a footballer's wife inside. A sports car that he didn't recognise which looked very, very expensive. If only for the fact that it was a unique almost pinkish colour. A couple of motorbikes and, hanging from the wall, a couple of kayaks and a number of differently styled bicycles.

Tilly pulled up in front of a set of shiny lift doors, she looked across at Adam and smiled a caring smile before she opened her door and climbed out. Adam was still getting out as he saw Sam approach, wiping her eyes on her sleeve. She tried to manage a smile before she reached him, forcing her arm out for a handshake and apologising again, "I'm sorry I didn't know you were there. Thanks for coming." He was shocked by the speed at which she grabbed his hand and pulled him in to a tight hug. He was considerably taller than her and found himself nervously looking over to Tilly for confirmation of how to respond as she buried her head which only just reached his chest. Tilly was smiling as he reached his arms around Sam and carefully placed them onto her shoulders. After what had felt like far too long, Sam let him go and all together they entered the lift.

A few moments of awkward silence passed before the doors opened at the second floor. Adam couldn't help but stare. This kind of place simply didn't exist in his world, the first shock was just the expanse of the view from the floor to ceiling windows. Looking out at a panorama reaching from the sea across the beach and onto the mountains beyond. As he tried to take in that view, he was distracted by the collection of furniture, the pinball machine, the statue, the everything - all positioned so perfectly except for the one box of papers that were halfway through being sorted on the floor, next to a rug that looked like it had been stolen from the set of Aladdin.

"Let me get you a drink" Tilly said and headed straight to the bar about twenty metres away. Sam indicated a sofa and they wandered towards it. He almost had to step onto the rug it was that thick, and as he sat down, he couldn't help but think that he could get used to a place like this. Then he looked at Sam and, seeing the emptiness in her eyes, Adam remembered why they were there.

She looked beautiful but he could see the lines where tears had been running down her face and the worry in her eyes had etched dark rings beneath them. He wanted to reach out, put his arm around her and tell her it would be ok, but he didn't know her, and he really didn't know what was going on. Surely only international arms dealers lived in houses like this.

Three hours had passed since they had arrived. Adam was

already feeling like he had known Sam for years. He knew that he would do anything to help her and completely understood why Tilly had left her desk that morning. He hadn't even seen a picture of Jada yet, but he also knew that he wanted the chance to meet her. Both Sam and Tilly had at various points told him that she was headstrong (apparently, she was always wanting to do more and forever pushing others) and she had characteristics that at times drove them both crazy but, he could tell that she was loved completely by both of them.

They were speaking in English for him, their language ability was better than many of those he had dealt with daily back in London, but they kept apologising for their inability before using a word like rancorous or capricious. He couldn't be sure if he'd ever actually heard anyone else use those words in real life but, both had appeared as if they were simple colours. Every now and then they would ask 'How do you say…?' and then use exactly the word he would have chosen before he had answered. Occasionally they would then get a little distracted by variations in the English language but over the course of the discussion Adam simply sat and observed two friends who both clearly needed each other.

As the sun set between the mountains on the headland across the bay, Adam excused himself and stepped out onto the terrace. Perfectly smooth giant tiles spread out for an area about the size of the garden he grew up in. He imagined for a moment the games he could play out here; he'd get a set of stumps and you could have a great game of soft-ball cricket, low shots only and they would bounce off of the glass protecting the fall to the terrace below, which would make fielding so much better. They could set up scoring zones, he quickly realised that his brain was doing this as a distraction from the seriousness of what he had been hearing.

He carried his drink to the balcony and took a swig as he

leaned against the edge and looked down to the gardens below him. A beautiful blue pool was surrounded by more perfect tiling which continued along pathways radiating across the gardens. A collection of beautiful flowers and shrubs surrounding the rocks of the cliff in such a perfect form that he wasn't sure if the rocks were there first or if they had been carefully installed to suit the garden. The widest path led out to the furthest point of the garden where a pod like building had been constructed to provide shelter from the sun, a large sofa was positioned to look out to sea. Adam was convinced that if he had the opportunity to sleep on that sofa, it would surely be the best night's sleep of his life.

He stood for a moment and realised the enormity of his situation. He had left his house, his job, his life. He had some money in the bank but not much and now, just twenty-four hours later he was stood on a balcony belonging to a millionaire, looking at the Mediterranean Sea knowing that behind him were two beautiful women discussing the kidnapping of the wife of one of them. So far, they didn't know anything about why she had been kidnapped. More worrying for Adam was the fact that they had mentioned several people that Sam thought it could have been.

Tilly had told him that Jada's family were interesting characters on the drive down, it was only now that he had learned exactly who they were. Her father had been famous across Europe, he had been in films, presented shows on TV and had several hit albums. Her mother was a Swedish singer who had always been told that she could have been as big as ABBA if she had sung in English. She had chosen that fame in Scandinavia was enough, realising that to have been bigger would have taken her away from her family.

They had both stepped back from the celebrity spotlight when the newspapers revealed that Jada's father had been involved in a few rather shady business dealings. He had decided that his business arrangements were far more profitable than his celebrity career and so had chosen that path. Jada had railed against his ethics and left them on her 21st birthday, taking with her the money that he had been investing in her name that had become hers on her birthday. She had immediately chosen to invest in companies that were doing the opposite of her father's. Luckily for her this combined with the global campaign for supporting local businesses. By investing relatively small amounts in hundreds of small businesses, she had amassed a fortune almost as large as her father's.

Jada had since been quite outspoken in her dismissal of her father and some of the governments and organisations that he had dealt with. Unfortunately, this presented hundreds of people who would be capable of 'taking her out'. The phrase had sounded strange spoken in Sam's delicate voice. She had obviously picked the phrase up from the movies, before she explained that they were more likely to be the people who would,

"…just make someone, how do you say it? Dissolve?" Adam guessed that she had meant disappear, but dissolve seemed to work just as well and decided that now wasn't the time to get distracted by describing a word like dissolve.

Sam had another theory that it could be a local drug dealer. They had approached her a while back wanting to buy the house. It was a perfect location. Secure and with limited access from the road, the mountain-side location meant that any other approach was very restricted except for via the staircase that Jada had had carved into the rocks. leading to a private dock at the base of the cliff. When he heard this Adam had just laughed, he hadn't even seen the staircase yet but, it was just absolute proof in his mind that he was on a Bond film set. Or Sam admitted the kidnapping could be because of something that they hadn't even imagined yet.

Adam stood enjoying the fresh breeze allowing him some time to process everything that he had seen in the last 24 hours. He looked over his shoulder and saw that Tilly and Sam were still talking. He wished he had been recording the whole event. He had thought earlier of the comment about being the star of the book of your life, well, that had changed, he was now a supporting actor in an action movie.

He stood looking out for another ten minutes or so before he sensed Tilly approaching him, she came and stood silently next to him, close enough for him to think how nice this scene felt but far enough away for them both to feel perfectly comfortable. After gazing up at the stars she reached out a hand to his and almost whispered "We are going to head to bed, do you want to stay up here? Sam has a room ready for you?" Adam looked almost longingly to the sofa by the cliff but with all he had heard tonight, he wanted to be somewhere he could feel as safe as possible.

Whoever it was that had got Jada hadn't got into the house. They hadn't even got near the house. The note that Sam had shown them earlier had been left in the cafe by the beach that apparently Sam cycled to each morning collecting that day's lunch. Adam had studied the note but, not knowing the language, he had only been able to confirm Sam and Tilly's comments that it appeared to be written very neatly and carefully by someone who appeared not to be stressed whilst they were writing.

Tilly led him back inside and across to a staircase that circled down to a cosier reading room, still with fantastic views, this time showing more of the gardens. A corridor led away from the open space, they walked along past three doors on each side before Tilly stopped with her hand on a door handle,

"This is your room; I will be in the room opposite and Sam is at the end of the corridor if you need any of us. Sam brought your bag down. I told her that I don't know what time you get up but, if you get up before anyone else, Sam asked you to help yourself to anything from the kitchen. Did you see the kitchen?"

He hadn't but the thought of wandering around someone's house and helping himself to their food seemed so wrong. He knew that he wouldn't eat before at least one of them was up but he nodded. She continued,

"The light switch is here but, it's like a hotel, you can switch everything off from your bed, I'm sure you can work it out and there is a bathroom here, there are towels and soap, shampoo, they might be a bit feminine but…" She laughed as she said that before adding "Thank you, for being so nice." She bounced up on tiptoes to give him a little kiss on his cheek and turned to head to her room.

Adam stood by the door for a minute before padding across the carpet. His bag sat perfectly in the centre of a table that stood subtly in one corner of the room. The biggest bed he had ever seen was laid against the wall to his right and again floor to ceiling windows spread across the room. The lights on the terrace area showed that he could open all of those windows and take a walk into the gardens if he wished. He looked to find a way to close the curtains. He probably wouldn't have needed to, but he wasn't ready to take his shirt off in front of an open window. He found a control panel on the wall, pressed a button and blinds suddenly appeared and slid silently down the windows. He looked around, assessing the six different armchairs he could sit on, each one looking like an example from a design magazine. The giant TV screen on one wall, the mirror on another wall and, above the bed a beautiful modern artwork that although he instantly had an idea of who might have painted it, he couldn't be sure but he didn't feel the need to search online to match the squiggle in the bottom corner.

Chapter nine
Tower Bridge Lit Up

In the cab home after the gig, Shy had asked Jo if she fancied a trip to Spain. Knowing that Shy had already been planning to go to the Valencia and Barcelona gigs on the tour, she had already wondered if there might be an invite for the whole office. They had done that a couple of times and nothing felt better than being part of a group flying to a gig as a 'work trip'. She had only just met the band but they all seemed like decent people so there wouldn't be the trouble that had occurred on some tours; she wouldn't want to have to talk to the Spanish Police through using her translation app. Particularly if the incident was anything like that one in Manchester on her last tour. The memory made her laugh before answering Shy with a smile. "Yes, why not". He nodded as he smiled his response and looked back out of the window, unable to resist the view of Tower Bridge lit up.

As the cab pulled up outside her flat, he wished her goodnight in the way that she always found so cute, and she smiled as he said "I'll see you in the morning". The cab door shut and drove away as she stood there realising what Shy had just said, he was coming too. She skipped up the stairs knowing that it was going to be a great trip. Desperately she tried to remember how many days the trip would be. How much should she pack? She knew that she could make time to shop if she needed so she made sure she had her essentials and crammed those into a bag that she knew she wouldn't mind throwing into the back of a van.

Jo had wanted to make sure that she was the first at the airport in the morning but by the time she arrived at the agreed meeting point, Jim and Paul were already there. Jim rushed straight over and gave her a hug,

"Is this real?" he asked like a child who couldn't believe it was his birthday. "Shy said I didn't need to bring my drums, but I've got eight sticks is that ok?" Jo managed to keep a straight face as she reassured him that they would have a choice of kits available, but she asked for a list of his favourite drums and sticks so that she could make sure that he was happy. She then turned to Paul,

"And if you can let me have a list of guitars, picks and strings". Jorge had already provided a list of kit that was in the studio already. Suspecting that the band probably would never have had the chance to see how they'd sound with different kit, she wanted to give them the chance. Some loved the most exclusive kit, others the worst. Was it Brian May who still played with a sixpence? And on a guitar he built himself?

Jo knew that they would be excited to play with the expensive toys, but she wanted them to play music with the same raw power that she had heard in those two gigs, and you can't do that if you are only thinking about how valuable your kit is. She had once been given one of those gift experiences where you get to take a supercar around a track except that you can't enjoy it because you are too scared of even just hurting one tyre.

Shy was next to arrive and ushered them all towards the food hall for breakfast, Leonard and Jack arrived together each carrying a rucksack and a guitar case looking like a typical pair of students heading to a festival. Jo made sure she took lots of photos which the band loved. She was always thinking of the biographies and the documentaries that would be made in years to come. So many things in life only happen once, she wanted to record everything.

The heat hit them as they stepped off the plane as Jo took more photographs. Making sure that she also got a picture of the guy holding the band's name on a card to lead them to the cars outside. The band were all led into the first of two people carriers and Jo and Shy hopped in the one behind. It was intended to give the boys a chance to be alone for a while on Shy's advice. He had explained,

"You don't want to become their mother always answering their questions and, equally, some of the feelings they are experiencing now we want to get onto the record."

Of course that made sense, although Jo knew that she would miss seeing the excitement on their faces.

They made some plans on the drive down from the airport before Shy asked his driver to overtake so that they could be the first car to arrive. Jo was out of the car and filming as the boys awkwardly clambered out of their car and looked around them. The whiteness of Leonard's skin clashing with the bright blue sky was alone enough to make them look completely out of place. Jorge and his assistant, Nicandro, came out of the studio welcoming the whole group. Shy got a hug from both whist everyone else was met with hearty handshakes. "Let me show you around before we eat" Jorge boomed as if he was inviting the whole of Spain.

The Band had literally dropped their bags in the bedrooms and rushed straight to the rehearsal room where Jorge had told them to come when they were ready. Nicandro was creating a direct replica of Jim's home drum kit. He had already created three kits from different manufacturers, all tuned to the same sounds, giving Jim the choice of which to play. This was always Jorge's favourite time. He had hosted a few bands that Shy had sent over and Jorge always gave them extra time, he knew that many of them would never again get this opportunity. He enjoyed the delight in the faces of each band member when he pulled out the cases full of kit that he had selected for them. It was easy enough for him to make an assessment of how their time together would go when he saw which instruments they went to first. It would tell him whether they were true musicians or just there for fun. Both could have their advantages and he knew he could make great music with each group. He and Nic had discussed the likely choices based just on the way the band got out of the car and he was usually right.

Jim had gone straight to the kit he recognised. It was a newer version than the one he owned and the colour was brighter, but it sounded the same. Paul too had started with his own guitar although during the evening he had had a play with each of the nine guitars that Jorge had selected. Jorge and Nic shared a knowing look as the first guitar he had picked up from the rack was the Ibanez. Jo had described the kind of music they played over the phone but despite that, as soon as Paul had stepped out of the car Jorge had said to Nic, "Ibanez". They weren't a metal band but, the 'metal' guitars were always the ones that the best guitarists wanted to try, wanting to see how fast they could play. Jorge predicted that the Gibson would be next. Leonard had gone straight to the most expensive Bass and played that all night long, Jorge had told Nic to help Leonard most in the first few days.

Jorge knew it was his job to essentially audition this band. Would they all be able to cut it? Could they all play to the necessary ability all night every night? Did they have the willingness to learn? The right attitude to succeed? Could they work together to make things happen? Many band members had left a band in the first week working with Jorge. Many more bands had split either during the week or, not long afterwards. Jorge himself could play most of the instruments well enough that if a band member left, he could step in until a permanent replacement was found. Nic was a brilliant drummer and bassist, far better than most of the players he supported, and Jorge had the phone numbers of all the best musicians in the area to help out if necessary.

As he left the studio that night, Jorge was feeling happy, he had lit up the stage lights to perform three songs to finish. He didn't want them to spend the whole night playing and had told them that he would be back at 8am. No one was to go into the studio before him. They themselves could decide what time to arrive, but he would be opening up at eight. He had a few tapes from a local band that he wanted to play with so if they weren't early starters, he could keep himself busy working on those.

Chapter 10

As Idyllic As I Remembered

Adam woke early as he always did, reached for his phone and checked the time. He exhaled as he saw it was still only 06:20. An hour earlier if he was still in the UK but still too early to be a reasonable time to leave his room. He stepped out of bed and was immediately reminded of just how luxurious this house was as his feet sank into the carpet. The carpet alone felt like a pair of favourite slippers cushioning his every step. He loped over to the place on the wall where he remembered the blind control being and without too much fumbling, he found the open button. He was surprised by just how dark it still was outside although the sky was a beautiful blue, and he could see a band of light appearing to form on the horizon. He then walked the length of the room looking for a way to open the door before coming back and finding an icon on the control panel that might, yes, it did, the doors slid for a fraction of a second before stopping whilst Adam stood confused for a second before realising that he had to keep his finger on the button.

The fresh sea air blew through and woke his smile up, he stepped outside to be met the scent of the flowers and the orange trees. He stood for a minute just allowing each of his senses to bask in the delights around him before walking further into the garden. Taking the long way round he knew that he was heading to the sofa he had spotted the night before.

As he approached the edge of the cliff, he saw the staircase which led down to a short pontoon with a giant RIB tied up on one side and what looked like a fishing boat on the other, glowing in the half light. From the pontoon there was also a bridge leading to a small beach with perfect white sand, Adam was lost in the beauty of the location when he heard a quiet

"Good morning".

He spun quickly to see Tilly poking her head above the sofa,

"Oh hey, are you ok?"

He almost stumbled with his words. She had been there for just over an hour herself,

"I woke up dreaming of the view from this sofa so wandered out to see if it was as, idyllic? Is that the right word? Yes, if it was as idyllic as I remembered."

"It is stunning, isn't it?" Adam replied perhaps too enthusiastically,

"Yes, absolutely stunning". He wasn't entirely sure if he was still talking about the seascape or, of the view he now had in front of him, Tilly had stood from the sofa. She was barefoot and, as far as Adam could see, she was only wearing that Mickey Mouse T-shirt. "Would you like a coffee?" she asked as she turned and headed towards the back of the pod, a fully equipped kitchen with a well-stocked bar and a state-of-the-art coffee machine were hidden away inside. He watched as she prepared him a black coffee.

Adam was sure that, when he woke up this morning, he would have been back in the London suburbs. Confident that this hadn't happened. Instead, he had woken in an even better dream. As he took the first sip of coffee his brain started firing again. So many questions and yet he knew there were no answers. Sam had simply received that note, "We have Jada. Await further instructions. DO NOT CALL THE POLICE" but written in Valencian. Adam had heard of Catalan but didn't know that there were other versions of Spanish. There had been a quick history lesson last night but, with everything else that was going on he wasn't too sure about the details. Apparently that had narrowed, quite dramatically, the number of people who could have actually written the note. Adam had pointed out, surely, they could have used an online translator, although he also admitted that this would have required a particularly deep-thinking character to have thought that necessary.

Tilly had beckoned Adam to sit down. She sat herself at the other end of the sofa tucking one leg underneath herself as she did. "I had said last night that you could leave first thing if you wanted to so, do you? I could drive you into town if you like or there is a station at Denia to go south, or at Gandia, that's about one hour away but you could get the metro to Valencia?" He looked at her, trying to assess if she wanted him to leave, he hadn't even thought of leaving, he had for a few minutes before he fell asleep wondered if he really should be getting himself involved in this. He had originally thought that it could have all been a set up by Jada herself although he had since been convinced that she wouldn't do something like that.

Adam looked at Tilly, trying to read exactly what was happening behind those eyes, "I don't know if I can help but I reckon that you might need someone a little less involved to talk to occasionally?" She looked like she might cry but she managed a little smile, "I think so too" she sighed into the top of her coffee cup and hugged her knee to her chest. Adam looked back out to the sea, a couple of fishing boats were loitering not far out and further away he could see a number of larger ships carrying everything everywhere. He guessed he was staying then.

They sat silently for a few minutes before they both turned as they heard footsteps as Sam approached, "Hola, Bon dia" she almost sang, they both smiled a greeting and Adam came back with a "Buenos Dias" which made them both giggle. It wasn't quite the reaction he had been hoping for, but Tilly quickly tried to reassure him. "That was perfect Spanish pronunciation but listen, Bon Dia, that's Valencian!" Adam apologised and stood to offer his place on the sofa, Sam smiled sweetly and said, "It's OK, let me be here" and she climbed into the centre of the sofa and sat on the back with her feet on the seat.

Sam propped herself above Tilly and Adam with her view across the bay,

"So" she expressed in a way that drew complete attention then, after a pause "Tell me something…" Adam was a little taken aback, what could he tell her? She was still looking out to sea. He didn't know if she was talking to him or to Tilly. He was sure she didn't want him to tell her some of the nonsense that he had currently in his brain. Thankfully Tilly spoke up,

"I told Adam he could stay as long as he liked, as long as he didn't mind listening to us."

Sam turned to him and smiled that warm smile that seemed to light up her whole face,

"Thank you" Adam replied, "If it's ok, I said to Tilly that I don't know what I can do but, if I can help in any way…"

Sam reached out and rested her hand on his head,

"Thank you she said, just having you here helps".

She paused looking like she was trying not to cry before adding "I'll just have my coffee then I'll cycle down to get pastries if that's OK?" Tilly leapt in,

"I'll come with you. Adam can look after the house", The fear of being left in the house alone struck Adam,

"Or I can go and get the pastries if that's better?" He was quick to add. He had been wondering what on Earth he could do to help, he had no knowledge of the criminal mind, he'd never even stolen a sweet from the pick and mix. He couldn't speak the language so he couldn't really go to investigate. What was he doing?

"Hey Adam, can you drive a boat?" Hearing Tilly's voice reassured him. It had been the longest thirty minutes of his life. Sam and Tilly had headed out to the cafe leaving Adam alone, just in case anyone came to the house. He had been petrified that someone would, a neighbour or a delivery guy wondering why this strange bloke, who didn't speak Spanish, was in this house. He had programmed some phrases into his translation app and had spent most of the time trying to say "Sam volverà pronto". His book had told him that he had to change some words, if it was someone he knew that he was talking to, but he had no way of knowing what the translation app had given him. He hoped he'd be ok. Adam had been relieved when he had seen them appear on the screen. Since they had left, he had been checking the screens regularly and, other than one dog walking by on its own, he had seen no-one. The screen had brightened as the camera had detected movement seeing Tilly and Sam cycling towards the outer gate. Adam watched them approach and the cameras had followed them into the lift.

"I don't know, why?" He thought about the question, he had driven a barge for a short period on a family holiday once and he had taken a rowing boat out more than once, but he wasn't sure if that met their criteria for driving a boat.

"There is an odd car just down the road. We want to know who is in it, they look like they are watching the house. If you come out from here, they will know that there is at least one other person here. If you could take the boat, you can run it into town and walk up. They wouldn't know where you had come from." Tilly had said all of that as if she was describing something completely normal. Adam had already felt his heart rate triple. He had said he was here to help, but he wasn't sure that he was really ready for it. He bit his lip and realised now was the time to show his commitment. This was his first duty.

"What kind of boat is it?" Adam asked confidently.

"Come, I will show you, Tilly stay with the cameras. Call me if you see anything." Sam had answered, they were both trying to act normally but Adam could feel that they were nervous. He grabbed his cap as he headed down the stairs and into the garden. Sam was well ahead of him on the steps down to the pontoon, by the time he caught up he was rather out of breath. Sam had the motor running already,

"The ignition is like a car but make sure that it is in neutral first, the key turns to start - the instructions are in English". She giggled a little but there was an urgency to her words,

"Once you have ignition it is simply forward or back, you don't need to go too fast, and the sea is calm today. If you follow the coast, as the cliff drops you will see the harbour. Go real slow as you enter and try not to hit the other boats. There is a low wall on, how do you say this, right side."

All of her descriptions were being given with appropriate mimes or hand waving. "If you bring it to almost stop before you hit the wall you can slide into the side - put these out to defend the boat on this side as you enter the dock, and the boat will be ok. If you need to stop quickly - push this into reverse. Jump out holding this rope and you can tie it to the posts there. Tie the front and back, do I need to show you how to tie…" It was Adam's turn to giggle. He had enjoyed ropes in the Cubs and still tried to tie proper knots whenever he could.

"OK. Take this, if you walk up to the car, you can ask the man for directions, look for as much as you can about the car but don't take photos, don't look suspicious at all, you have just taken one wrong road."

He had felt nervous taking the boat away from the dock under Sam's watchful eye and felt the weight lift off of his shoulders as she had waved a cheery "Well done" and turned to head up the stairs. He gained more confidence as he headed along the coast, feeling like a proper tourist watching all the beautiful houses pass by. The gentle sounds of the waves lapping against the bow turned to smacks as he realised he was speeding up a bit. Easing the throttle back to where he had originally held it, the gentle lapping sounds returned. He was sure that anyone watching would be asking why he was driving so slowly, but he'd prefer to be slow than careless.

He was rushed back to reality by the sight of the dock coming into view, he slowed the boat down, probably far slower than he needed to and put out the fenders nice and early. He thought to himself that he probably looked quite natural. Just as he was thinking that he could get used to this, he realised how expensive some of the boats around him looked. A group of men sitting at a table on the back of one of the boats had paused their game of cards to watch him approach. He wondered if they knew Sam or Jada, would they recognise the boat, did anyone else know that she was missing?

"Try to act casual and just fulfil the task" he told himself out loud. Surprised by how well he brought the boat alongside he couldn't resist looking back at the men, two of which gave him a knowing nod of recognition. His confidence was almost lost completely as the rope caught a little as he jumped ashore, but he thought he disguised that well enough. Double checking that the boat wasn't going to float away, he set off following Sam's directions.

Chapter 11

To Tie His Shoelace

He found the footpath behind the open-air gym where two young mums sat chatting which led past a couple of waterside properties before reaching the old town centre. The street immediately narrowed alongside the church, the sun disappeared as the houses grew taller and closer to the edge of the road. Happily for Adam lowering the temperature too. He hadn't felt the heat with the breeze on the boat but stepping away from the beach he had noticed the change dramatically.

The cafe on the corner, where he presumed Sam had bought their breakfast, was empty except for three cyclists each clad in florescent Lycra. The street led onwards, there was another store on the opposite side of the road, but what it sold Adam couldn't tell, and it certainly didn't look like the kind of place that would welcome customers who were just browsing. Turning the corner he recognised the junction ahead of him from their original drive in.

The sweat started to form once again on the nape of his neck causing him to pause and use a tissue to mop his face and neck as he stepped out of the shadows and the road began to climb steeply. He could already see the back of the car he was looking for, but he knew it would take him a good couple of minutes to reach it. As he neared the car, he tried to create a memory story to remember the plate, he didn't know if they knew anyone who could identify the car for them, but it couldn't do any harm, "PGC 0187G" How on Earth would he remember that? Was he far enough away that he could write that into his phone? He thought so and bent down as if to tie his shoelace whilst he typed. He stood and approached further, feeling his chest tightening but not knowing if that was because of the climb or the fact that he was getting closer to the car.

Three people sat in the car, all the windows were open, unsuccessfully trying to alleviate the obvious discomfort caused by the early summer heat. As he reached the rear window he looked in at the occupant, he guessed aged twenty, maybe twenty-five, already balding a little. He had a magazine open on his lap with an advert circled, Ram Disco Garden and today's date was all he could see before the person turned towards him, "Hello," he panted, hardly ably to speak, "Hablas Inglesi?" He was sure that wasn't quite the right thing to say but he thought it was best to try to be polite, "I'm sorry I don't…" The man was just looking at him quizzically but, as he got halfway through his second sentence the driver turned to him, "What do you want? My friend doesn't speak English."

This chap was obviously used to being in charge. Adam took a step forward to stand alongside the driver's door. He took the chance to look across at the third person in the passenger seat, surprised to see a young woman who turned to smile at him. She was trying to hide a camera behind her leg and there was another bag by her feet. Adam felt his back run cold as he thought that he recognised what was in the bag. The driver leant forward to make Adam look at him, "Oh I'm sorry, I was looking for this bar, do you know where it is?" He was relieved that he had remembered how to speak. Reminding himself to be focused, he showed the man the leaflet that Sam had given him earlier. The man took it, checked both sides as if scanning it for clues before handing it back and gruffly saying "Yes, go back down here, go this way and take the next road" as he finished speaking, he made it clear that the conversation was over.

Adam thanked the window as it closed and gave a little wave to the passenger in the back seat, he would have liked to have thanked the girl in the front but that really wouldn't be subtle. He had all he was going to get and headed back down the road. Almost running down the hill, he was unsure if it was his body acting entirely on its own to speed up his escape or if it was simply the effects of gravity. He was relieved when the road began to level out a little and was able to at least feel as if he was in control of his feet. He made one final check behind him to see if he had been followed before heading in the direction he had been given. He wanted to at least walk to the bar now to justify his question. He had decided that he didn't need to go in, if he was asked, he was going to say he had arranged to meet someone there later and wanted to make sure that he knew the right place.

When he saw the bar was open, he desperately felt the need to go in for a drink but knew how Tilly and Sam would be feeling waiting for him to return. He turned and half ran back to the dock, relieved to see that the boat was still where he left it. Quickly, he untied the ropes and leapt aboard before remembering that Sam had told him to make sure to switch the engine on before untying, else he would drift. He already found himself a foot away from the dock and was frantically trying to get the key in the slot, it slid in perfectly and the engine fired in a way that Adam hoped made it look like it was all intended. Turning the boat towards the sea, he gave a wave to the men still up on their boat 'Montaña de la luna'. Adam thought he could translate that himself as he sped the boat up and headed back along the coast. This time feeling a lot more like James Bond than the tourist he felt he was earlier.

He saw Tilly, standing on the pontoon, and felt very glad to see her. They had only met less than 24 hours earlier but there was a sense of security about her. She had taken him in when he had needed someone, and now she looked genuinely pleased to see him.

It was a long time since he had felt that feeling. More likely that she wanted to know if he had learnt anything than the look was out of genuine affection he felt but, he was happy she was there and that was enough.

Before he stepped off of the boat, he was telling her what he had seen, he realised that he was babbling as she stopped him. "Wait, tell us both together! How are you? I didn't mean to get you involved, you don't have to, I can take you to the station…" she left the last comment open. Adam was still smiling from the first question. He paused, feeling temporarily overwhelmed. She seemed to genuinely care. "Thank you" was all he could say, she stopped, turning to look at him, "Thank you for the offer, you might have saved my life by offering the lift at the airport, if I can do anything to help in return, I will do absolutely anything I can." He realised he was blabbering again he might have been exaggerating a little bit but, genuinely, he had felt that he really wanted to help her. She smiled again, a caring smile. They stood for a second, Adam could hear the waves gently rolling against the cliff, a little nod and she turned and carried on up the stairs. Adam followed behind, trying to stay focused on the information he had.

Sam met them on the terrace, she ran over and gave Adam a quick hug. He really didn't know where to start… 'OK, so there are two blokes and a girl." He had only just begun when he was first interrupted, "Blokes, what is blokes?" Sam asked,

"Oh sorry, Men, blokes is like a kind of, oh I don't know but… the man in the driver's seat is in charge, maybe 50 years old - ish, a greying moustache. He looked quite strong, not unfriendly but, like a bull, you'd want him on your side. The other guy is younger, not more than 25 and the girl even younger, maybe 18, 19. She was carrying a camera and I think that she had a gun in her bag." He wasn't sure if he should mention the gun, he didn't want to scare them, but he also thought that it was probably important to know.

He had read an article about how guns were more 'normal' in Spain. The look between Tilly and Sam however suggested that it wasn't that normal. He chose to carry on, "the car is a Megane, registration PGC 0187G"

"That's a Guardia plate!" Tilly interjected, "What the…" Sam looked at Adam, "The Spanish Police. Did you get anything else?"

"The only other thing was that there was a magazine open on the back seat, it had a page open with an advert circled. It was for an event at a place called Ram Disco Garden and it had today's date on it."

Sam and Tilly looked at each other again, Tilly nodded.

"OK Adam, come with me." Sam spoke with authority and a steeliness in her voice. Adam looked across at Tilly for reassurance as she stood to follow Sam. Adam genuinely felt nervous for the first time. "In Spain, we sometimes have a problem with squatters, particularly homes by the coast for holidays. The police take the side of the squatters - it is easier - so you need extra protection. If you have a gun in the house the police have to get any squatters out immediately because they don't want the guns out. So, it is useful to have a gun cupboard." As Sam was speaking, she had led them down a corridor that Adam hadn't even noticed before. She opened a door and stepped into what looked like a well organised office, a tidy shelf full of files sat above another full of happy photographs and little mementos. Jada and Sam at Disneyland, a sand sculpture from Dubai, Sam turned the computer on and placed her hand onto a pad alongside it. Within seconds the screen on the computer flashed into life and then faded so that Adam couldn't see what was on it. Sam clicked through a few pages and then strode further down the corridor.

"Adam, place your hand here please", it wasn't an unfriendly tone, but Adam knew that he wasn't going to argue. As he placed his palm against the panel, he felt the warmth of the ray of light as it passed over his hand. He now felt the feeling when the shoe measuring device squeezed your foot as a child or the feeling when his friends had all photocopied their hands in the staff room at school. The light changed colour and another door opened. Sam stepped into the room. A dull blue light shone eerily across the room's contents.

"This room always keeps this light so if you come in at night without your eyes adjusted you will still be able to see easily." Sam was now speaking like a tour guide, bored of giving tourists the same speech but he felt that this was a place not many had previously been. The room was not large but that did not stop Adam feeling like things had suddenly ramped up a few levels.

"Have you ever fired a gun?" Sam asked in a way that sounded as simple as 'have you ever had a glass of water?' He thought of the few shots he had taken at a target on a Scout camp aged 12 and the few he had taken with a cork gun at a tin can at the fairground but,

"Like this, No." He answered, hoping that his voice didn't give away his feelings. She reached behind her, and lifted the gun from the top shelf,

"Tilly, can you grab 6 and 12? Here, Adam, take this." She passed him a bag that felt far heavier than a bag that size should have and a smaller gun. He wanted to be able to say something cool like John Wayne would, 'Oh a Lee Enfield 101, you spoil me' but he knew his ignorance in this situation probably wouldn't be funny. Before he had a chance to speak at all, Sam had passed him and was heading down the corridor. As he stepped out to follow, he felt the door slam shut behind him.

Sam looked completely natural carrying the huge gun, and Tilly, now striding along with a pistol in each hand looked like she had stepped straight out of a computer game. They reached the edge of the garden and Sam placed her weapon on the floor. Adopting a teaching pose, she addressed both Adam and Tilly, "I hope it won't be necessary but…" she went on to explain that she'd rather, if the worst did happen, that her friends would be on her side and wouldn't shoot her by accident.

It was an intense lesson. Adam had truly never felt so alive. He thought of his old colleagues as they would be looking at their watches now, desperately hoping for the hands to reach 5pm. Here he was standing on a cliff edge with two beautiful women firing bullets into the sea. Sam had asked him to aim at a seabird but had laughed when he had missed by a long way. Adam didn't know if she had realised that for a fraction of a second, he had aimed at the bird before realising what would happen if he hit it. He wasn't sure that he was ready for that guilt. Sam put the bag of ammunition down and cheerfully stopped him, telling him it was time for lunch. He looked at his watch and saw that it was 2pm already. After returning the weaponry, Sam checked the CCTV and saw that the car was still waiting there. Tilly offered to go and talk to them, Sam shut her down quickly,

"The note said don't call the police and yet they are watching the house, we don't know enough about what is going on, they must contact me again soon."

"So, what are we going to do?" Adam asked,

Sam simply smiled,

"Do you want to go and see a band tonight?"

Chapter 12

A Particular Melody

Jorge arrived at the studio at 7:50am and wasn't really surprised to see Jim and Paul already stood waiting to be allowed in,

"Morning boys" he called, "It's going to be a great day!"

Jorge loved mornings, Nic didn't share the love of mornings and so he wouldn't appear until half past ten at the earliest. Paul immediately started talking about the last piece that he had spoken with Jorge about last night. Jorge slowed him down and asked if they had had breakfast. Jim nodded heartily, Paul gave a simple nod to the cup of coffee he still had sitting alongside him,

"Jack is in the Gym and Leonard promised that he would be here by nine, he doesn't really do early starts!"

Jorge laughed as he confirmed that nine in the morning is still incredibly early.

With care to shield the code from the boys Jorge unlocked the studio. Knowing that if these guys had access, they would burn themselves out within the first two days. He had to teach them discipline, not in the way he had to with most bands but the opposite!

"Take a break, live your life!"

That thought alone made him chuckle,

"You guys will be ready for a gig before Shy realises."

He happily called back as he headed to get himself a black coffee,

"I might put you in for a gig early!"

He listened carefully for a response, half watching them in the reflection from the studio windows.

"That'd be great" was the response in unison,

Paul went on to explain that they had just done ten gigs in three weeks, the last two of which were the ones Jo had seen,

"Great so you are match ready? Let us see how today goes." Jim and Paul almost bounced to their instruments.

Jim spent three quarters of an hour setting up three kits to the same specifications, one Maple, One Birch and most interestingly for Jorge, the acoustic set with the electronic triggers, Nic usually set this one up to show drummers how things could sound with the help of tech but must of the drummers these days instantly refused. Jim had often been told that he needed different kits, living in a tiny flat in London rather made that impossible. His drum kit was also his dining table as it was. There was a different kit at the rehearsal studio they used but it was so old that he wasn't certain who had made it.

Jack burst through the doors with a really loud "Good Morning Spain" and seeing Jorge at the desk he came straight over with a collection of paper,

"You said I should write everything. So, I have". He almost cried with pride like a child just collecting his first star from a primary school teacher, Jorge slowly took his headphones off and reached out for the notes. Large sections had been scribbled through but over the next few hours, he would make sure he read those too. In his experience, often the early rejected notes had come back to create a hit. He would have to remind Jack not to delete anything.

When Leonard arrived, five minutes before nine, Jorge hit save on the files he had been working on and turned to the band.

"OK guys, listen up. I have a mission for you this morning, I'm going to give you five songs. I know you aren't a covers band, but I want to hear you do these songs. It's just so I can work out what sounds you like. You might tell me what you think you sound like, but those influences will have come from a variety of places, this is the quickest way for me to work out what you really sound like.

"Once I give you the songs, no arguing, those are the songs I want to hear. I'll give you until two o'clock this afternoon when I'll be back to hear them. Nic will be here soon and so if you want any changes to the tech or advice on any of the instruments, he'll give you everything. At two o'clock I want a performance of all five songs. Do what you want with them, I'm going to leave you to it, remember, they need to be ready at two." He flipped a folder onto the table and left the room.

They all rushed over and stood as Jack opened the folder, He took a second, reading the titles himself before exhaling slowly. Looking around at the others, he slowly read the list of five disparate songs, a classic blues track, an 80's track with a solid beat but a rather dark twist, a pure pop rock song, a dance, pop hit and the latest hit from the biggest American female singer of the time.

"What the… How on Earth are we going to do those? I only know one of them."

"I know them," Jim said "but…" he left the sentence trailing. Paul had picked up the folder and out fell a memory stick,

"I guess these are the songs let's have a listen", Paul inserted the stick into the computer and a whole load of files popped up on the screen, the finished songs together with a demo version and each individual instruments' part isolated. He played each song through, every one of them listening intently in a way that Jim didn't think he'd ever listened to music before. Paul had suggested that they each made notes as they were listening, and he and Jack were both scribbling frantically. Once they had listened to all five Jack asked for their comments,

"So, what are we going to change?" Paul was the first to respond.

"OK five songs, let's just make it like a gig. First two have to be fast, the middle songs and then a pile-driver to finish."

"Sounds good" agreed Jim, Leonard was nodding,

"I remember a cover version of track two that made it more industrial, can you play that?" Leonard asked. Paul searched and found the song and the sound of teenage angst leapt through the speakers.

"I like that version, we could open with that starting slowly with just Jack doing the spoken word intro or, even just a bit of guitar and build up, if we get the rhythms right it might even go straight into the Shake song, he didn't say we had to do the whole song." Paul was taking on his usual role of leader.

"Yeah, that'll sound great, clashing both of those works, ok, let's try two, five, one four three and see if that works as an order. Does anyone have any other ideas?"

"I might need to play with some of the lyrics a bit" Jack added,

"Right let's take an hour or so, let each of us practice through our parts and then we'll play them all together and see where we are at, that will give us another couple of hours to refine them further.

"As for the merge, let us all think where and how we join those first two and we'll see if we all agree." They all nodded and headed off to their own corners. For the next hour they all worked, they didn't have long to learn five new songs. Occasionally one would call over to the others for an opinion on a certain part or, most commonly to ask Paul to tell them what notes something was, Jack had asked Nic if he could use the piano and had been led away to a separate room, by the time he returned he had earned himself the nickname Elton.

Paul was watching the clock and at 10:45am he called them all together,

"OK, I don't know about you guys but, I reckon we've got this, the only decision is where we merge those first two, has anyone got a strong want?"

"Did anyone else get Guns N' Roses vibes from the bridge?" Jim picked up, "we could pretty much copy the cover until there and then bring in the GNR style chorus and go straight into the pop but keeping that vibe running?" As he finished talking, Paul started playing the chorus and he saw Jack and Leonard's approval, Nic was just sitting back, he knew that Jorge would watch all this later, there was always a camera and a microphone running in the room, not only for security but so that when a band said that they wanted to do something like they had last week, even if no-one remembered exactly how it had sounded, they would be able to find it. It might take most of a week to find but, they'd find it. Nic knew that Jorge really enjoyed seeing the results of this test. It let him know more about how much work a band needed but he knew that this band were the real deal. At two minutes to two, Nic flicked the switch as he had done with all of Jorge's previous new bands.

All the lights in the studio went down. The projector screen at the back lit up with the message, "Two minutes to stage time, band to stage positions please" and a clock started. The band hadn't noticed that Nic had been quietly setting up the stage, throughout the morning. Certain instruments were located at appropriate places together with screens containing either the music, or the lyrics for the songs they had been working on. They raced like children to the stage area and immediately picked up and adopted their stage personas. As the clock reached zero, a single light lit up on Jack.

He sang. As the rest of the band kicked in the whole studio lit up with a display worthy of Knebworth. The band were buzzing with energy and flying around the stage giggling at each other whilst absolutely nailing the songs. Jack forgot the words at one point, Jim dropped a stick, even Paul made a couple of mistakes but they were so wrapped up in the noise they were making that it really didn't matter, the volume, the heat of the lights and just the pure joy of the experience carried them through the next 15 minutes. As they reached Leonard's 'Massive Ending' to their finale, Nic played a recording of a huge crowd cheering for more as the band rushed to hug each other. Above all the noise they could hear Jorge shouting and clapping

"More" he kept booming - "What's your encore?"

"Tube station" called Jack and they all raced back to their kit to run through it but this time with just the normal fluorescent lighting. Jorge looked across to Shy and Jo who had arrived spot on 2pm as ordered and had stayed hidden by Nic's desk.

"What can I do with them?" He called, "They want to play!"

Shy walked over and shook Jorge's hand,

"You like them?" he asked. The response he got was just a laugh as he boomed,

"They are playing tonight at Manuel's, the set you just heard." The band looked at him, "Yes, you heard me, you are on stage at 11:30pm, there is a local band first, they will have lots of fans, you come in and blow them away with exactly that set, Nic arranged the lighting rig to match theirs so that will be the same except for a few little improvements and we'll arrange some lighting for your encore. You might want another couple of songs in your heads if you need more but, I want you just to do those six as your target. You can work until five, we'll stop for an enforced sleep then meet again at nine for food and then go there. Enjoy boys!"

Paul didn't know whether to be happy or angry, he had loved ripping through those songs with absolutely no pressure, feeling the joy of playing with the lights and the sound but, they had never played a gig without enough rehearsal, he always found playing in front of an audience much harder. Jorge had tried to reassure him,

"You boys can all play, some things come better without practice, don't refuse to improvise, make things happen, don't wait for things to occur and react, just go with how it feels." Paul wasn't sure if Jorge was referring just to the gig or to life as a whole, he had always worried more about the details.

Paul thought through the flow of the songs, they had messed up the transition from one to another a few times, but he thought that they had settled into the rhythm. By the enforced curfew he was feeling more confident. Jack was absolutely buzzing with excitement. He was always energetic but Paul hadn't seen him this excited since that time the ice cream van appeared at a summer fair where they had agreed to play a few songs. Whilst the band kept playing, he had run over, ordered a '99 and then continued with the song using his ice cream cone as a pretend microphone.

"Who knew I was better than Taylor Swift?" Jack laughed as they left the studio for their enforced rest.

Jo had had little to do all day except for a quick run down to the local shop for a few extra bottles of 'pop'. She thought that she was probably the only person in the world to still call soft drinks pop, but that was an element of her childhood that she didn't want to let go. Knowing that she wouldn't sleep during the curfew she took a shower, checked the time and, realising that she still had three hours before she would need to get ready to go out, went to look for Shy. There was no answer at his door, so headed out to the gardens. Shy had warned her that Jorge would insist on his afternoon break but, apart from that, they knew he was the best in Europe at what he did.

The smell of the flowers in the gardens amazed her, everything smelt so inviting, giving her the feeling that this was the only place to be at that moment. She had been told to make sure the boys did not know that they could leave their rooms, but the rules did not apply to her. Shy was prowling along the far side of the gardens. An orchard of orange trees stretched far into the distance behind him, his laptop and a drink were sat on a wooden table under the shade of a large, old, wrinkled tree. It looked a little like the willow tree she remembered from the pub garden that she grew up with.

Every Sunday during the summer the family would head to the country pub where she would be given a proper bottle of cola and a straw. She would sit at table 6, under the willow tree, alongside the pond and she would watch the ducks squabble over the crisps. Too many people would throw them food - and the rats that would clean up afterwards. At least the rats would usually wait until the people had moved back. She would sit and wait for her father to come out with his friends, they would play all the latest hits from the outdoor stage on the far side of the garden. Every now and again a barmaid would come out to admire her drawings and bring her another coke, each time asking her if she knew her table number and she would point to the number crudely hammered into the wood and she would draw her finger around the figure.

"Something good?" Shy asked as he appeared at the table, Jo smiled,

"How are you?" She knew the answer, they both knew the answer, this band were exactly what they had been hoping for and she could tell when Shy was happy. He sat down and nodded to his phone,

"I've just spoken to the office, we're going to do the whole country but just the cities, we don't want to burn these guys out and they don't need the practice, do you agree?"

It was exactly the plan that she had had in her mind. They

needed a profile and needed to be seen but didn't need to experience any of the negative sides of touring now. The band had told her they had about 30 songs of their own. Half of which they admitted that they had either never performed or had stopped performing live. Jo knew that a good producer should be able to find enough there to get going with a record. The band were dedicated enough that an album would not take long to produce so it was important to create that buzz quickly.

"I was going to see if Mick would let us have a live set on the radio when we get back" she suggested. Shy agreed,

"The story is simple, back from Spain and ready to go, Mary is booked to come out to do photos next week. We can move really quick here."

They were both still discussing work when the boys appeared. Jorge was just behind and the familiar sound of a delivery boy on a scooter appeared at the very second Jorge stepped into the sunlight.

"Pizza, the ambrosia of the Gods" he announced as if calling to the Gods themselves.

The bike came straight up to the table before unloading a whole tower of pizza boxes. Jo went to get more drinks as the boys set about their meal. The evening was full of joy. It was more the vibe of a high-class university barbecue than a wild rock and roll party. The sounds of the birds singing in the trees was only disturbed by the honking of horns as two people carriers and a transit van drove across the garden.

"Nic has packed your kit, if you need anything personal,

get it now, and then if you could give Nic a hand, has Jo given you outfits?" Jorge asked looking over at Jo, she blushed realising that she hadn't even thought of costumes. She had a whole folder of 'rock star' outfits and designers ready to call to dress her bands but there was something about these guys that just didn't need it. She thought quickly,

"I think they should just be themselves tonight, no need to try too hard, they are just having fun."

She almost convinced herself that she had planned that, but Jorge just shrugged his shoulders and turned to the van. It would only be Shy that knew that she hadn't planned it that way. Once they were all packed up, Nic, Jo and Shy hopped into the second car, leaving the first for the band knowing that Jorge would drive himself. Jorge had one of the best collections of sports cars in Spain, he would choose his car based on the venue that they were heading to. Shy was pleased that the band did not know that as he saw Jorge pull around to the front of the convoy at the wheel of his Humvee.

Chapter 13
A Seat at the Table

Adam had had a shower and got dressed for the gig, He had been asked if he had any clothes in which he could hide a gun. That was something he had never considered before. It was easy enough for Bruce Willis or The Rock to tuck a weapon into their jeans, Adam had never considered that it might have been with the help of the wardrobe department. The best he could think of was his jacket, it had pockets on both the inside and outside but, the weight of a gun might be a bit obvious. Sam took his jacket and returned having secreted a small pistol in one pocket and a box of bullets in the other.

"I'm afraid you'll need to keep your jacket with you, it might get hot but, whatever you do, keep this safe" she laughed as she handed the jacket back, "Unless you want to borrow a handbag." He considered a bag for a nanosecond but,

"No, thanks."

Sam came out of her room, "Do I drive, or do we get a taxi?" She asked, "I really could do with a drink but, that leaves us stranded if we need to drive somewhere else" she added.

"I think we should have a car", Tilly agreed.

"I'll drive" Adam leapt in, regretting it as soon as he did. He had never driven on the wrong side of the road, he had never had a reason to drive 'much' above the speed limit and, he had seen Sam's collection of cars which scared him more. The girls looked at each other weighing up their options,

"OK" Sam said, "let's pick a car for you." They headed to the lift and Adam hoped that no-one could detect just how scared he was,

"I think I have the right car for you, it's the easiest to drive". She headed to a cupboard and, placing her hand onto the pad, the door swung open revealing the keys. She threw him what felt like a pretty old and fairly basic key before leading him towards a corner of the garage.

"Here, do you like it?" Sam laughed as she asked the question, it was a van which, with only a few small amendments, could quite easily have been taken from a film version of Scooby Doo.

"There is space for all of us and some luggage, and, if we all decide to drink, we can sleep and drive home tomorrow!"

This now felt more like a holiday, they were all laughing as Sam shouted at him to stay on the right side of the road but not too close to the kerb and to go faster, he was driving like a tourist. Tilly was giving directions from her phone, they thought it better that Adam didn't try to look at the map. It had taken him a couple of roundabouts to get used to going the 'wrong' way around but otherwise Sam didn't have to shout too many times. He hoped that Tilly wouldn't drink too much because he didn't fancy his chances of finding his way back in the dark.

Eventually the venue appeared on the horizon and a nice big space allowed Adam to drive straight into a parking spot. The car park was about two thirds full. There were an awful lot of scooters but also a selection of other motorbikes, and just a small number of cars. The music was throbbing through the speakers at the front of the bar where a small handful of people were sat around picnic tables. Behind the villa, waves of purple, green and yellow light rose above the roof line pulsing with the beat of the music. The genteel country villa, with its hand painted signs and wrought iron fencing, looked like it was under attack by an army of UFO's. They walked through an archway wrapped with bright plastic flowers into a large garden full of picnic tables and chairs.

Whilst some tables housed the debris of previous drinkers, most were full of groups with pitchers of cocktails, beer and baskets of food. At one end of the garden stood a stage which appeared to have been created from anything that could be scavenged from the local allotment. Scaffold poles held a lighting rig above the stage and speakers that looked powerful enough to send the stage itself flying into the middle of next week. A crowd was beginning to gather in front of the stage in a space probably big enough to accommodate more than a hundred people Adam estimated, at least one hundred and fifty more were sat at the tables around.

As they took their seats, a waitress appeared at the table, Tilly ordered drinks for them all, asking Adam if he wanted a beer or not, her comment that they could sleep in the van sounded almost like an invitation,

"I'll just have a diet Coke please," he offered half to Tilly and half to the waitress. "I'm not a big drinker and just in case we have to drive" he explained. Tilly smiled and confirmed something to the waitress which made her look at Adam and smile too. He really wanted to know what she had said but thought it better not to ask. Sam had been scanning the faces around them for anyone she recognised. There were a couple of faces she knew, not well enough to talk to but people who would get a nod if they came close enough.

There were a couple of local celebrities, the girl who did the weather on the local channel was at one of the closest tables to the stage and on the other side, a couple of the less great footballers from the local team. Adam was fairly certain that he had spotted a couple of footballers from England at another table, but he couldn't be certain, he had more noticed the number of young ladies milling about the table before he had noticed the two men with expensive looking shades and tattoos. Sam gave Tilly and Adam a brief history of the venue before their drinks arrived.

As the drinks arrived cheers broke out at the front of the stage as an elderly man with the skin of a raisin walked out onto the stage. A pair of bright pink trousers held up with a leather belt exactly the same colour as his skin and a bright yellow hat were all that he wore. He strode to the front stage with a Liam Gallagheresque swagger and, after adjusting the microphone to his height, he addressed the crowd. Adam took a sip of his drink, confused by the one giant ice cube that sat on top. He turned to see if either of the girls had noticed him spill a little as he pulled the glass away, thankfully, they were both watching the stage.

The man was still babbling on and on, getting quicker and a little louder with almost every sentence, occasional cheers were all that slowed him down, "El Clima" he called, half the crowd looked to the table where the weather presenter was sat and a small cheer erupted. It seemed as if every attendee was going to get a welcome, some more chat and he heard "Valencia" called before a bigger cheer and the footballer's table lifted their drinks in recognition, more chat was followed by "West Ham" Yes thought Adam, he had kind of recognised them but they weren't big enough stars for him to be able to name. More chat followed from the host in a rather hushed tone before Adam heard Sam's name being called, a babble then a cheer broke out as a few hundred necks started spinning looking for her before almost everyone was staring at their table.

Sam gave an embarrassed wave and half blew a kiss at the old man on stage, Sam immediately turned to Adam and apologised,

"I thought they wouldn't spot me."

Adam was shocked, yes, he knew that she was rich, but he hadn't guessed that she also had this level of fame. He thought that he really ought to ask more questions but before he could think, the man had shouted another two words. The entire site was rocked by the sound of drums and trombones.

The music was infectious and within a few seconds even those seated at the back were nodding their heads and tapping their feet. The rhythms had been joined by guitars and trumpets and a host of other instruments and there seemed to be at least three singers. Adam wanted to enjoy the music. He knew that if they had a record out he would be downloading it tonight but he was also nervously watching everyone around him. He had almost forgotten why they were there with the party atmosphere but now that Sam had been identified he felt even more protective of her, and Tilly.

Sam clearly hadn't wanted the attention and she too seemed on edge. She was trying hard to look like she was having fun and enjoying her drink, which had been refreshed by the waitress. If the people all knew her then surely, they would all know Jada too, and perhaps they would be wondering why Sam was here and Jada not, or maybe no-one knew Jada and that was why there wasn't more fuss as to why she was missing at all. Adam had so many questions. He hadn't liked to ask too much but as he was getting more involved, he felt that he needed to know more. Maybe he needed to know just to keep himself safe.

He now felt like a personal bodyguard and was scanning

every face in the crowd that turned towards them, every person that walked past, which was awkward as it seemed that they were almost in a direct line between the stage and the toilets. Girls would glimpse as they passed, Boys would look harder, each one trying to look extra cool for Sam and Tilly. Then they would look at Adam and he could feel them wondering how he had earned a seat at the table.

The energy in the venue was rising with each song. A haze was appearing in front of the lights as steam rose from the throng at the front. Adam was still scanning the crowd as his attention was taken with the arrival of a new group, maybe ten people were being ushered through the crowd by a number of the venue staff. They were fighting their way to a space on the far side where three pristine white tables had been kept clear. The area was separated by the kind of rope that Adam had felt if it were at Boxpark Croydon wouldn't have kept even the quietest of attendees from crossing and helping themselves to the bottles and food that had been left on the tables.

Adam had been analysing the group, trying to work out who they might be and what they were doing. Sam had denied recognising any of them, as had Tilly. They certainly weren't film stars or sports people although the one at the front could probably have been either. He guessed they must be a band although none of the crowd had shown any real recognition. Another diet coke had appeared alongside the one he still hadn't started which was itself alongside one he had only just begun - although the Titanic sized ice cube in it had now shrunk to a more regular ice cube size.

The band onstage had shown no sign of letting things slow down at all, he now understood the need for the three singers, each one of them had been jumping and running across the stage and each one was drenched in sweat. Adam had had to remove his jacket but the look from Sam as he had done so reminded him of how close he needed to keep it and so it was now laid gently across his legs. The weight of the gun in the pocket feeling both reassuring and scary in equal parts. He had always expected a gun to feel cold, but he suspected that cold steel probably related to swords and cold blood, well blood was always the same temperature, wasn't it?

His attention turned back to scanning the crowd as he checked that Sam and Tilly were both still watching the band. He suddenly felt the icy chill that he had previously only ever felt watching films on tv. He reminded himself, this was real. The three from the car were all sitting at one of the tables. Near to the plastic flower gateway they had walked through earlier. They can't have been there long. Adam remembered seeing a group of six at that table but now it was the three he had seen earlier and a new fourth person, an older woman, a little older than the moustachioed driver dressed in a perfectly white suit and oversized sunglasses. Adam nudged Tilly and gestured, trying to whisper in her ear who he was pointing out and why before realising that even talking at a normal volume he would not be heard over the band. He chose to write a note on his phone which Tilly read and immediately passed to Sam who read it and then looked in the direction Adam had indicated. She quickly deleted the message before checking to see if anyone else could have seen the screen. Assured that nothing looked out of the ordinary she wrote a name into the phone and reaching to hand it back to Adam she called out "Google."

With his fingers almost quivering, Adam nervously misspelled the name twice before realising that he could just copy and paste Sam's text into the web search. That coldness returned as he looked at the first result. The picture on screen looked back at him with the confidence only found in a model's head shot. That of a person who believes that everyone will love them so of course they will pose for this photo. Lieutenant-Colonel Bally, Guardia Civil.

The next story leapt out even more sharply. Adam quickly read the summary of the article before looking back to the table where they all looked in a very different mood to those around them. The band had finished a particularly fast and energetic song which most of the crowd had chosen to shout along to. It was the kind of song that Adam felt really should be closing a set. The singer started speaking to the crowd again, lots of cheering ensued, and many in the crowd started to look across at the group that had arrived earlier. Adam looked to Tilly,

"They are saying that they'd normally go off and wait to be called back for an encore now but, apparently Manuel has asked them to just play their encore straight because they have these special guests from England…" she explained pointing to the late arrivals.

"Wow, bold move" he said, "following this band will not be easy". He looked back at the Lieutenant-Colonel who also looked surprised. The band accepted the crowds' cheers as approval and played on.

A team of staff approached the new band and escorted them back to the Villa although, this time leading them behind the crowd rather than through it. He was only distracted for a brief moment before looking back to the Colonel's table. The girl appeared to be watching the band, the younger man seemed to be more interested in watching the table of footballers, the Colonel and the woman in white were both engaged in what looked to be quite a difficult discussion. Adam wasn't sure if their discomfort was caused by the topic of conversation or simply because they probably couldn't hear each other above the cacophony coming from the stage. Within a couple of minutes, the crowd were cheering frantically as the band gave a final blare. The brass players looked fit to burst, the guitarists had their instruments above their heads and all three singers were rushing across the stage thanking as many people as they can.

Chapter 14

You Dress Me Up

Shy had told Jo that Jorge had arranged most things but the moment she had met Manuel, she knew that she was dealing with someone who could fix anything. Manuel himself had appeared the very second their car had pulled onto the drive. Unmissable in that bright yellow hat and pink trousers, he had rushed to shake Jorge's hand before waving his team of six men towards the van. Each one of his staff looked like they had spent the last thousand days lifting weights and the last thousand nights on a tanning machine. Jo had a new venue and cast to add to her 'promotional videos folder' she already knew that this would certainly not be her only visit to this venue.

Jorge brought Manuel straight over to meet her and Shy. She had been expecting to receive a kiss on the cheek, but she laughed as Shy received one too, he certainly had not been expecting it. Manuel enthused about how much he had heard about Shy and how much he was looking forward to seeing… he floundered then for the first time. He could not pronounce the band's name with his heavy Spanish accent and Jo immediately registered that they needed to consider another name promptly.

The band had clearly enjoyed the drive, Jo knew it was her job to keep that vibe going, it had taken them a little longer to get out of the van but as soon as they did Manuel rushed over and kissed each of them in the way that he had kissed Shy before expressing how pleased he was to see them. He waved at the villa and three of the prettiest girls Jo had ever seen appeared to show them to their table. Jack immediately went into full glamour rock star mode with the full emphasis on the STAR, reaching out his hand willing to be led by the blonde with long legs who took control of him. The others appeared a bit more hesitant but, looking around at the appearance of the venue and of the welcome, Jo knew that each of them would want to repay Manuel's hospitality with a great gig.

They were led into the villa and shown their 'area' of three rooms. The first room was almost empty except for mirrors, a couple of dressing tables and a couple of clothes racks, the second had amplifiers and instruments laid out and a third had a table full of bottles and food. A collection of sofas and armchairs, a pool table and a pinball machine completed the perfect space. Within seconds and before they could settle, they were led straight outside into a scene that Jo had only ever believed happened in films or music videos. A cast of beautiful people were dancing and jumping and generally having a wonderful time as a band that visually looked like a cross between the Beach Boys and a German oompah band played very, very loudly. The three girls had now been met by four boys who were clearing the crowd for them to walk to their VIP area.

By the time they reached their seats, the whole group were just laughing. The band were carried along with the joy of the crowd they had been taken through, the heat, the energy and the sound coming from the stage was enough to get the dead dancing. Jo was in no doubt about why Jorge had wanted to bring them here, tonight was going to be amazing. She turned to Shy who was grinning from ear to ear and obviously enjoying the attention that he had received as they followed the band. He would tell anyone who would listen that he was happy to be backstage and let the bands take the limelight. Anyone that knew Shy also knew that he wasn't afraid of standing in front of either a crowd or a camera and, his smiles always let everyone know that he enjoyed the buzz around him and his bands.

"Wow, what an ending" Shy thought as the oompah band reached their crescendo. Shy had been starting to worry more about whether his band were ready for the atmosphere in front of them. He was always like this when one of his bands were near stage time. He had seen plenty of hugely confident people get nervous before a gig and he knew that if he were going onstage, he would be feeling awful now. He gave himself confidence however by claiming that his nerves were simply because things were out of his control. Although he was then dependent on the band to cope, he knew that it was his responsibility to ensure that the band would be ready and able to deal with any eventuality. As the band had been taken back to their area for their final preparations, Shy had given all of the control to Manuel and Nic, he knew Nic had every eventuality covered with the sound and lights and Manuel certainly knew how to run a venue. Right now, between worrying about how the next 20 or 30 minutes were going to go he was also wondering if the oompah band had ever played in England. Would they want to? Would a British crowd need to understand whatever it was they were singing about? Shy certainly didn't think so after that gig, but crowds in Camden had a very different vibe and as for Liverpool. Maybe some things were best left on holiday.

Manuel appeared on the stage, still looking like a mad uncle who had got too carried away at a wedding, and the crowd cheered louder. Shy studied the scene. The area around him looked like a scene from any town centre the morning after an England world cup win, plastic chairs were waiting for a passer-by to sit in them, drinks were waiting for someone to finish them and flowers sat forlorn, desperately waiting for someone to present them to another to cement their love for the night. He looked at Jo on the other side of the table, she had stood with expectation; ready for the band to appear onstage. Manuel was laughing as he reached the microphone, his team in black shirts, smarter than any road crew and certainly healthier than any crew Jo had seen previously, were rushing to clear the stage of microphones, amps and the flags that had decorated the stage previously. They left the stage looking completely bare but, Jo thought this simply added to the rock and roll vibe, a bare stage, no frills and the crowd were already warmed up, they hadn't been expecting extra entertainment, so they had nothing to lose.

Jo was confident that the energy found in the heat tonight would far outweigh the response of a crowd who hadn't heard of them at King Tut's in Glasgow and therefore was probably the best way to see the band as she was certain they would appear in a few years, when surely everyone will be jumping to their songs. Manuel was still excitedly chatting away and the crowd were laughing and cheering. Jo hoped he was saying good things. She felt relieved to see Jorge approaching her, smiling and laughing, "He's the best, I'll translate it all for you later - but he never just does what I ask him to!" Jorge grabbed a chair and spun it towards the stage and sat down in one smooth movement with a confidence and panache that was noticed by a number of the people sitting nearby. Manuel was enticing the crowd to get even louder. Jo saw Jim take his seat at the drum kit, he looked nervous but, he had always looked the most nervous of the group, she hoped she hadn't given them too much. Shy now came and stood next to her, they had both seen the shadows moving at the side of the stage and knew the band were now just waiting for Manuel. Finally, he raised his hat, looked to the wings and announced… "My English Friends'"

Jo laughed, he had been professional enough to not try to pronounce their name, she will need to work on a name, the crowd were already cheering as Jack slowly ambled onto the stage as cool as you like, rolling all the way across to the furthest corner looking at the same time as if he was completely lost and didn't know that three hundred people were watching him and, looking like this was his front room, he had personally invited every one and he was now just looking for the one person before he would speak. He turned back towards the microphone in the centre of the stage and as he did so he spoke the intro to the first song. Nic's light show had burst into action by the time he screamed 'I FEED IT' and the crowd were completely trapped in his web. Jo hadn't even noticed Paul and Leonard appear alongside him but, if the previous band had nailed their closer, this was how you opened. By the time they had hit their second song, the whole crowd were moving as one, there was surprise as each individual recognised the song they were now hearing quickly followed by delight. Hands were raised, drinks were spilt and legends were made. Jo and Shy were both just laughing at all they could see.

The change in the lighting effects had made it harder for Adam to see around the crowd, he guessed with the number of people on stage the previous lighting had been fairly steady, that and the brightness of the moonlight meant that he had been happily able to identify all those around him but now, he could only see shadows. The lights would occasionally shoot into the crowd but now that was so bright that by the time his eyes had adjusted enough, they had shot past again, all he knew for sure was that the team of Police were still there. He was trying hard not to be distracted by the music, he had to admit that he had loved the first band, but this second group were absolutely phenomenal. As he looked across to Tilly and Sam he dreamed that they really were his friends and that this was just a normal night but, he really couldn't help remembering that he had a gun in his pocket and he was expecting something to happen at any moment.

Jim had been trying to get the attention of the crew, he was kicking so hard he was worried that he was going to fall off the back of the stage, he couldn't believe how amazing this gig felt, he had only been in the band for a couple of months. He had played drums in a variety of Indian drum groups at weddings, celebrations and 'cultural events' and for a while he played with a jazz quartet. It was a meeting with Leonard at a council event at the local Town Hall that led him to go to watch the band where he first offered to play drums for them.

He had been brought up playing traditional drums with his family and it was only after 'Uncle Shyamal' had bought him his first kit that he had ever considered that he might be able to play 'western drums' too. He remembered Shy telling him that he had rhythm and to imagine the power he could have with more things to hit. And now here he was. He could see Uncle Shy standing proudly and he wished that his father could see him now, he looked at the rest of HIS band and felt a wave of emotion that he had never felt before. There was nothing difficult for him as he was rocking the standard beat through their last new track and so was taking the chance to look all around him, he wanted to remember every face, every smile.

Everything went black, pitch black. He heard the sound of his sticks hit the drum skin, but it was no longer amplified. He heard Jack's voice, a little huskier than it had been earlier in the day. He tried to look to see if he should keep playing but all that he could see was the very feint outline of the buildings in the distance. He didn't want to move for fear of falling off of the back of the stage.

Adam immediately grabbed his gun and moved closer to Sam and Tilly, an instinctive move to protect, he knew that he had no idea how he should respond, his instinct was to just sit and wait for the lights to come on, but something inside told him that that was what the old Adam would have done, he had to get them moving, it seemed that Sam was already thinking the same thing. They both grabbed Tilly and led their way back towards the villa, Adam was searching through the darkness for the police table, he saw in the darkness at least six people wearing helmets come through the gateway and surround the Lieutenant-Colonel who had stood and looked like he was giving orders. Adam had paused watching this occur when he felt a tug on his sleeve from Tilly. Turning towards her he saw that they too now had a group of attendees, all taller than him and all dressed in full military terrorist chic with their faces fully covered, helmets, body armour and big, big guns pointing straight at them. With one word shouted at them Tilly and Sam both dropped to their knees. Adam was slower to react and felt the crack as he was hit in the back of the head.

Chapter 15
How To Roll Down The Stairs

When he awoke, he felt the roughness of the rudimentary hood catch on the stubble on his chin. He felt the plastic digging into his wrists where his hands were bound with a cable tie in front of him, he tried to move and found his legs were similarly bound. He had no idea where he was or whether he was alone, he lay still trying to listen for any other sounds, a clue as to where he might be. Hooded, cuffed and very hot. Adam sensed rather than felt the sweat covering his back, he had always hated the way his back got sweaty, but he stopped himself from thinking about that.

"If I make a sound, they will know that I am awake, but who are they? What if there is no-one there and I am just waiting for someone to release me? If I try to move to see if I can loosen the ties then, well, if I am being watched then they might think that I am trying to escape, and they will shoot me. What if the girls are here too but they are injured? Then I am just laid here whilst they are bleeding to death."

He thought about that for too long before realising that there really was nothing he could do about that unless someone else was there. In fact, there was nothing he could do about anything unless someone was able to help. He pulled his legs across to stand up before he felt the sharp edge of the cable pull tighter around his ankle. He tried to sit himself up but couldn't find the leverage in his shoulder. Laughing out loud he imagined someone watching him rolling around like a fish in a bucket. As soon as he had that thought he realised that that was exactly what he was. He had no experience of guns or investigation, kidnapping and millionaires. He had thought that he was running away from London to find out who he was, not what he wasn't. His aim had been to have an adventure but that to him was seeing a different view and eating in a restaurant that didn't have steak and ale pie on the menu. How did Bond or Bourne know how to respond to these scenarios? Was there a training course, were they taught by escapologists how to escape from handcuffs? Was there a big gymnastics room where they could practice the exact kind of run and somersault to avoid gunfire and then how to roll down the stairs?

Or did they just make it up like he was now doing? More pertinent to Adam was the fact that, now that he had moved even just a little bit, he wanted to visit the bathroom. How long would it be before he would allow himself to embarrass himself completely? He took stock of his position. Someone had tied his hands and legs, he had something over his head, but it wasn't tight and, with the right angle, he might be able to shuffle that off. He hadn't hit a wall yet, so he wasn't in a coffin, would a coffin be hot or cold? He was definitely hot but, he was in Spain so that wasn't surprising. Well, perhaps he wasn't in Spain, he could be anywhere, they could have taken him anywhere. No, he realised that he was still in his clothes and, if it had been that long then he would have surely needed to urinate previously. He didn't feel wet so that was just one positive. Oh, but now he thought of that again.

Deciding that dying would alleviate any embarrassment of wetting himself, he decided to act before he couldn't control himself for any longer. Pushing his head against the floor caused enough friction to move the hood a little, and with the limited use his arms were allowed, he discovered that not only were his hands tied to each other but that something was holding them to his belt too. Within a minute or so, he had lifted the hood enough that he could see around him. Alone, the bare concrete floor led to what looked like plasterboard walls, but this wasn't just a cell or a storeroom. Posters and framed prints were on the wall, he could see two desks on which stood a pot plant and an open packet of biscuits as well as computers and the usual office paraphernalia. He looked for anything that might help his situation.

From his position on the floor, he could see the quantity of chewing gum stuck to the underside of the battered desk, above which he could see a phone. He didn't know who to call and even then, what would he say? His first thought was the police. It always would have been but, why had Sam been so against calling them and why were they being watched by the police? Tilly had explained that Spain has two separate police forces but, he hadn't really been paying enough attention to understand what the differences were. Even so, if he called 112, he had no idea which department that call would go to. He snaked his way towards the wall. How did they make this look so glamorous in the films? He knew that he wasn't exactly film star, six pack material but he didn't think that he was that unfit.

Leaning against the wall he managed to get into a position where he was able to get onto his knees, now, separating each knee as far as he could with his ankles tied together and with his hands on the floor in front for balance, he managed to waddle to the chair and, pushing the chair against the wall, he managed to use that chair to push himself back onto his heels and then stand. He looked to the ceiling and sighed in relief but that only made his desire to urinate stronger. He was wary about stepping too far from the wall, but there was no toilet here, so he had to reach the door. He stumbled as he reached the door frame but was able to keep himself upright. Placing his shoulder against the door frame, the door swung open with the slightest of touches.

The clamour in the hallway and the shouting both surprised him and hurt his ears with its volume. He stopped, wobbling a little for balance, "I'm terribly sorry but I need to visit the bathroom." he found himself saying. "Terribly sorry?" he thought to himself, why should he be sorry? And visit the bathroom when you think of it is an odd phrase too. There were two guards outside his room and another two a little further down the corridor. The corridor itself looked like he would expect any office block to look like. The only thing making it look any different to England were the posters on the wall and the fact that through the window he could see a scene that definitely wasn't Milton Keynes.

The guards nodded and whilst one picked up a pair of scissors and cut through the tie around his ankles, the other reminded Adam of a Spanish Ed Sheeran with the same haircut and the same cheerful looking face. The face was rather incongruous with the ease with which he held that gun. Once his feet were free Adam looked to his hands and the guard cut those free too. Eduardo, as Adam had named him, gestured him along the corridor. The other guard, who didn't seem to suit any name, followed too after picking up his gun.

"Here" the grunted command came. They had reached a door upon which Adam was relieved to find had the common pictogram he was so happy to see. Opening the door he stepped inside, immediately worrying that they would follow him in. He knew that he needed to go but what if he was being watched? Was he desperate enough? He took another step and was pleased to hear the door start to shut behind him. He instinctively headed towards the urinals, but he thought, should he sit down? It had been a while, he never usually used public toilets, but he never usually found himself in any of these situations.

He walked to the sink almost fixated by the look on his own

face. Wanting to know the answer to so many questions but, he didn't know how long he would have to think. First things first he thought and headed to the urinal. The relief that he felt was almost enough to take him away from the whole situation. At the sinks afterwards, he was looking at himself in the mirror, his hands now getting cold from the water that he was just letting run over him. He had washed his face and his hands, all the way up to the elbow, he wasn't sure why he went so far up. He hadn't needed the hand washing lessons when the pandemic had arrived but, he didn't usually wash all the way to his elbows. He washed his face again.

The door swung openly violently, well, as violently as a door can when it has a heavy self-closer on it. Adam knew what the guard had meant the effect to be but, the disappointment in the guard's face made Adam laugh a little. He had always thought that perhaps the humour the heroes had found during films may in real life be pure bravado and now he knew for certain that that laugh was.

He felt his bravery growing though, he was telling himself that he had no reason to feel scared. Yes, he was surrounded by heavily armed people. Yes, he had no idea where he was and, even if he did know it would only be a name. He barely knew the name of the country he was in and, yes, he was possibly in a whole world of trouble but, was that the worst that could happen? They could kill him but, although both of his parents were still alive, he hadn't actually told them that he was leaving his job and running away. They would read the story in the news and maybe wonder how things had led to the situation where their son had died, and they had no idea that he wasn't just doing his regular job.

He hoped that at least a couple of people would raise a glass and nod his way as they thought about him when they read the news. He and the friend who had driven him to the airport would share news of celebrities that died that way, a name, a nod and a raising of the glass. Although over recent years that had become more the 'clinking beer' emoji followed by the name. The nicer the person was, the more beer emoji's they got. He wondered how many he would deserve, probably only one maximum. "Ho Hum, let's see what I've got coming." He felt tall as he wandered down the corridor, the guards were no shorter than him, but he felt tall, maybe because he now saw them as his guard rather than his captor. He was momentarily distracted by a poster before he turned the corner, entering a room where he felt even more like a celebrity.

As he stepped into the room, at least thirty faces turned to stare at him. A stage stood at one end of what appeared to be a dusty old dance hall although one that now looked like it was more often used for gatherings where no one cared if a few sandwiches were left on the floor afterwards.

Five heavily armed soldiers were loitering on the stage. Adam had decided to call them soldiers because that is certainly what they were dressed up as. He had a feeling that these guys would never cut it doing a shift standing outside Buckingham Palace or marching back and forth across Horseguards Parade on a hot June day, but then he also had a memory of the guards at the eternal flame in Rome who had just stood chatting whilst tourists took photographs. The men around him now looked like they struggled to stand up straight. Other than that, they had the outfits and the weaponry of a fairly serious army.

There were three soldiers by the doors he was now walking through and his escort stopped to talk to those, their gestures suggested that he should join the civilians mingling in the middle of the room. Most of the people in the room were sat on the floor in small groups, there were a few who had been brought chairs but they themselves looked like they felt guilty for having such luxury. If you hadn't seen the soldiers, it could have been a waiting room for a theatre audition where the casting call had obviously been 'attractive young festival crowd in an atmosphere of fear'. They had all turned to look at him. He scanned the room, looking firstly for Tilly and Sam and then for any face that he recognised. Realising that he knew no-one, he held his arms open wide and addressed the whole room.

"Well, hello everyone, does anyone here know what is going on, I appear to have just woken up." Most of the crowd just looked at him fairly blankly but he noticed a few almost smiles. Enough to realise that at the very least he had been understood, he headed to a group he had seen standing on the outskirts of the main huddle, three girls and two men. The men had both looked at him as he arrived as if they were assessing him as either a threat or someone useful.

Chapter 16

A Villa On The Coast

"Hello, I'm Adam" he announced with a confidence that he hadn't previously had. The taller of his new acquaintances reached out a hand,

"Hi, I'm Matt, this is Jamie, Lenka, Ceri and Sofia." Every one of the names sounded very foreign, coming as they did in a very Birmingham accent. Hands were shaken and smiles shared. Adam felt like he had immediately taken control of the group and wanted to keep the upper hand,

"Who's in charge here?" The question had been quite general, there was so much that he wanted to know. He knew that in all the best films someone would explain the plot to the hero before the final scene occurred, so he had decided to be the star in his own film. He just had to play the lead role and ask the right questions. Matt took the role, immediately answering the unasked question as to who the alpha of this little group was before his arrival.

"There's an old couple, yer man in a black suit and a woman in a white suit, they appear every now and again and pick people to take out somewhere else. These guys here don't seem too interested in what is happening until they appear." Adam looked around the room again, it must have taken some logistics to get this many people here but, if the couple in charge were the police, surely they would have somewhere more suitable than this to hold them in he thought. He presumed that Tilly and Sam must have been already separated, but he was here now, alive for the moment. He needed time to think, "So what are you doing here?" It was a corny line, but he hadn't had time to script anything better. Matt responded,

"I've got no idea mate" Adam felt good to have been called 'mate' like he belonged as part of the group. "Me and Jamie here are just on holiday. I have a villa just on the coast and we met these girls at the bar. I've known Manuel for a few years, and he always makes things happen but, nothing like this."

He had spoken as if Adam should know who Manuel was, but Adam decided just to let that go for now. "Is Manuel here?" Adam asked.

"I've not seen him" Matt responded and looked to the group for assurance,

"No, there are just the people in this room, and they have taken six others, four women and two men." It was the shorter of the women who had answered, Adam was never any good at remembering names from introductions, but he was fairly sure that this one was Ceri.

"So, when they are collected are there extra security?" Adam didn't want to use the word soldiers yet to describe their captors and thought that security sounded quite professional.

"Yes, the woman has three men and the man just one, but they are all heavily armed. They all look bored though except for the one with the glasses who looks like this is his greatest dream."

Adam looked to the stage and immediately saw the guard she meant, he was stood away from the rest of the group scanning back and forth across the room as if he was expecting a revolution any second and he was going to be the hero that prevented it. He looked the weakest of the guards, and Adam decided that he would be the one he would speak to if the opportunity or reason occurred. Adam was gaining information, but he still didn't know anything that gave him a clue as to what they were doing here.

"So have they said why we are here?" They each shook their heads. Matt looked sincere as he said,

"Look I haven't got a clue what's going on, they don't seem to know who they've got here, either that or they don't care."

"What do you mean" was Adam's genuine response, "Look, they've got footballers from three of the biggest leagues in the world, there's a couple of actors, there are some big names in this room, if they wanted money, I wouldn't still be wearing this watch." He proudly showed the lump on his wrist as if it was a battle scar which didn't impress Adam at all, he only looked at it for a second and he immediately realised that it wouldn't be easy to tell the time with it, so it served no purpose. Matt continued,

"They are obviously after something so, as long as none of us have done nothing wrong, I reckon we just play the good guys that we are and soon enough we'll all get out of here, making a fuss only makes things more dangerous."

What he was saying felt like it made sense except that Adam knew that odd stuff had already been happening and somehow, he was involved. The chat continued before bizarrely drifting away from the situation they found themselves in and onto the band they had watched.

Matt was full of enthusiasm for the band, asking Adam if he remembered their name as he wanted to book them for a party back in England "before they get too famous!" Adam confirmed that the band were introduced as "My English Friends" and that Manuel certainly would be able to put them both in contact. Adam was about to ask Matt more about himself before stopping. He guessed that if he was famous as Adam had thought he probably got bored of basic fan questions, he instead tried to pose a more interesting topic for discussion but as he started to speak the old man and woman with came into the room with all four extra guards.

"Adam Cook" the woman called almost joyfully as she sped across the room towards him. Adam took a step back crashing into two people as the woman reached out and embraced him fully. He was immediately aware of the strength of the woman. He was sure that he was absolutely going to do whatever she asked him to do. He was also aware that the rest of the room were now looking at him as if he was the biggest enemy. He felt her breath against his neck as she leant closer into him and whispered into his ear,

"Come with me like we are old friends, we need to walk quickly." He was still being held uncomfortably close, feeling every part of her body against him and he felt his own body reacting to the proximity. She smiled and released him before grabbing his hand and leading him towards the doorway. Now he knew that the whole room saw him as an enemy, he was dealing with a professional at the very least, she had fooled him completely. He was now wondering if he did indeed know this woman although he was absolutely certain that he would have remembered.

They returned along the corridor but turned left before he had reached the poster, a second left and they entered another room, far more luxurious than any he had seen so far. An expensive looking display case, full of antique looking, dusty volumes of books and a couple of very old portraits clashed with the modern artworks positioned on the wall in the way that said, you will not know these people or understand this modern art but, you will know that they are all very expensive pieces. The room was furnished to impress, the three large blue leather Chesterfields set in the centre of the room did nothing to reduce that feeling. She turned to sit on the first sofa but rather than sit, she lifted one leg considerably higher than she needed to before placing it onto the sofa and twisted it beneath her as she half sat, half lounged into position.

Adam sat himself on the second sofa and it was only then that he registered that the man had also followed them into the room, he went and sat on the third sofa.

"Hello Adam" he said in a heavy Spanish accent. "I'm sorry I did not introduce myself properly the first time we met. My name is Alfredo, I am the Lieutenant-Colonel of the Guardia here, my colleague Mercedes here will tell you why we were outside the house of your friends but, first, I'd like to know how you are involved."

Adam wasn't sure if he was expected to answer before she spoke but, either way, he didn't know the answer. After a moment's silence, Mercedes took over.

"Your friend Jada has been getting too close with a man called Per Hafidi, do you know him?"

She looked him deep in the eyes as she said the name and she seemed to know his response before he even had a chance to answer. She carried on,

"He is a smuggler, he brings things from Africa, sometimes straight to Valencia, or to a number of spots along the coast as far as Gibraltar.

He wants to use your friend's house. We think that she probably said no and that he has taken her until she says yes."

"So, who are you? Adam Cook? Born in London, you have lived in London all your life, never been in trouble with the police except for a speed awareness course for travelling at 55miles per hour in a 50mph limit. You have very little presence on the internet, you left your job last week and now you appear here in the centre of our investigation.

"We found no links between you and Jada, or Sam or even Tilly. We have spoken to them, but we want your story." Apart from a couple of pauses to look at his notes, Alfredo had been looking straight through Adam's skull all the way through his address. Adam needed more time to think.

"How do I know you are telling the truth? If you are the Police, why would you bring all of us here at gunpoint the way you have? Why did you choose those people in the hall? Just what on Earth is going on?"

Adam could feel himself getting increasingly angry and knew he should calm down, but he needed answers,

"You tell me about Per Hafidi and I'm expected to know everything. I don't even know any of the people in that room. I don't know anyone in the whole bloody country, I don't even know why I'm here."

He had started simply thinking that he wanted an answer, as he went on, he realised that he now had so many more questions, why was his sister always more popular? Why hadn't his teachers encouraged him more at school? Why hadn't he found a career?

Why hadn't he found a wife? He suddenly just slumped back into the sofa and sobbed, years of frustration flowed out of his soul, he could feel the awkwardness in the room but, well he hadn't cried like this for years and he felt he needed it. Don't stop he told himself, get it all out and then you'll be better, he wasn't sure he believed that but, he wasn't going to try to stop, he couldn't. All the events had built up and here he was, sobbing into his hands on the most comfortable sofa he could imagine.

He didn't know how long he had sat alone, he had sensed Alfredo get up and leave the room but he hadn't heard Mercedes move. He wondered if he should look to see if she was still there but, would that look like he was seeking attention, if so, he didn't want attention from her. Who would he want? He allowed himself to be distracted by his thoughts, maybe that girl from the poster. He almost laughed. He thought that it was sad that he couldn't actually think of anyone, maybe that girl from school that he had been too scared to even talk to. He had imagined a long happy life together, but she never knew. Or the girl from his first workplace about whom he had had almost matching thoughts. He couldn't even think of a fictional character that matched the need he had now. He simply sobbed some more. Slowly his shoulders started to jerk less. His ribs hurt from the way he had been trying to stop his whole body racking with each sob unsuccessfully. Eventually he was able to wipe his eyes and prepared to see who had witnessed possibly his lowest public moment.

Mercedes was still there, sitting with one leg still half under her body, she now had a glass in her hand but other than that, she appeared not to have moved. Everyone else had disappeared. As he wiped his face more, Mercedes reached forward and let her arm indicate that a box of tissues had been placed on the coffee table in front of him. "Please" she said. He reached forward and after starting with a very weak nose wipe which did more to annoy him than to actually help, he realised that he had no dignity left so he blew with all of his strength and disgusted himself. She waited until he had finished and then a little longer. "What brought you to Jada's house? We need to get Jada and now we are just wasting time. Per Hafidi is not a patient man it is possible that she is dead already but, we think that if she was, well, then he would have taken the house already."

"Adam, how are you here?" The use of his name shocked him, it was sharp, almost aggressive but said in a way that she did not really care about him at all. "I'm just travelling" he said, "I accepted a lift and a night's stay from Tilly, I have never met Jada, I don't know who she is, I don't even know where I really am." Mercedes stood up and barked at the guards, "He is useless, take him to the exit room and send him away quickly." She left the room at a pace and the guards shabbily roused themselves to carry out her order. They led him down the corridor again.

Adam allowed himself a last glance at the poster before he found himself outside. He was being led across a large car park where the lines were painted so brightly. It looked almost as if no car had ever driven across the perfectly smooth surface. He was being led to a smaller building, looking more like a shoebox, left in the corner of the car park. A good pair of shoes though, a sturdy smart box.

As he stepped into the shadow of the building, he immediately felt cooler. The sweat on the back of his neck immediately condensed and a trickle ran down his back. Stepping into the dark he was led further into the building and into a side room where he saw Tilly, she looked up as he entered the room and immediately leapt to her feet. He froze, unaware of how she was going to react as she threw her arms around him, burying her head into his chest as she held him so tightly. Adam just stood there until she released the grip, still holding onto him, she leant back looking upwards. He realised that he hadn't seen her since he had been hit at the concert. How long ago was that, was it last night or longer? "I'm ok" was all he could mutter. He wasn't sure how true that was, but he tried to sound ok. "How are you?" He asked. She looked at him for a bit too long, "I don't know Adam, I don't know anything." He pulled her close. Knowing that anything he said would sound pathetic. He stood there as upright as he could whilst it felt like Tilly was melting into him.

There was a clatter by the door, a guard walked in and announced something sharp in Spanish and handing them a bag each containing their mobile phones, as expected, without any photographs from the night before. The guard came close and whispered threateningly in Adam's ear. Adam looked across at Tilly, who looked desperately back at him. "My taxi is here, they have told me to go home, what are you doing?" He spoke without thinking, "Come with me." It sounded more like an order than a question and Adam was worried that he might have sounded too harsh, but she looked relieved as she answered, "Let us just go somewhere."

Chapter 17

It's Ok

Adam stood feeling confused as Tilly spoke to the guard who kept looking him up and down whilst she spoke. Adam tried to exude an air of strength and confidence that he had completely lacked just ten minutes previously. The guard looked to his colleague who shrugged his shoulders, "Come on then" Tilly cried almost excitedly. They settled into the back of the taxi, and both sighed as they drove out of the car park. The blackness of the tarmac and the width of the lanes was almost as impressive as the fact that there was absolutely no traffic.

"The taxi is going to take us back to the house to collect our things and then we are being taken to the bus station to get out of here. Whether the Lieutenant-Colonel is working officially or not his budget wouldn't stretch to a taxi to the airport and I told him I had very little money." Winking as she said that last sentence seemed like her way of telling him not to say anything else here. He didn't know if it was a genuine taxi or another mystery in this bizarre story. The taxi dropped them at the pedestrian entrance to the house. Adam hadn't seen this before and although he had expected it to be grand, he hadn't quite been prepared for the amount of money on display. Tilly quickly opened the door and, ushering him in, was careful to lock it fully behind her.

"Ok get your bags and anything else that you might want, it might be worth bringing some snacks and the like, I don't know when Sam will be back. I don't want her to find a load of mouldy food."

That seemed eminently sensible, so he rushed straight to his room to collect his bag and then headed to the kitchen, as he reached it, Tilly was coming the other way with her bags. Her eyes were puffy, she had obviously been crying, he reached out to hug her again and this time more tears fell. A pointless and incorrect "It's ok" was all he could offer.

Trying to form a plan with such little knowledge wasn't easy but he was desperately thinking. "Do you think that we should take something else with us?" He asked. Tilly stopped and looked at him coldly "What are you saying Adam, you want to steal Jada's things?" Adam was shocked then laughed, "No. No, not at all" The look on Tilly's face changed from anger to complete bewilderment, he just looked at her, noticing the angles of her eyebrows in a way that he hadn't previously, "No, but I thought that it might be prudent to borrow something, just in case."

She still looked confused, "Adam, I do not understand, what do you mean?" He knew he'd have to explain everything.

"I had a gun on me at the bar, I don't know what happened to that but, there are obviously some dangerous people about." Tilly didn't look any less confused,

"But they won't let you on a plane with a gun, you won't need a gun in London."

"Who said anything about London? I don't want to go there, and this chapter will be really odd in my life story if I don't find a happy ending." He was looking straight into her eyes, willing her to understand what he was saying.

"You don't want to go home? But where…" She let the question hang as she suddenly realised what he was saying, her head dropped as she reached into his arms again. "I don't know Adam, there is nothing we can do, the police don't know where she is so how will we find her. Also, without Sam, I don't even know..." she clung to him for some time. Adam wasn't sure if she had given up. He had no idea where to start with any investigation or search, but he felt that at least he had a few clues and, if the police couldn't find her, then surely it couldn't do any harm if he just asked a few questions somewhere.

He took a deep breath and prepared himself, "Look, this Per Hafidi wants somewhere to land drugs I'm guessing. Jada doesn't want to let him use here, surely there are enough English fools with holiday homes in the area, why don't I go straight to Per and offer my place?" Tilly snapped away from him,

"How do you know about Per?" she asked angrily. He immediately felt cold with the way she looked at him, "I don't. But that's what Alfredo and Mercedes were saying" Tilly's eyes narrowed at his use of those names too but he continued, "Per Hafidi won't know me, I don't know him but surely I could ask a few people, it can't be that hard to get a message to someone like that, particularly if it is a message that they want to hear. It's got to be worth a try?" She held his gaze. He felt like she was trying to tell if he was serious and so he tried to hold his strongest face but, it was no good, he cracked and started giggling.

He had just signed up to go and meet a notorious man and offer him a service that he could not provide. But he was glad to feel that this was the new Adam, perhaps he had always been there. She was still looking seriously at him and obviously had no idea why he was laughing, "So do we borrow a gun or not?" She cocked her head to one said, assessed him again and thought for a second, "Seeing what happened to you at the bar, I think that a gun is more likely to get you into trouble than out of it but I think there is something we might need." She led him towards the gun room and opened a drawer at the bottom of the cabinet, she reached in and grabbed a white tote bag which seemed to be full of wires when she handed it to Adam. "Do you have room in your rucksack for this?" He nodded and immediately headed back to pack it, sneaking a look in, he could see that at the base of the bag there seemed to be a couple of boxes but certainly not enough to let him know exactly what was inside. He would find out later. He picked his bag up and met Tilly by the front door. She had a final look around and opened the door.

Chapter 18

Shuffling Closer

Jim enjoyed this part of the set. All too often Paul got the focus through the songs but on this one, Jim felt that he and Leonard really ruled the stage. The drum part was relentless, the steady rhythm allowed him the chance to enjoy the crowd. He had spun his sticks and had taken the chance to scan the whole crowd. The lighting set up allowed him to see to the back rows where the seating areas were. He had noticed the group of girls hanging around the spot where they had earlier been sat which he found hilarious. For some reason, back in London, it had seemed that the only people who wanted to talk to the band after a gig were only interested in Paul's effects pedals. The only girls that ever came were asking Jack about his haircare routines. His mind switched to how on Earth they would unwind from this performance when he saw the line of helmeted militia come into the space. Two seconds later and everything went black, he carried on hitting his drums for a few beats until he realised that the sound had gone too. He was blinded by the adjustment from the brightness of the full lighting rig to the darkness he was now surrounded by.

A little moonlight shone but there was no emergency lighting from the venue at all. In the temporary silence he heard a sharp barking shout and, as his eyes adjusted, he saw sections of the crowd had just collapsed to the floor. Other areas were frantically shuffling closer to themselves. Unsure of where to go they were acting like a shoal of fish surrounded by a shark and just crowding together. Each trying to avoid being the outermost person.

The swarm of invaders had focused on the sitting area surrounding them. Within seconds ushering them away from their seats. He saw at least two people being knocked to the ground as they had been trying to move away. The next thing he knew, Manuel was on the stage calling the band to him. Jim grabbed a new set of sticks and leapt from the kit. The rest of the band all joined him, following Manuel off the stage and away from the villa.

"Listen - I don't know what is happening but please, follow this path, at the end you will reach the road, wait there and I will arrange for someone to come and pick you up. If no one is there within thirty minutes, start walking away from the house." He handed them a small stage torch but told them not to use it until they were well away. He then turned back to where the band could see people already being loaded into coaches.

They all remained in silence until they reached the road and found themselves stood in a circle, all breathing heavily from the exhilaration of the concert and then the immediate extra adrenaline hit of whatever was happening now. Jack was the first to speak,

"What the effin eff was that?" That released the gates and they all joined in a chorus of profanities. After at least two minutes of just cursing the night sky they had quietened enough for sanity to return.

"Well, that's a good scene for the film" Jack said, and they all burst out laughing,

"What just happened?" Leonard asked, both he and Paul still had their guitars around their necks, "I couldn't see anything. I'd been posing right in front of the spotlight" the whole band laughed as Jack said,

"I haven't got a clue. I had my eyes closed when everything went black and when I opened them again, I just heard loads of shouting. I turned back to look at Jim thinking he must have pulled something" Jim then took over and explained what he had seen.

"So, what about Shy and Jo? Or Jorge and Nic?" Leonard asked,

"Well Shy and Jo were in the seats so I presume they will be on a bus, Nic was at the rig, and I hadn't seen Jorge since we went on, so God knows where he is."

The realisation of what had occurred was only just hitting them,

"Does anyone have their phones?" Jim asked, he knew that normally when they were on stage none of them had their phones in their pockets, Paul had been insistent even at rehearsal that phones could only be used to record sections or to use one of the apps they sometimes used to add a keyboard part or to experiment with different sounds. They all looked blankly.

"Ok so we wait, anyone got any idea how long the walk took us?" Both Leonard and Jack looked shocked to have been asked. Paul thought it had probably only been five minutes or so and Jim agreed,

"Let's wait for twenty-five minutes before walking." He was just reiterating Manuel's instructions but this time it was more like a question. The others just looked at each other,

"Why don't we just start walking, it can't do any harm, the, the baddies..." Leonard had been running on adrenaline but now, he felt those powers running out. He had paused when trying to find the word to describe the people who had just rather bulldozed their way through their gig. He continued to gabber,

"Until they arrived, things were amazing. They must have gone by now. It was an amazing gig. Surely if anyone goes past, they will help us?" He realised that the longer he spoke, the more desperate things seemed although he couldn't help feeling so proud of the gig itself. Jack stood looking at every second like the true rockstar that he had always wanted to be.

"I don't know, Manuel is pretty switched on, you don't get to his age running a venue like this without knowing a few people, he'll be sorting things out and, I trust Jorge. If he trusts Manuel, then I say that I don't think we'll have a better option. We don't know where we are going so, we might as well give him some time." He was still standing as if he was on stage, Paul had noticed that he always seemed to grow as a person as soon as he stepped on stage, it would be some time after a gig that the usual Jack would reappear.

Jack's suggestion made sense to the rest, they had been very well treated since their arrival and this certainly wasn't normal, but they had no better ideas. At the side of the road a stack of plastic boxes had been left, maybe for collecting oranges, but Jack went and collected a few throwing one to each person, "We might as well get comfy." As he said those words lights appeared further down the road. The band scattered back into the trees clearly in fear. The van pulled up at the side of the road, the door opened and out jumped Nic. The band reappeared and with a quick group hug, they all piled into the van and the van sped off.

The journey back to the studio passed as speedily as the driving appeared to be. Each individual telling their version of events. Nic had been at the mixing desk. He had seen a helmeted figure cut the power cable at which point he had jumped into the general crowd and stayed amongst them whilst the 'targets' were rounded up. Once they had been taken away, he had gone to try to fix the cables to get the light back on for those who were all in shock from what they had seen. It seemed that most of the attendees were purely focused with filming events which Nic guessed would be useful for the police later, but he was more worried about the now. After he had managed to connect at least a few lights, he had gone to the stage to make sure that the bands kit was being looked after. It was there that he found Manuel who told him where the band were. Manuel was going to look after the kit and once the soldiers had left, Manuel sent Nic to get the band with the driver.

No one had seen Jorge, but people had seen Shy and Jo being taken away, so they had to presume that Jorge had gone too. As the van arrived at the studio, they all stumbled out and instantly collapsed onto the picnic tables. The relief of being safe and the adrenaline from the gig was hitting and when Nic arrived with a coolbox full of beer, the battle began to get through the contents.

Back at the gig, Shy had seen the movement early too. His friends had always thought it odd that he could enjoy a gig or indeed any event just as much without actually watching anything that happened on the stage. He would watch how the lights lit up a particular piece of kit or the way that seating affected a crowd's response. He was always looking at the technical aspects of entertainment. He knew that no lead singer could ever just walk onstage and be the star. There are lots of fantastic singers, but the biggest stars are often not the best singers.

By watching for those little details and passing that information on to his artists Shy ensured that all of his bands had a great live act and so he never stopped watching. Each new act he worked with could teach him something new and so he'd been watching. How the band reacted to a situation in the crowd could also hugely affect a gig. The days of just playing on and letting things happen had long gone, the band had to know when to stop and when to potentially step in. As soon as he saw the first soldier arrive he had thought quickly, his first fear had been of the Bataclan incident in Paris. That was different to this though. His immediate thought here was that this was not an indiscriminate act.

He knew he had not done anything wrong so he decided that he should stay still and calm. He grabbed Jo close and called to Jorge. They all stood still as they were surrounded quickly and efficiently. Kneeling when told and then complying with their captors. Jorge had been able to whisper that Manuel was a good man but that he sometimes allowed 'others' to use his facilities "so" he said, "don't worry, this will be linked with that and, when they know we are not involved, a release will be arranged." It felt strange to be so calm but both Shy and Jorge felt no need to fight. Jo had started less compliantly complaining at the guards and wanting to resist. Their refusal to respond to any of her comments in English soon had her just accepting the situation in the way that most of the locals had.

The Spanish football players had been rowdy, though it had seemed to be more about looking like they weren't scared than actually threatening to do something. Jorge had seen one person being hit on the head apparently quite violently but all the other reports when they reached the buses were that everyone was being treated as well as you could ever hope to be when you had been abducted from the middle of an amazing concert.

The crowd were being separated and guided towards coaches in a way that Jo could only connect with a sheepdog trial but with human sheep and heavily armed dogs. As they settled onto the coach, they were driven off at a fairly sedate pace which reassured Jo, unless they were driving slowly to avoid looking suspicious. Was she overthinking things? She hoped that enough people had been filming on their phones. As soon as she could, she would get a message to the office to ensure that someone found as much footage of the events as they could and saved it. This could be gold dust for media coverage, as long as no one gets hurt. Their phones had been collected so she assumed that the person who had come and collected the passwords had then been going through and checking the camera reels to delete anything involving the incident. She hoped that the majority of the crowd were cleared to get away and that people had at least posted something, she wondered if anything had been broadcast live.

Shy and Jorge turned the waiting room into a business meeting, they were analysing elements of the gig, as far as Jo was concerned up until the incident it was possibly the most professional show that she had ever seen, everything seemed to work perfectly. Paul didn't exactly move like a guitar hero, but they would work on that. She let them carry on talking and went herself to try to find someone else who spoke English well enough to speak to.

Chapter 19

A True Cacophony

The journey to the bus station was almost in silence. As soon as they had driven away from the house he had reached into his pocket, dug his phone out and started searching Per Hafidi online. What he read didn't fill him with confidence. Whilst he didn't exactly have his own page, the search certainly threw up enough mentions of his name. Most seemed to be associated with photos of various celebrities who appeared to be enjoying the hospitality at a nightclub or a restaurant. Per Hafidi himself looked fairly small, but sharp, both in his fashion taste and his physique. Everything looked angular, he was someone who didn't look like he had much time for modesty.

Adam then searched each of the locations and noted the fact that each and every one of them were linked to a number of complaints from neighbours about the noise and general 'activities' that occurred at those locations. His translation page had struggled with some of the terms that it had been offered but, Adam was confident that the translations were giving enough information for him to make a judgement of the man. Now he just had to work out a way to meet him.

He looked out of the window, taking in the beauty of his surroundings. It wasn't long before the beauty of orange tree orchards and distant mountain views was replaced with an open industrial landscape. Large brick and corrugated iron cubes literally dropped onto the landscape. Soon the industrial units became blocks of flats. They took a left turn and the roads immediately narrowed and darkened. The atmosphere in the car seemed to darken too as both Tilly and Adam were alone in their thoughts. He guessed that neither Alfredo nor Mercedes thought that he was anything to worry about, but he still didn't know what they had said to Tilly. Adam hadn't thought beyond the very rough outline of what happened next. His perception from the films was that one action scene instantly falls straight into the next. He never imagined how the action heroes coped with sitting at traffic lights. Or if they too had extended periods of indecision about where to go or worries about where they would spend the night.

He felt the sun hit the front of the car as they pulled into a square, all of the buildings looked brighter. The world looked nicer. On the far side of the square, he saw three bus stops. If this was the bus station and the driver hung around, then they would have no choice but to get the bus towards the airport. They need not have worried about that as the second they were out of the car, the driver sped off.

Tilly took Adam's hand,

"Are you sure about this?" Adam wasn't sure whether it was because she cared about him or if she simply didn't feel that he could cope. He sounded assertive as he spoke,

"Yes. We need to head to the city, find somewhere to stay tonight. I need to buy some clothes and we are going out tonight." Tilly breathed deeply, nodded and turned towards the bus shelters. She had been using the internet too during the journey and knew exactly where to head.

"The next bus will be going from here we have twenty

minutes. Do you want a drink?" He did, but there was no way that he was going to leave the bus stop. He wanted to get away from this small town where he felt that everyone was watching him. They stood awkwardly, each of them regularly checking their watches. They were alone at the stop except for two old ladies, both dressed in far too many clothes for the ambient temperature. Adam felt their eyes as they studied both himself and Tilly.

Was just that natural fear of strangers that he expected in a place like this? Similarly, the stares from the group of three men at the cafe across the road? He felt he was perhaps getting paranoid, but he also told himself that he had a good reason to. An engineer sat on his toolbox next to a low brick box at the side of the road, in front of the flower shop a few doors down. And then there was the woman in the white Sandero parked just around the corner in front of the brightly painted steps. She herself was giving a good impression of waiting for someone but, she looked too pretty for the location and the car, and surely no one would keep her waiting.

Adam realised that he was now just staring at people but couldn't help himself from feeling suspicious of everyone. He looked back to the engineer who still had his head buried in the cupboard. Either he had a camera watching them or he really was an engineer. Another car went past, and another, as each car passed both Adam and Tilly nervously looked to see if the driver was watching them. Adam stopped breathing as he saw the door open of the small white car. Out stepped the woman, taller than he had expected and graceful. Her movements were incredibly careful. She closed the door and checked twice that she had locked it before carefully placing the key into her bag with a distinctive little dog design on it. Adam was sure that he had seen that style before but couldn't quite place it.

He was watching so intently that he was shocked when

Tilly suddenly stood alongside him and grabbed his arm. The bus had arrived. The two old ladies made it clear that they were going to board first. Adam would have of course allowed them in front of him regardless of when they had arrived, but their presumption angered him a little. He then stood back to allow Tilly to board and do the necessary talking. He heard the word Valencia, loving the way it sounded. She turned to him too at some point and the driver nodded, recognising that she wanted his ticket too. As he handed over the little paper ticket Adam copied Tilly's "Gracias" although he still felt really awkward letting the final sound roll in his mouth in the way that she had taught him, but which still felt completely unnatural.

They headed down the bus. It was larger and cleaner than Adam had expected but it was also busier than he had imagined. He had always tried to avoid buses in London, happier to walk if he could. Looking around him he realised that he was one of only three men on the bus if you included the driver. Most of the others were of a similar age to the two women that had angered him. He tried desperately to lift his bag over the knees of those sitting along the aisle. None of the passengers even paused their conversations as he passed.

"Here?" Tilly asked as she paused by the first of the empty seats.

"No, a little further" was his response, there was another empty pair of seats towards the back of the bus alongside a small section where Adam had already decided he could fit their bags. It also meant that he had fewer people behind him. He had never liked having anyone behind him and today he certainly wanted to be able to keep as many people as possible in his eye-line.

He had just settled back into his seat and the bus jumped forward before the brakes were heavily applied. Tilly was rocked forward in her seat, Adam with years of practice on London's tube trains, managed to hold himself steady. He looked, as did the rest of the passengers, forward to where he saw the woman from the white car looking a little bothered and behind her another lady. A little older but dressed in clothes that would have suited a teenager.

The doors opened and the driver spoke a few words. The woman boarded, looking a little flustered and behind her, the other woman climbed up into the carriage looking particularly unflustered. They reached the seats that Tilly had first paused at and sat themselves down. The driver heading off just before their bottoms hit the seats. The woman had looked straight at Adam before she sat. Adam had been looking straight at her and the way their eyes caught had made Adam think many thoughts but mainly sympathy with her obvious distress about making the rest of the bus wait. He was watching the back of her head, she was sat perfectly upright in contrast to all the other people on the bus who had appeared to become almost part of the bus, her shoulders held square in her striped shirt.

The bus only made a couple of stops, each one made entertaining by watching the fuss made by at least one passenger struggling to collect all of their bags. Each character had only started to prepare for getting off, after the bus had opened its doors. Tilly had been looking for hotels close to the two clubs that they knew Per Hafidi had links to in the city. Thankfully both were in the central area. Albeit according to Tilly not quite in an area that she would have visited if she had been heading for a night out. Her wording had confused Adam, he suspected that she was being deliberately vague about her opinion of the location to avoid worrying him. He simply chose to ignore those concerns. She showed him a few photos of possible rooms, each of which looked more than acceptable to him, but something made her keep searching.

He was worried about his budget. They hadn't spoken about costs and he knew that Tilly worked in a different pay grade. In all of his planning for this journey he had only ever expected to stay at low grade hotels. He figured that he had already saved money from a couple of nights' accommodation so he surmised that he would be able to raise his budget appropriately. There was no way that he would ask Tilly to stay in the kind of places that he was prepared to. He had offered her the money for the bus ticket, which she refused, he already knew that he was going to insist on buying lunch. He couldn't really believe that, in the middle of all that was going on, his stomach was still telling him that he was hungry.

The landscape was changing again, the villages were getting closer together and the industrial units were starting to look cleaner and shinier. Through the front of the bus, he could see the city starting to emerge in front of him. Two things that always excited him on a journey, the first view of a city and the first view of the sea. Here he had both. He had no knowledge of Valencia so he wasn't looking for any particular landmark but that just made every view special. The way that the motorway carriages only appeared to be split by a row of vegetation, the footbridge over the road. He was looking into the windows of all the shops. Places that he knew he would never visit, selling things that he would never need and, many things that he simply would not know what they were.

The buildings stood higher and grew smarter as they obviously approached the centre of town. His head bouncing from side to side like he was watching a tennis match as he spotted places of interest on each side of the road. He was desperately trying to see everything but still found his eyes returning to the back of the head four rows in front. She had sat facing directly forwards for the whole journey except for a couple of moments when her friend (colleague, sister?) had spoken and she had leant closer to hear or had turned to look at something that had obviously been pointed out.

Adam had been shocked at the level of noise on the bus, people talking to the person whose ear was no further than thirty centimetres away as if they were a mile away. Others on the phone seemingly giving a running commentary of the bus journey but as if the journey was being carried out at 300 miles per hour. He had tried to identify particular individuals with each voice but the level of noise and the number of people speaking had made that impossible. Each voice had disappeared into the fabric of the bus before being charged full of electricity and amplified through the seats creating a true cacophony. This time she turned to the left looking out of the window, Adam followed the view and was pleased to see the giant frame of the Mestalla stadium wrapped in a huge image of a bat and a sponsor's logo.

Another of Adam's thrills. He remembered the days of travelling to football matches when the sight of the floodlights would guide you to the stadium. The advent of better lighting meant that stadiums now far more often suddenly revealed themselves in the way the Mestalla just had. Adam closed his eyes for a second knowing that this trip must soon be over, and he had a vision in his mind of the floodlights of the county ground in Chelmsford. He was a long way from cricket now, he tried to switch his brain back into secret agent mode. He decided that he didn't know what that really meant so he went back to looking out the window, trying to get his bearings so at least he would have an idea of the geography of the city if nothing else.

Eventually the bus lurched to a sudden halt at the side of the road. A huge bustle occurred as each passenger emerged from their cushions and the noise grew even louder. Adam looked at Tilly who just gave him a nod to recognise that they were both thinking that it was worth waiting for everyone else to get off before they attempted to do so. As the crowd around the doors thinned, he was not unsurprised to see that there were two other people on the bus who were doing the same. Tilly gave him a nudge and he stood and reached to collect his rucksack, as he did he saw the woman rise, she half turned and caught him looking again, a smile crossed her face as she looked down quickly and leant across to help her 'friend' stand and they left the bus just in front of Adam and Tilly.

Chapter 20

Ice Cream In The Park

The bus had been hot and crowded but that really hadn't prepared him for the atmosphere as he stepped off of the bus. There seemed to be no air on the street. The hoardes of people passing him were all just floating in one mass. Seemingly they were all controlled by a central rod like in some giant table football game. His immediate thought had been to aim for a small eddy in the current on the other side of the pavement from which they could get their bearings. Instead, he found himself being ushered immediately further down the road, bustled by an army of elderly women all carrying unnecessarily large bags of fruit, surely far too much for any family to possibly eat. Adam couldn't actually honestly remember finishing a bunch of bananas without throwing at least one away. He battled his way through the throng and turned to Tilly to ask,

"Is the whole place this mad?" She laughed as she told him,

"Market Day, it will be quieter around the corner." She took his hand and led him into the current where he was immediately swamped by the plastic bags and the smell of fruit.

Adam was looking to see if the woman from the bus was following him. He didn't know whether it was because he was still on full alert for everything around him but, every sense in his body was wide awake and for some reason he felt as if there was some connection. He wasn't sure if he should feel disappointed that he couldn't see her.

Tilly dragged him onwards until sharply ducking through a space between a fancy bakers and a very grimy looking mobile phone shop, the pathway was not wide enough to walk side by side and, even if it had been, the quantity of litter that had piled to one side would probably have prevented that. He could not see much past Tilly as the pathway climbed, the basic graffiti clashing with the deliberate pieces of public art that he had seen as they drove in. Tilly took him left, ducking under a metal staircase. Adam was certain that they shouldn't have been on this path.

They escaped onto the next street, the air flowed once again, and the light came back into the city. Tilly offered her hand, Adam really had no choice but to take it, confused as to whether her hand should feel that good. He was nervous to hold it, he knew his palms would be sweaty, he didn't want to horrify her but then he was also wary of holding her too tight. She smiled at him,

"It's ok, the hotel is just up here a little bit. I've just booked one room, I hope it's ok, I thought it would look a little less suspicious but it's a big room. If you want a separate room, we can get it I'm sure." He smiled and gently squeezed her hand as they walked on.

The hotel appeared to evolve in front of him, a giant wall of marble glinting in the sunshine. Red and yellow glowing from the flags of Spain and Valencia that hung above the doorway. Intricate carvings stood in relief and an immediate calmness overtook the environment surrounding the hotel itself. As they approached the door an arm appeared from the shadows and a perfectly attired man followed the leading arm to open the door. Adam immediately felt scruffy, he had been lucky enough to stay in a couple of nice hotels in the past but had never truly felt like he fitted in. Tilly, however, looked in her element. As Adam was busy looking at the artwork on the ceiling, she had already almost waltzed to the desk and was collecting their keys.

Adam was asked to sign a form, he had no idea what it was, but he signed it regardless and within no more than two minutes of walking through the door, they were directed to an elevator. Not from the main bank of four he had seen as they walked in but to a private one. They had to walk behind the desk and around a corner to where a lift stood with its door already open, waiting for them. Tilly led him in and pressed the lower of the two buttons.

"I'm sorry, the Presidential Suite was booked so we are one floor down, I think, I hope that you will like it."

The lift opened into a wide hallway that alone was considerably wider than any room that Adam had been expecting to stay in during his trip. To the right was a life-size statue of a roman goddess, they tuned left and towards the end of the corridor was the only other door. Adam was surprised to see that it had the same kind of hotel lock as any travel lodge on any motorway. Tilly entered her card and opened the door. Adam felt the glow as the light spilled from the room into the corridor. Tilly stepped back and indicated to Adam that he should go first.

As he stepped through the door, he was immediately struck by the view of the beach that filled the glass wall a distance in front of him. A full kitchen, bigger than the one in the house he had grown up in, spread to his left. The shiny mahogany dining table was set beyond with a huge central ornament that looked like a giant multicoloured bird's nest. To his right was a sofa, set to look out at the sea, beyond that a further two sofas were positioned facing each other. He dropped his bag on the first and went straight to the window. Tilly placed her bag next to his and silently came and stood alongside him. Adam once again felt the emotions building up and he could sense his tears forming. If he wiped his eyes now, she would know the reason. He chose to ignore them and hoped that they would dry enough for him to not show her.

Adam stood, unable to speak but desperately trying to think of something appropriate. Time passed until he felt her hand on his back,

"Are you ok?" she asked in the softest voice he had ever heard. He could feel the texture of her voice and let it wash over him, he could cry, or he could bluff.

"Yes, this is pretty spectacular, isn't it?" he said in too loud a voice. She let her hand rest there for an extra second before heading back to her bag,

"Shall we look at the bedroom?" He turned and watched her as she swung her bag onto her shoulder walking towards the door at the far end of the room. He went and collected his holdall, taking the time to look around the rest of this room, a bookshelf had a collection of various ornaments as well as the kind of books that surely no-one ever buys to open. Books on art and furniture and random historical figures.

He approached the door and could see that Tilly had put her bag down on the corner of the biggest bed that he had ever seen. He was more familiar with hotels that would clip two single beds together to make a double. This must be at least two king-sized beds together, enclosed in a sled frame that would ensure that Santa had plenty of room for all the presents. It would certainly require more than his usual quantity of reindeer to pull. A chaise lounge was positioned under the plush footing of the sled and another laid out alongside the window looking out at the marina where a windsurfing lesson was being held. Adam looked at Tilly, this is the sort of place that you should be walking into on your wedding night with the woman of your dreams, he couldn't help but look at her and question why she had brought him there.

"Would you like a drink?" she asked as she opened the fridge door revealing a wider selection than he'd find at the local petrol station. They had moved back to the main room and Adam was sitting at the dining table. They had sat down to plan their evening but quickly realised that, other than going to one of Per's clubs then, if necessary the second, they really didn't have any plan in place. Much of the evening was going to have to be decided on the fly. They had researched the footballer's villa and taken a few screenshots from the online maps. Enough to prove to Per that they had what he was looking for. If they could find him.

The plan was to lure him into a conversation about their property but then question him about his professional conduct stating that they had heard rumours of his involvement in the disappearance of Jada and then to basically see how he responded. They both felt that it was too simple and neither knew how they would proceed once they had said that but neither had any better suggestions. If they had told each other the truth they didn't really expect to get the chance to see Hafidi, the rest was really just irrelevant. They just knew that they had to do something and going to his club was at least doing something. Tilly had acknowledged that she had more knowledge of the area and negotiation than Adam would so his role was just to try to arrange that meeting. Tilly felt that his English accent would hold more credit with those lower down the food chain so was more likely to spark an interest than she would, and from what she had read, Hafidi would find talking to her a greater challenge.

Adam advised Tilly to leave the keys to the hotel at reception just so that if anything happened to him there would be no link back to the hotel and she would at least be able to get back to the safety of the room. She had assured him that it wouldn't come to that, but Adam knew that if necessary, he would do absolutely whatever it took to ensure that Tilly would be safe even if it meant putting himself in greater danger to buy her time to get away. He would have preferred it if she could wait at the hotel, but he knew that had no chance of doing this alone. Adam picked up the key and spun to walk to the door,

"Come on let's go shopping, I don't think they will let us in either of the clubs in these clothes." He called.

Adam immediately felt his body reacting to the heat as they left the air-conditioned foyer. Tilly rushed straight over to a waiting taxi and within seconds they were back into air conditioning. Before Adam had taken his seat, Tilly was instructing the driver to take them to a particular store. There was a further bit of talk before Tilly turned back to him,

"There are better smaller shops but, it is the best place in Valencia to get outfits for both of us. Do you have an idea what you want?" She asked.

He hadn't thought of what to wear, he didn't really care too much for clothes but knew that he'd need to look smarter than anything that he had brought with him.

"A shirt and maybe I'll be really radical and get some trousers too!" Tilly laughed adding,

"OK I'll help you". She reached out and rested her hand on his forearm and smiled before turning to look out of the window. Adam sat looking at her hand, wishing the journey was longer. It took just a few minutes before the taxi was pulling over on the edge of a roundabout. Tilly reached forward and paid for the cab whilst Adam had to wait for Tilly to get out before he could clamber across. There was no way that he was going to open the door on his side, he could guarantee that he would knock a scooter over. He tried not to look as Tilly bent forward as she stepped out of the cab before she then hesitated by the door, waiting for him to step out. She reached out her hand, and seemed genuinely happy as the words burbled from her mouth,

"Come on, I haven't taken anyone shopping for ages" she was giggling as she approached the doors to the store.

He was relieved to discover that it looked like a fairly normal department store, he still wasn't entirely sure exactly what he had let himself in for. She had already decided that they would get his outfit first, rightly suspecting that he wouldn't take long. She wanted to buy something that complemented his outfit, explaining that although they weren't a couple and they weren't going to this club for fun, she didn't want that to stop her feeling good about heading to a club with an attractive man. Her words had confused him. He was never certain if he was reading more or less into her words because of her accent. She would sometimes put emphasis on different words and Adam wished that he could tell if she was doing that deliberately.

He had turned his nose up at a couple of shirts that she had held up to him before he had actually asked her what she thought of a pale blue shirt. The colour made his eyes shine brighter and the tan that he had gained over the last few days added to make him look even more like he belonged there. He hadn't wanted to try it on, she convinced him. Although he resisted her desire for him to come out to show her how it fitted. He had hated that as a child, when his mother would insist that he came out regardless of how bad the clothes had fitted, and then she would subject him to standing as still as he could whilst she tugged the clothes (and him underneath) in all directions before agreeing to his first comment that it didn't fit.

As they approached the womenswear department, Tilly asked him what she should wear. He honestly didn't have a clue. During the days they had spent together he had realised that the smile that originally captured his attention had since been added to by a number of other features that he had tried not to get too enraptured by because of the circumstances. But now she was directly asking him what he thought she should wear. He self-censored his first thought before deciding that the best course of action was just to ask another question.

"What would you normally wear to that kind of event? Do you have anything at home that you'd wear if you had it here?" She smiled and thought before answering with a simple yes which left him with a whole load more questions that he suspected would not be answered quite yet.

As they approached the next escalator to ascend, she playfully turned to him.

"I've been told I've got pretty good legs; do you think?" She rushed onto the escalator to stand above him and was watching, almost daring him to look. Of course, he had to agree, and now, he could not help but look. It was true. He had noticed her poise, enough of a sign of her education and gene pool but this was the first time he had really taken the chance to look.

When they reached the top of the stairs, she took his arm and pulled him closer, she spoke straight into his ear,

"How about a very short skirt but, a bit floaty so that it doesn't stop me from moving my legs quickly if I need to?" He almost blushed at the words but before he was able to respond she reached out and picked up almost exactly what she had described. She held it up against her and looked in his direction. He could only nod, imagining what it would look like on. Tilly kept hold of it and almost skipped onwards. It was one of those environments where time simply didn't exist. Adam simply followed in a daze. Looking at garments in a way he never had before and just allowing himself to be led around the store. It could have been minutes, hours or days before she had decided that she had enough outfits to try on. Adam was guided to the husbands and boyfriends waiting area. Two comfortable looking chairs sat alongside a small table containing the store's autumn-style magazine and a lingerie catalogue, both of which had obviously never been touched by anyone waiting there.

He sat there and habitually went for his phone. There were the usual collection of emails from companies he had once bought a pair of trainers from, the ticket agency letting him know which concerts were coming up and then just one message that he wanted to read. He wondered why he still always looked to email first. One of the first to have his own private email address, he remembered when you had to get a CD to do that sort of thing, he guessed he still felt an affinity with the medium. He knew that very few people would contact him that way, but they always felt more important. Nothing today though and so he closed the app.

He looked up to see if Tilly was ready yet and noticed that he could see more at the edge of the curtain than he should. Embarrassment immediately made him look back to his phone. The other messaging apps all merely contained spam from people he had no interest in anymore or groups he should have left months if not years ago but which he felt was rude to leave. He then he opened the text message app, he had seen that he had four messages, far more than he would have expected to have but, he had put off actually opening them as he knew it would take him back to an old world. As he went to open the first his jaw hit the floor.

Tilly danced in front of him in a dress that made her shine. As she saw his reaction, she laughed but didn't stop dancing,

"Do you like?" she asked, obviously already knowing his answer. All he could do was nod, she turned her back allowing him to watch the way it clung to her hips before turning to face him again. She nodded and then half ran back to the changing room. Adam looked around the store to see if anyone else had just witnessed the display. He sat back and then, feeling like he hadn't breathed for too long, tried to breathe and act normally. As he exhaled, he truly felt content. He knew that none of this was real. Things like this didn't happen to Adam. He was never going to be famous, but in this moment, he felt content. He closed his eyes and felt all the stress, all the pressure, all of his history, just disappear, here he was in a Valencian department store and life started now.

Tilly reappeared, seemingly, just seconds later and reached out to take him by the hand, leading him to the pay desk. As they left the store, she looked at her watch,

"We still have a few hours to pass. We should have dinner before the club. What would you like to do?" She looked at him and although she had changed back into her jeans and T-shirt, Adam could still feel that glow of life around her. His first thought had been to go and find the club and have a scout around in daylight, but that could ruin their story later and, right now, he just wanted to enjoy the way he was feeling.

He had researched Valencia earlier online and it seemed that the city seemed to have two characters, the old of the cathedral and the market area and the new, the marina and the architecture around the 'City of Arts and Sciences'. For the next few hours, he wanted to be free, and enjoy the fresh air. He had looked at the map in the taxi on their way in and had seen that the store itself was close to the Jardín del Turia. He took her hand and as casually as he could said,

"Let's walk".

His nervousness with taking the lead soon disappeared as a huge gap in the traffic appeared, allowing them to cross the wide expanse of tarmac. Having been used to London's narrow streets for far too long, the wide avenues here seemed to give the city more freedom. Adam was glad to be walking, he had spent most of his time in Spain so far sitting down. He could see a building ahead which rather reminded him of one of the machines from an early series of Robot Wars. That was a programme he enjoyed watching, probably more than was cool to admit, and also a reference that he suspected Tilly simply wouldn't get.

The stunning architecture continued through the gardens. The park itself seeming like it was laid alongside a queue of spacecraft that had landed and, whilst they were there, it appeared that the locals had chosen to give them a purpose. There was an aquarium, a concert hall, cinema, all designed by an architect who Adam presumed had spent their childhood dreaming of exploring for alien life forms. As they entered the parkland a kiosk appeared in front of them, the idea of an ice cream on a hot summer's day was just too good an image to refuse. Tilly laughed when he first asked her if she wanted an ice cream. She told him she'd love a waffle which confused him as he approached the counter but, only speaking English sometimes had its advantages and he managed to order what she wanted. After he had paid, Tilly thanked the server in Spanish and added some further words which made them both laugh before they continued through the park.

Tilly looked at him and laughed with every bite before asking him if he had a tissue that she could use to wipe her face. They spent the afternoon admiring the architecture, laughing and playing but as the shadows lengthened, they both recognised that they had needed the break. They both knew that it was now time to play their different roles. Tilly summoned a taxi and they headed back to the hotel. It was a pleasant relief to get back into the air-conditioned room, Adam took his new clothes from the bag and asked Tilly if she wanted to shower first. With a flick of her leg, she headed to the bathroom.

Chapter 21

The New Song Spinning

The band hadn't slept. All night had been spent discussing the whole gig. Their feelings before, through the intro, each song, the chat that Jack gave between the songs, and then, the details of the 'event' as they were calling it. Leonard had studied psychiatry and although he had never practiced it, he still knew enough to convince the others of the benefits of talking. Since day one he had encouraged them to talk through each gig as his group therapy session and so far, it had worked. At about 3am Jack, Paul and Leonard had got their guitars and started writing a song. By 5am, the first of them had raised the possibility of trying to sleep when they heard the doors burst open and Shy's voice boomed through the halls.

"Hello, anybody here?" They all cheered at once and ran to meet Shy, Jo and Jorge. Hugs were exchanged and drinks were recharged. It took some time for the stories to be told and retold. The band played their newest song as the final act before each heading to their rooms. Jo closed her door, kicked off her shoes, sank into her bed and just sighed. If those few hours had not been as scary then they would have been perfect. The gig was amazing and if the 'event' hadn't occurred, she would have guaranteed that this would have been the start of the best period of her life.

Jo had spent most of her time whilst she was being taken away on the coach, and then while she was waiting to be questioned, worrying that this would be the end of the band. She worried that perhaps she should have been more focused on the obviously important matter of her direct safety. But now, having spent the last three hours talking with the band, she was sure once again she was ok and that this band were special.

The song they had just written was brilliant as it was even though they had said they wanted to spend more time working on it. In the first hours after the event Jo had expected the trip to be over and that they would all want to go home. She was pleased to see that, if anything, it seemed that they were now even more determined. Tomorrow was going to be spent going through the preferred setlist of their own songs to allow Nic to create the lighting effects. There was a big discussion about the songs that Jorge had given them, taking someone else's music but putting their spin on it had excited them. The familiarity that the crowd had with those songs had lifted the audience even higher. Jo had also been replaying the gig in her head and was again enjoying the sights of those around her singing and dancing and living their best lives. This band were going to be the soundtrack to that.

Most of the next day would be spent deciding their setlist before they would head down to Marbella for the first gig supporting Convoke - the band that up until now everyone in the office had been most excited by. Jo had filmed some of the rehearsals herself on her phone. Shy had told her to keep the new band under wraps until they knew exactly what their next plan was but, she wanted to get things moving quicker. She was too excited not to release some of these videos but, knowing that they hadn't yet fully agreed to the plan she written for them, she posted a couple of 'teaser' clips without the group's name or any details and with only brief glimpses of each of the four members. Short 30 second clips of people simply having fun was exactly the sort of thing that her social media following would enjoy. She was sure that by hiding the band a little, she would be able to start the rumour mill rolling. She jotted a few more words into her notebook before falling asleep with the chords of the new song spinning through her whole body.

The next two days had flown by. The gigs had been exactly as she had expected, the only issue she had had to deal with was the frustration that Convoke had raised,

"These new guys are just too good" had been their collective statement to Shy. To their credit they had offered to swap to support them and, if everyone was honest it would probably have been better for the audiences if they had but, as Shy explained, their name was on the tickets and,

"If the new guys are good, you just have to be better."

Jo had then been sent in to try to massage their battered egos and so far, it had worked. Both bands had had photo shoots on the beaches, and both had thoroughly enjoyed the attention that they had attracted walking onto the beach with all of their instruments. The bands had merged to provide a little acoustic gig on the beach which would be one of those moments that Jo would never ever forget until a police car drove over the beach to find out what was going on and then told them to move on. Jo was really looking forward to the Valencia gig, the last two nights had been far better than she had expected. In her younger years, she had avoided the typical teenage holiday locations because she had never been interested in drugs or typical nightclub music. Jo and the band were all pleased the see that the holidaymakers that they had attracted to the gigs had also had enough of the noise coming from every other door on the strip and the sounds of guitars had attracted a good crowd who were all full of enthusiasm.

Now though, they were heading into Valencia, the city.

Jo loved city life; she wondered if she could think of any good band who truly came from the countryside. A city had a mixture of influences an opportunity to hear something new, music from all parts of the world, and all styles of life, the super-rich and the destitute and all those trying to hold their positions between the two, the conflicts that raised inspiration. The opportunity to become either completely anonymous or known by everyone, the opportunity to sleep all day and live all night. She could feel the excitement building as they drove onwards. Jorge had asked the driver to take 'the tourist route'. Showing them the modern opulence of the city, the shiny architecture, the boats in the marina. From there they headed towards the old town, past the Bull Ring and into the narrower streets towards the cathedral.

The band rejected the opportunity to visit the Holy Grail which the cathedral claims to hold, that disappointed Jorge, but he soon perked up as they headed back out of town. Passing the developments surrounding the Nou Mastella which, despite work starting many years ago, Jorge assured them that it would be completed any year soon and the collection of new buildings going up in the neighbourhood certainly seemed to justify his optimism.

The journey continued onwards towards the area that Jorge told them was the 'most dangerous in Valencia' although looking out of the bus windows and comparing it to the streets that they had grown up on, no one on board the bus saw anything that looked even the slightest bit menacing. Friends were sat at cafe tables in the street, families played in the parks between the apartment blocks and although most of the graffiti wasn't quite as artistic as it had been elsewhere, the overwhelming feeling of the city was of serendipity.

Jo wanted to pick the city up and shake it, she wanted to see the energy but it appeared that, other than the occasional disgusting stench of cigarette smoke in the air, Valencia seemed to live up to all of the reviews she had read that described it as a 'lovely friendly city!' They continued through town and headed back towards the outskirts.

They were first going straight to the venue for a soundcheck and would then head to the hotel for some rest before the gig. As the bus pulled up, Jo's first thought was that this must be a mistake. They had arrived in an industrial estate, opposite a giant self-storage warehouse. Looking out of the other window she was relieved to see a giant guitar pointing up from the roof of a building giving a clue that this was indeed a music venue. The vans with the kit in drove around the back but Jorge took the bands through the audience entrance, in his words,

"To understand how the fans feel to see you."

Both bands headed through the doors and soon found themselves in an environment that felt much more familiar. A large black space with a fairly low roof, the stage set at the end. A raised ceiling level above the stage allowed for an impressive lighting rig. To one side behind a velvet rope was a VIP seating area. Jorge was keen to emphasise the bands need to perform to the people in here,

"It will be worth your while. And mine". He didn't say any more about who he expected to be there but the idea excited both bands.

Jorge took them onto the stage and then off to the changing area, He apologised immediately.

"The only bad thing about this venue is this room here, there is not enough space for everyone so I suggest that you dress at the hotel, bring a change for after the gig and you can decide afterwards if you have a quick shower and change here or go straight back to the hotel." Jack quickly responded,

"Mate, if you think this is bad" and left the rest of the sentence. Back in London, they had often just had a towel to wipe their sweat off before a whole can of deodorant and a new T-shirt and they'd be back out into the main bar.

Coming back into the hall, Nic had already connected his computer to the lighting desk and was testing the programme he would be running. He called out to both bands asking if they wouldn't mind helping bring the kit through whilst he got the desk sorted. Convoke were a little more reticent to help but they all headed to the vans and started unloading the kit. Convoke had just begun their soundcheck when the doors to the hall burst open and, from the stage, it looked like Darth Vader was about to arrive.

Five perfectly choreographed giants had entered the hall led extravagantly by a very petit woman. The men all dressed in sharp black suits, black shirts and black ties. The woman in the purest white and then at the rear of the procession a man in perhaps the most ridiculous sparkly green jacket anyone had ever worn. A knowing look between Jack and Paul agreed that they weren't going to mention it.

The procession parted allowing him to walk through to where the girl was stood with her held arm out for him to take. Convoke had stopped playing as the parade had begun leaving an awkward silence in the room. Broken by the most ridiculous voice that the bands had ever heard, sounding like a Spanish Joe Pasquale, he announced,

"Welcome to Club Vale, The grandest house in our wonderful

region. Where is Jorge?"

Jorge stepped out from the side of the stage,

"Per Hafidi, you old rogue, good to see you my friend" they met in the centre of the hall and shared an embrace.

"Per, may I introduce two bands who will both sell out your room here on any day of the week. Convoke and a band for which the name might change". Per looked to the stage and waving his arms extravagantly called out as if to the whole room

"And you are welcome my friends, I am sure that Jorge has looked after you, but I know he plays safe so, if you want anything more just ask Maggie here, Girls, Boys, Dancers, Drugs, whatever you want we have it here." The band laughed, not sure whether he was serious or not, but Maggie was already on her way to the bar.

"Let me hear you play!" Per Hafidi ordered. He was used to having his words obeyed and the look of the people behind him suggested that it would probably be a good idea not to refuse. The whole performance seeming like a Victorian circus with Hafidi as the ringmaster. The band quickly confirmed the next song and started playing. Per instantly turned and walked towards the VIP area. Maggie reappeared with a whole tray of green drinks, walking straight to Per who took the first and a second, Maggie then went to Jorge, then Jack and everyone else in the room before placing four on the stage for the members of Convoke. The boys were all standing together, and they all automatically took the drink. Knowing that they always made a rule of not drinking before a gig, Jack, Leonard and Jim all looked to Paul,

"Look, Jim isn't going to have his, I reckon either we all refuse and face the consequences, or we just suck it up and accept that we are in a foreign country." Jack spoke next,

"Well, I don't fancy having to explain our lack of Rock and Roll credentials to him before he has seen us play" taking a sip, he laughed, "I haven't tasted that for years! It's just Limeade."

The others looked oddly at him before Paul took his and agreed, Leonard chose to down his in one and Jim simply chose not to take the risk. They sat back down at the trestle table which had been set up towards the side of the stage and picked up the soft drink cans that Jo had arranged for them. Looking across at the VIP area, Per had trapped Jorge in the corner and Jorge had summoned Shy. The group were sure that Jorge looked scared, and it almost looked like Shy had been brought in as support. Per Hafidi's entourage were positioned around the entrance to the VIP area despite there being no other people in the building. Maggie had taken a seat at another table a good distance away, it seemed like an act from performance theatre was taking place and the band couldn't help but watch before realising that Convoke had finished their song.

The sound of a single person clapping is a very sinister sound and it certainly sounded such now. Per was on his feet clapping slowly and calling out

"Very good, very good, now let me hear noname."

"Noname" Paul chuckled as he headed straight to the stage, He picked up his guitar and strapped it on

"Let's do 'Yours' and then 'Tube Station.'" The group nodded and Paul called the instructions to Nic at the sound desk. They took their positions. Nic gave the signal and, although the regular lights were on in the hall, the lighting rig shone brightly. Jim counted them in and their sound filled the room.

Immediately it felt right. The band thundered through their first song, Jack was performing as if he was on the Pyramid Stage at Glastonbury as always, Paul knew it was good, he took the chance to look around him at the watching faces. Maggie was almost dancing on her chair, even the suits, who looked like they were made of concrete, appeared to at least want to be moving a little.

In the VIP area, Per had his arm around Jorge and kept hugging him closer and tapping him on the shoulder. At the end of their first song, Nic shouted across to the venue staff to just adjust something on the stage and asked Jim to just play a little on his snare before giving the band permission to continue playing. By the time they finished with the abrupt ending to 'Tube Station' Maggie wasn't the only one dancing. A round of applause came from everyone in the venue and Per was on his way to the stage.

The suits were a little slow to react but Per was up on the stage shaking hands, telling them all that they were the best. Nic approached the stage and fiddled with a bit more kit but everyone else seemed happy. Per announced to the whole room that he would be back for the gig and disappeared. With a flash of the green jacket, he was again engulfed by the suits and with Maggie leading the way, they left the building.

Jo and Shy had both also come over to congratulate them. The band fiddled about a little just checking their kit and had another little chat before Jo was able to usher them back to the bus for the journey to the hotel. Both she and Shy had been impressed by their approach to everything. Both were sure that if they could manage these four individuals well, then they easily could be big. Tonight, they weren't going to the hotel they had originally booked, instead it was a gift from Shy to the whole touring party, a cleaner, shinier, more spacious hotel alongside the marina. They walked in as Tilly and Adam were heading out, Jack and Paul both pausing to admire Tilly as she stepped out through the doors, held open by the immaculately dressed attendant.

Chapter 22

You Will Get Stuck

Tilly had thought about taking him to her favourite restaurant in Valencia but, from their conversations she wasn't sure that he was quite ready for the Michelin starred place. The next place she thought would be perfect, she conveniently knew the maître d' and it was the place with the best view. She knew that even if he didn't like the food, the ambience would make up for that. Looking along the road and seeing that no taxi was available, Tilly looked back to the attendant who nodded and stepped back inside. Within seconds, a car was pulling up and the driver was out to open the door for her. It was only a short drive before they were once again stepping into the heat. A short hop across the pavement and through an almost secret doorway, the kind that Adam would have never dreamed of walking through if he was on his own. The doorway merely opened onto a lift and as they waited for the doors to open, Adam once again looked around.

He knew that he probably looked better than he had looked for years, well, if you overlooked the undoubted sweat patches that would have been starting to appear and just the general out of shape-ness that was typical of a lot of the people of his age back in London. Here, everyone looked healthier, more relaxed. Adam was sure that he had made the right choice to come but he had absolutely no idea how he would feel later.

The sound of the lift arriving disturbed his thoughts and, although it was obvious that the lift was at the ground floor it took too long to open. When it did finally choose to do so, there was a rather awkward screech from the doors, the kind of which seemed to Adam to shout 'Don't get in here. You will get stuck'. He looked across at Tilly who was just herself looking at the doors and smiling as if the whole world was perfect. Once the doors fully opened, she stepped in, seemingly unaware of Adam's distrust of this lift. The bright light and the mirrored walls showing views of Tilly on three sides made him realise that it wouldn't be the worst place to get trapped inside. He stepped in and Tilly pressed the only button available inside, once again, the doors screeched, the motors whirred and just at the point where Adam was certain that it wasn't going to rise, they felt a clunk and there appeared to be movement.

He didn't know if he was going up or down, surely if there is a lift to purgatory then it will sound like this he thought, the whirring sound increased, followed by clunking, a shudder and an abrupt stop before the doors opened as smoothly as jelly on ice.

The light filled the lift as they stepped out into the full glare of the evening sun. A light breeze blew, and Adam stepped out onto the rooftop garden. It felt like a scene from the Chelsea flower show but with a Valencian sky, Bright white sails tied with equally bleached ropes brought patches of shade above a collection of tables dotted amongst the foliage. The perfect linen on the table clashing crisply with the greenery. The staff all dressed in the cleanest white glided across the ground as if they were on rails.

As Adam looked in awe around him a perfect specimen of humanity appeared at his shoulder and greeted him with a flurry of words and smiles. He had no choice but to just smile and step backwards as Tilly took over. He understood Tilly saying something about 'Inglese' as the angel looked at him and in perfect English apologised before asking him if he would like a view of the city or the gardens. Of course, he didn't know, and once again he looked to

Tilly to answer. He had no idea what she chose but the two women looked knowingly, and he was led to a perfect table positioned in the corner of the building. He held the chair for Tilly to sit before settling himself into his chair and sat back, just taking a moment to enjoy the atmosphere, knowing that whatever happened it was unlikely that he would ever have an experience like this again.

Before he had a proper chance to look all the way around another waitress had appeared at the table with a basket of small perfectly formed miniature loaves of bread, a small plate with immaculately presented pats of butter and a jug of iced water. He looked across at Tilly who was just sat smiling at him. They both acknowledged the waitress with a smile and a gracias before each looking to the basket. A hasty discussion about how great it all looked and a first taste. All Adam could say was thank you as he sat back with the warm bread in his mouth. All was good with the world.

The meal passed so quickly and after the main course, the dessert menu arrived and they both read each entry carefully, trying to imagine the glory of the flavours on their tongue. They both were hoping that the other would not want a dessert, eventually it was Adam that spoke,

"What would you like?"

"Oh, they all look so lovely but I'm really not sure that I can." Tilly spoke gently,

"I know what you mean, this place is fantastic. Thank you. We should come back another day". Tilly smiled at his words,

"Yes, yes we should, let's hope we can come with Jada and Sam".

Adam knew what was ahead of him, but he had tried not to notice the sun dropping in the sky. A quick check of his watch confirmed that the club would be just opening. It was a little out of the main city centre, and according to the website, it provided a nightclub from 9pm to 4am from Thursday to Saturday with live music provided on Friday and Saturday nights.

"Ok, let's go." He looked at Tilly trying to sound as confident as he could and as authoritative as he ever had. She nodded professionally and, with a speed that he had never experienced before, one look at the waitress caused the bill to appear at the table and they had paid. Tilly took one last look around the rooftop before asking,

"Shall we walk, or do we play with the lift again?" Adam too took a look around but this time he was trying to estimate just how many flights of stairs it might be, too many was the simple answer,

"Let's play in the lift." He said the sentence cheerily and Tilly raised an eyebrow interrogatively before she reached out to press the button.

The lift doors both opened and closed very smoothly but as soon as the door had closed completely the clunking started, and they both looked at each other and laughed. They nervously giggled all the time through the variety of sounds that clunked and whirred and chirped before the doors started opening, delivering them back to the ground floor. They stepped out, Adam took Tilly's hand and led her across the pavement to where a taxi was waiting. He opened the door, poked his head in to give the name of the club and stood back to let Tilly get in, holding the door for her and then closing the door behind her. He half trotted around the car, scared that it would drive off without him before he was then able to enter from the other side. The second he hit the seat the car lurched around and sped up the road in the opposite direction. The driver had said something quickly in Spanish, but he hadn't caught what and Tilly wasn't telling.

As they pulled up outside the venue on the outskirts of town, Adam stepped out, somewhat unsure of his surroundings, the building looked like a version of a DIY store that had been closed for some time albeit with a crowd gathering outside. Most dressed almost like it was a polo ground in the middle of summer. Chinos, short sleeved shirts and sunglasses for the men, short summer dresses and sunglasses for the ladies. An antiquated van parked to one side was selling cocktails whilst on the other side the smell of burnt cheese filled the air from a pizza oven.

Tilly looked at Adam, nodded and headed straight towards the black glass doors, as she opened them, they felt as much as heard the music and they stepped into the darkness. A desk to one side of the room had two people sat on it whilst directly in front of them three bouncers stood next to a tiny booth. They approached the booth and Tilly spoke simply in a voice that Adam had not previously heard. She commanded the attention of everyone within earshot. She elicited a short response from the baldest of the bouncers and he quickly led them through to the main auditorium. Adam was simply in awe as they were led to the VIP area and guided to a table, a hostess approached with drinks for them both and they settled back into the green velvet chairs.

Once again Adam looked around himself and wondered what the old Adam would have thought. There were two other people in the VIP area, both very attractive girls and two bouncers stood guarding the entrance to the area. It was up a short flight of stairs giving a perfect unhindered view of both the stage and over the heads of those who were already filling up the dance floor.

"What did you say to them?" He asked,

"It isn't what you say as much as the way that you say it to people like that" was Tilly's response, she took another sip from her drink and just looked at him, he felt like she was waiting for another question but he really didn't have a clue what he could say so he held her gaze and just looked back. She continued,

"My father played rugby, he was pretty good so people of that size really don't scare me, I have seen far bigger men than them in far scarier situations and I haven't had too many scratches so, it seems to work, I'm ready for whatever happens and, if all else fails, I have a few useful names in my phone. I haven't called on any of them because I really hope that I don't need to but, with a couple of calls, I bet I could contact someone that this Per Hafidi is scared of."

Adam let this information soak in, he knew that there was so much about her that he didn't know, he didn't like to pry so hadn't asked many questions believing that any information that she wanted to share she would. Now they just sat, they hadn't really discussed a strategy other than telling Per that they knew he was looking for a property. They still hadn't decided how to broach the Jada issue other than by suggesting that for her safe release they would come to an arrangement for him to use the house. They were sure that he would want to visit the property before releasing her, but they would sort out access to the property later. They both agreed that it wasn't the best of plans, but they hadn't thought of anything better, so they were following Adam's philosophy of just seeing where they lead.

The stage was set up for a band, to the right of the stage was a DJ booth where a character who looked like he had modelled himself on the cartoon image of a rock star from 1988 was waving his hands in the air enthusiastically, his long blond hair was perhaps not as thick as it had once been, the bandana covering the receding hairline and the leather waistcoat pulled tight to try to hide the weight that he was now carrying. The dance floor, however, was full of incredibly attractive young people. At the bar were the original bikers and cowboys who had been there when the bands the DJ was now playing had first been rocking the world. They all now seemed quite happy to pose with their beers whilst the younger crowd danced in front of them. Tilly and Adam both agreed that the music was brilliant.

The music was at that happy volume, loud enough to feel through the seats and to avoid having to listen to the conversation at the next table but still quiet enough to hear the person you were with. Adam asked about Tilly's youth. She told him about her father, as soon as she mentioned his name he saw the way that her face lit up, it was clear that there was so much love. The name was familiar to him, but he wasn't enough of a rugby fan to properly identify him but the fact that he recognised the name was enough to tell him that he must have been a very big deal. She told him in the briefest possible way about his successes on the field and then of his work on the coaching side of things.

It seemed like he was still heavily involved in the game and the names that she mentioned were almost all names that he knew. She briefly told him about things that had happened to many of his friends who had stepped away from the game whether due to injury or just age and she was saddened by the number who hadn't coped with the process, hence why she knew some names that might be worth dropping if the need arose.

Tilly asked Adam not to mention her father to Hafidi yet. Although he had been a warrior on the field, apparently too many people knew that he was a pussycat off it and therefore he wouldn't give them the credibility they might need if the need for strength arose. She then gave him a few names that, she told him,

"If I mention these people, just look as tough as you can." She laughed as she said that last line, of course he couldn't look tough, he hadn't been in a fight since he was in infant school.

As they were chatting, a young girl approached with another tray of drinks, placing the drinks on the table the girl bowed to Adam and deferentially spoke,

"I'm sorry Mr Hafidi is very busy tonight. You know we have two bands from England and Mr Hafidi has a lot of business. He will be coming to watch the band shortly and he says he will talk to you when the first band have completed their set. He hopes that you will enjoy the band, he is very sure that you will. He has asked me to bring you these drinks and, if you need anything whilst you wait, please just let me know."

She placed the drinks carefully on the table in front of them and, as she stood to leave, she had one more instruction.

"He will be coming to sit over there very soon but he has asked if you would not approach him until I take you to him. He will be with other businesspeople and he does not think it appropriate to mix, he hopes that you will understand."

They both nodded to her and accepted the drinks, Adam would have preferred a pint, but he wasn't brave enough to ask for one and, despite the girl being terribly polite, it was clear that the instructions were not a request.

"Well, we might as well try to enjoy the band" Adam laughed,

"Do you like to dance?" was Tilly's response which just made him laugh more but perhaps in a slightly more embarrassed way.

"I'm not sure I can dance and look tough" he pleaded which brought Tilly into a fit of giggles,

"It's ok, I have never gone for the strong boys - we just need to look relaxed." Adam took a sip of his drink and once again scanned across the room, he liked the seating position, he had always liked to fully assess his environment. Making sure he knew where the exits were and how he would escape if ever he needed to. He had always told his friends on a night out, that it was better to leave early than to leave in an ambulance. That might have been useful advice to follow now, but, he mused, if he left now, where would he go? Without an answer to that question, he was here and now and que sera.

The lights lowered, and the music volume rose. A doorway on the far side opened and Per Hafidi's procession entered the room. Adam had seen the movement and noticed the way the crowd parted to allow the most delicate girl through first before the henchmen ensured that the space was wide enough for the lapels on Hafidi's bright yellow jacket.

"I guess that's our man" Tilly offered rather stating the obvious. Behind Hafidi followed Shy and Jorge. Jo had chosen to stay side of stage. She had taken an instant dislike to Per and although he had repeatedly tried to encourage her to join them, Jo had stuck to her feelings. She had spent enough time with seedy men to spot a wrong 'un and he was certainly in that category. She was pleased that Shy had always ensured that he would not tolerate any of his staff being made to feel uncomfortable and he had enough credibility, certainly in the London area that people knew how to behave. Sadly, that wasn't always the case elsewhere and right now, Shy was doing his job of having to deal with the creep. She was not going to tag along just to keep this guy happy and Shy would never ask her to.

Chapter 23

O Fortuna

Jo had a final walk around backstage, asking Jim and Leonard if they were ready. She had learnt that she didn't need to ask Jack, he was ready at any moment to be a rock star and he certainly looked the part right now. A nod from Paul and she aimed her laser pointer at the agreed mark at the back of the stage, Nic would be looking for the signal and he in turn would send the signal to the DJ. She could see the booth from her position at the side of the stage and he held up a finger, one more record. As the current track came to its end, the lighting in the hall changed and the volume of the music roared as Carl Orff's O Fortuna filled the room along with a huge cloud of smoke. Jo almost laughed; it was too Spinal Tap for her but at the same time it kind of felt right.

She sensed the crowd prepare themselves and she could see a number gathering at the front of the stage. Jack in the wings bouncing, Paul and Leonard were laughing too. As the crescendo rose at the end, Paul let his guitar wail, Jim ran to his drums and with a huge burst of noise and energy the gig was underway. The classical introduction had taken Shy straight back to the excitement he had felt at his first ice hockey game. The darkness filled the room but Shy had simply become part of the room. Shy felt the sounds rumbling inside him and washing over him. The lights igniting every one of his synapsis as his brain and his body reacted to and became part of the environment.

He was relieved it was loud. He had had enough of listening to the precocious clown next to him who was constantly spouting his opinion but who would not listen to a word that was said in response. If Jorge had not been trusted as much as he was Shy would have made an excuse and left already. Instead he had spent the last few minutes listening to how the government of Spain were making things too easy for immigrants and that this new wave of immigrants were only interested in petty crime and girls and that he had had to put on extra security at all of his clubs to prevent them stealing phones or spiking drinks.

Shy hated every single word that Hafidi was saying, not only because of what he was saying but also the way he was saying it. Jorge had already told him that he suspected that Hafidi was heavily involved in both drug and people trafficking. Jorge's suspicion was enough to tell Shy that it was true and having spent just minutes with the man Shy knew that they would never be friends. It went against all of Shy's morals to even put a band in a room with this man but, according to Jorge, here, if you don't stay on the right side of Hafidi you have no chance to operate any kind of business. Shy resolved that, when he was rich enough, he would set up a competitor and advertise his credentials as a clean operator. He had already told the band that as soon as they had finished playing, they were to leave the venue, they could have a drink in the hotel bar, but he wasn't going to accept any more hospitality here than he had to.

Hafidi was excited for the music though, it was impossible not to be. Shy had now seen the band four times in front of a crowd and for many hours in rehearsal and each and every time he had been impressed. The buildup was perfect, Nic's lighting was superb and the band, well the band played their set. Hafidi kept tapping Shy and Jorge on the back offering his unwanted thoughts and praise.

Shy had had enough and made an excuse of needing to visit the bathroom. Hafidi uncomfortably insisted that one of his goons went with him. If he had intended it to make Shy feel important then it had the opposite effect, Shy felt like a prisoner, the hulk led the way and once again the crowd just stepped back out of the way as they crossed the hall, slowly returning to their places after they had passed. Shy noticed a girl stood just outside the Gents as they approached, as she saw them, she leant around the corner calling something and almost immediately about six people came out of the door. The henchman ushered Shy in indicating that he would wait there.

Shy walked to the sink and splashed water on his face then just looked at himself in the scratched and stained mirror. He read the stickers plastered over the mirror and for the first time this evening, he felt comfortable, for that second, it didn't matter who was outside, he was at a gig. The sounds he could hear, muffled through the walls, were a great band, a band he wanted to see and a band that everyone there loved. He was doing his job by bringing this band to a wider audience. He looked once again at himself and said out loud,

"Ok, let's enjoy the gig."

As he walked out of the toilets, a queue had developed because the brute had been holding people back. Shy ignored him and tried to make his own way towards the stage. Shy's unexpected direction obviously confused his shadow who was now desperately looking towards Hafidi for an instruction. Shy continued until he reached the point where the crowd thickened and then he stood watching the band like a fan. The guard caught up with him and placed his hand on Shy's arm indicating that he should head back towards the VIP area. Shy simply nodded then pointed to the stage and started nodding his head to the music before just turning his focus back to the band on stage. He knew that they didn't have many songs left and so he would just stay here and watch the band for the remainder of their set.

The guard just stood at his shoulder. Shy was trying his best to ignore him when the small girl who had led the procession earlier appeared dancing alongside him. She moved in front and with the sexiest look he had ever received she simply told him that,

"Señor Hafidi would like you to come back to the selected area where you can watch the rest of the concert." Shy looked back to the area where Jorge was looking at him pleadingly. Realising that there was no other answer, he turned and followed his security back towards the VIP area. Once again, the crowd parted as if they were the Red Sea. When he retook his seat, against his best wishes, he apologised to Hafidi and explained that he had just wanted to experience the atmosphere from the floor. Politically, he followed his apology with a compliment on how good the sound was in the room.

Over the years, Shy had needed to butter up enough club owners and had learnt that they all wanted to hear how good their sound systems were. Either they were the item in the building that had cost the most amount of money or, the owner would have had their system for far too long and, being told that they sounded great was their justification for not spending any more on a new system. He knew he was cheating the paying public each time he said that, but he knew what the owners wanted to hear. If they then asked an honest question, he would respond but, if he was being completely honest there were only a small number of clubs that he had refused to go back to because of the quality of sound, it was rock and roll that he sold, not the Royal Philharmonic. He sat back down and chose to watch the crowd. The majority of faces were like those he had seen on every night of this run. Shy though watched the older crowd at the back. Shy was interested in them, they would have seen bands here maybe every week.

The thrill of live music might never recede but with age, Shy had noticed that it took a little more to be really impressed than it had so he would gladly listen to the old heads whenever he was watching a band. He was pleased to see that almost everyone was watching the stage, and that included those behind the bar too. Heads were nodding and feet tapping and the applause began before they had even finished their song. Shy had spent a fair amount of time the day before on the phone with various journalists and radio people trying to engage their interest for when they went back to Britain. It was never easy trying to describe a band without seeing or hearing them and, although he had the few early videos that Jo had taken, and a few other pieces that they had got a crew to film at Jorge's studios, he needed to be sure that his contacts would watch the videos.

Of course, whenever he had done that, he had worried, hearing the voice of his mother when his father had first told him about the church in Dhaka,

"Why do you tell me of these strange people singing their songs about someone you cannot see". His father had spent the rest of that evening trying to explain how the music had made him feel but Shy's mother couldn't understand. Shyamal had since made his career out of trying to tell people how their lives could be better if they listened to this band or that song, and trying to find the band that would make the whole world better!

Trying to explain the power of music to others never makes any sense, it has to be heard, and felt, but that was his mission. He really thought that perhaps this band were the best he had found. Everything so far suggested that they could be huge. Shy looked around him, thoroughly studying the faces of everyone close. Sadly, this wasn't a meritocracy, this was the music business. For every person like Jo and Jorge, there were ten like Hafidi that could destroy a band and a life without the slightest hint of remorse.

Hafidi had made space for Shy to sit alongside him, he sat down and once again Hafidi wrapped his arm around him, but this time pulling him closer for a full hug as he told Shy that these were,

"The Band of the Summer." Shy was torn, he wanted the gig to last longer but at the same time, he was relieved to hear the band strike the chords to their last song. Jack had the crowd following his every command, the front half of the hall were all waving their arms as if they were at a Taylor swift concert, Paul was stood on his monitor at the side of the stage with a sea of hands reaching into the air, he saw Jo coming onto the stage to take photos. Hafidi saw that too and immediately put his hand on Shy's knee.

"You'll need to pay me if you ever publish those pictures." Shy looked at him in disgust first before remembering the warnings Jorge had given him,

"It's business my friend" Hafidi said before he stood and walked to a table in the corner and sat next to a couple who had been sat there since Shy had arrived.

Shy had noticed them throughout the gig, they seemed to be enjoying the music but there was a strange atmosphere about them. Shy had kept an eye on them. In the way that he was always alert for anyone that seemed uncomfortable. If he hadn't been surrounded by Hafidi's gang he would have tried to talk to them, they looked like they needed a friend. He perhaps understood why they had been feeling like that, they had been waiting for their audience.

Chapter 24
The Duck And The Seahorse

Tilly and Adam had been keeping themselves occupied by trying to imagine the names of the people in Hafidi's entourage, and then assigning them with the animal that they most resembled. They had the Badger, the Chipmunk and one that could only ever have been a Rhinoceros. Jorge had been designated the Seahorse for the way that he had seemed to float above everything that was going on and if anything touched him, he just seemed to bounce away. Shy had been the duck - his beak never stayed in one direction for any length of time, his head would bob to his drink then look left, then right, then ahead, then drink again. He seemed to be fully in control of the one square foot in front of him but fearful of attack from any side. In the moments where Hafidi had got closer, he looked ready to fly away. And then there was the Sheepdog who had been sent to follow the duck on its walk and made sure that it came back and didn't stray too far. But now the Ostrich was approaching their table, sticking his neck so high and making sure that everyone saw him despite the fact that if you looked properly, it was rather unpleasantly ugly.

Tilly and Adam both sat up straighter as he grabbed a chair from the table alongside theirs and he sat. Adam immediately offered a hello, but he just sat and looked at them, carrying out his own assessment. Eventually it seemed that they were worthy of conversation,

"I have been told that you might have something I need." There were no niceties in his approach and he only spoke in Spanish, so Adam merely sat and tried to look relatively tough.

"We represent someone who might" was Tilly's response not wanting to give too much away too soon. That approach lasted until the end of Hafidi's next sentence,

"I don't have long so don't waste my time, what do you want, I either do business or have fun and right now, this is neither." Adam saw Tilly reposition herself, she could tell by the cold look on his face that she hadn't yet got him interested. Tilly had thought that she might need to go direct so hit the ground running,

"OK - I know you have Jada Arrazola. You want a house on that stretch of the coast where you can allow boats to come and go with privacy. Is that right?" He did not answer but cocked his head suggesting that she say more.

"My friend here is the agent of a football player. He has a property that will provide everything that you could want, the footballer uses it for no more than six weeks a year so my friend is looking for a way to ensure that the property is looked after and that he receives some benefit for the taxes he pays on it." Tilly and Adam had discussed using the tax line, no one likes paying taxes and Tilly was sure that Hafidi would be the same, but she was also sure that he would pay the taxes properly on some of his businesses to ensure that others remained hidden. Why would a footballer not be the same, telling him that everything was properly paid for and clean would make it more attractive she felt. Hafidi nodded, she was starting to connect.

"So, tell me, where is the property?"

"Close to Jada Arrazola's, just the other side of the bay."

"And it is clean?"

"Yes"

"Who is the footballer?" Adam was following the staccato rhythm of the conversation like a tennis match. It was clear that information was being shared but without either party giving too much. And it certainly was more business than friendly.

"That is not relevant, you do not need to know."

"You know that I can find out in seconds don't you, I already know every footballer here."

"I don't doubt that and once you visit the property you will I'm sure know the individual. If we do business we will ensure that his, how shall I say it, his fingerprints will be clean from the property so you will not be at risk from anything relating to him" She didn't really know what she was saying here but she felt that it was probably the kind of bluff that he was wanting to hear.

"So do you have photos of the property, if you know what I want?" Hafidi asked. Tilly turned to Adam and speaking in English asked him for the photos, He opened the album he had prepared on his phone, with a bit of basic photo editing he had made the pictures that he had stolen from the internet look a little more like genuine photos and had ordered them in a way to make it look like they had planned the pictures purely to show what he needed to see rather than looking like they had been taken by an Estate Agent. Adam insisted on holding the phone, positioning himself a little closer to Hafidi. He had noticed that Hafidi had sought physical contact throughout the evening and Adam thought that he may be able to break down some barriers in that way. Adam also commentated throughout the display. Although Hafidi had been speaking in Spanish only, Adam had heard him speak to the duck in English so knew that he could.

Hafidi studied carefully, assessing the dock and the garden more than any of the photos taken indoors. Once finished he turned back to Tilly.

"It is not as perfect as the other house that I want, why have you bothered me?" He had swapped back to Spanish and stared intently at Tilly who did not blink before responding.

"You know that you will not change the mind of Jada Arrazola on principal and kidnapping her has only made her friends more resolved, they do not like your business and they will not change their minds, you have got yourself into a battle that I don't believe you want and that I don't think you are prepared to die for. I heard about the situation, I have a solution, you tell Jada Arrazola that you have found a better solution, you thank her friends for not being too upset but now, you are happy to let her go and you will not disturb her again."

Tilly knew that she had to be careful, she didn't want him to think that she cared about Jada, but also needed to ensure that she would be released. She knew that she couldn't just ask for that to happen, she wanted to look like she was only interested in the business, and she wanted to offer him the business solution.

Hafidi sat back, looking around the hall, the stage was being cleared, the DJ had returned to his booth and was playing records again for those who were still spread out over the dance floor or now sitting on the edge of the stage but most of the crowd had either headed outside to the smoking areas or were queueing at the bar.

"I have business tomorrow in Barcelona. Give me the address, I will get my associate to see if your offer is viable and, if he agrees I will come to visit the property on Monday." He raised his hand in the air and the girl came running, well, as much as she could in those shoes,

"The address." This time he was looking straight at Adam and spoke in English, Adam looked across at Tilly who nodded. So far, the script had been followed perfectly. Adam gave the address perfectly with appropriate Spanish intonation.

Tilly had taught him that even though he couldn't speak the language well enough, if he was anything like most of the British people she knew who had bought property in Spain, they would have made the effort to at least give their address with a Spanish pronunciation, either just to impress their friends back in Surrey or because of the need to give a Spanish delivery company very clear instructions. He recited the address as the girl typed it into her phone, when he had finished, she showed him the phone highlighting the property on the map, Adam nodded and she put the phone away.

Hafidi looked back at Tilly and added, I need your number too and passed his phone to his assistant, Tilly gave her number and the girl looked for more, "

You don't need my name" Tilly responded. Adam and Tilly had discussed names before, recognising that if they used their real names a quick internet search would raise far more questions than they answered. Her online profile was filled with newspaper reports of her business successes and investments and his with a fairly poor batting average in the London East cricket league. The girl nodded as if it was a perfectly acceptable answer. She looked at Hafidi who nodded in response.

"Good, then we will meet again on Monday" he announced as he stood, adjusted his jacket and by the time he had straightened himself out, his entourage had appeared behind him. The girl had already taken her position at the front of the group, and they sped across the hall.

Adam and Tilly watched them leave and, as they left the room, they looked at each other and stood up to leave. As they were heading towards the exit of their VIP area the Seahorse (Jorge) and Duck (Shy) were heading out too. The Seahorse was a little ahead of them and nodded before heading down the steps onto the floor, Duck paused, looking at them both,

"Are you ok?" He asked with a voice far softer than could have been expected. Adam smiled,

"Yes thanks" it was his automatic response, Tilly smiled too,

"I hope so" was her rather more realistic answer.

Chapter 25

Open The Champagne

They said almost nothing in the taxi back to the hotel, Tilly had warned Adam that it was likely that the drivers would all be working indirectly for Hafidi. He was the kind of character who would want a cut from any business that anything he did could benefit from. Adam was relieved to reach the privacy of the lift, he leant back against the mirrored wall and breathed out like he had held his breath all night, Tilly smiled at him, placing her hand on his forearm and sensitively asked,

"Are you OK?" Just hearing those words brought a tear to his eye. He had been thinking how difficult this must have been for her, her friend was still lost somewhere. He knew how emotionally exhausted he was by the situation, he could only imagine the effect it was having on Tilly, and yet she still was caring for him. It should be the other way around he thought, he should be the brave one doing the talking and keeping her safe but, he didn't know the language, he felt useless. All he could answer was a

"Yes thanks", he looked at her, "and how are you?"

Before she could answer the doors slid open, Adam hadn't even felt the lift stop. Tilly led the way to the door, but Adam had the keycard which he proceeded to enter upside down again before opening the door and walking in. He remembered being told that the man should always enter a hotel room first in case there was anyone already inside. It went against his idea of chivalry and he would have probably been useless if anyone had actually been there but, whether Tilly noticed or not, he did it for that reason. That is why he walked in first, which made the bouquet of flowers, the bottle of champagne on the table and the candles a surprise. Tilly laughed when she came in, Adam was looking confused, he was torn between the thoughts of 'this must be a mistake' and 'oh my goodness, does she really...' his mind was spinning in hope then fear then just pure awe. Tilly walked to the flowers and picked up the card that Adam hadn't even seen. She turned it over and read the message,

"Welcome to our hotel, we hope that you enjoy your stay" she laughed again knowing exactly what Adam had been thinking before asking "Shall we open the champagne?"

The next morning Adam woke early, he had not pulled the curtains and so the sun streaming through the windows had awoken him. It took him a few seconds to work out what he could feel against his back before opening his eyes and seeing the coffee table in front of him, he was reminded that he was on the sofa. He stretched his legs out, feeling the blood reaching his toes before working out exactly how he should position himself to stand up.

He stood slowly, pausing for a moment to look around the room. Everything looked so exquisite and he wanted to be sure to take everything in. He took a few steps to the window and spent a good couple of minutes just watching the traffic on the roundabout below. Once he was sure that he had seen every colour of car pass by, he turned back to the room. Opening the fridge, he took out a bottle of orange juice and then put the kettle on. He took a swig from the bottle and sat on the high stool. The bedroom door had been left just slightly ajar. Through it he could see the bright white sheets on the bed just slightly ruffled by the form of Tilly sleeping beneath. He wanted to look more but left the stool and wandered to the couch where he sat and, as with people in hotel rooms all over the world, he then started the search for the remote control.

Finally spying the controller on a little side table in the corner of the room it took him an extra few moments to build the motivation to head over to get it. He flicked it on and had to desperately search for the volume control as it blared immediately. On screen, three brightly coloured women in only slightly less brightly coloured clothes were sat at a table in a much more brightly coloured room. Adam laughed at how universal daytime television formats appeared to be worldwide. The discussion may have been about anything from the grieving process to the terrors of starvation, but he suspected that whatever had occurred in the world, this programme would be the television equivalent of the post nuclear beetle and it would continue to broadcast its special kind of reassuring chatter and nonsense. He watched for a minute or two, unable to work out what they may have been discussing but he was sure it was of vital importance. As he always did, he hit one on the remote and started scrolling up through the channels knowing that, if nothing else, he would eventually find a sports channel.

It was channel 22 before he found sport but kept looking for anything in English. On Channel 44 he recognised a celebrity chef and paused until he heard the dubbed voices. And then, an episode of Poirot, again with dubbed voices which he watched for a couple of minutes just enjoying the scenario of a Belgian, who notoriously has a bad accent, talking to an English old lady (with what he was sure a very typical Oxford English accent) both talking away in Spanish.

Eventually he found the full sports section, baseball first, then some indoor football which he watched for a few minutes before deciding that both teams were awful, there was horse racing from maybe China or Japan before finally he settled on volleyball.

He had been watching for a few minutes before he sensed he was being watched, he looked up and saw Tilly stood at the doorway with her sheet loosely wrapped around her.

"Morning" they both said at almost exactly the same time, Tilly laughed, Adam stood immediately and offered her a drink, switching the kettle on even before she had answered,

"Coffee please, and can I have a shower?"

"You don't need to ask me" was his quick response before he worried that he may have sounded too sharp, but her smile reassured him,

"I'll have my coffee when I come out, it will be ok to drink." Adam merely nodded, desperately trying not to look anywhere he shouldn't. He guessed that she was just behaving in a more European manner where it was perfectly normal to see people topless on the beach but for him, from his background…

He busied himself with her drink, making sure that it was perfectly placed on the counter, he had found a plate and arranged the small packets of the complementary biscuits neatly on the plate alongside it and finally selected a flower from the bouquet to lay alongside. He stood back wondering if he had done too much, and now that it was done, what should he do?

Adam sat back on the sofa and continued through the channels to find BBC news or, if not that, he guessed he would find some other news channel in English, sure enough he was soon relieved to find the reassuring sight of the BBC logo filling the screen as a montage of newsworthy stories flew around it seemingly advertising itself. When the presenter reappeared, they started droning on about the upcoming Australian elections, Adam managed to listen for approximately 45 seconds before realising that not only did he not understand Australian politics, he also had absolutely no interest in the subject either. Adam went back to the volleyball channel except now the volleyball was over, he hadn't known how many sets (?), games (?) There were in a match, and he now would never know if it was the reds or the yellows that had won. They were now showing swimming so, given the choice of Australian elections or swimming, he selected music. He turned the volume down a little and let a low-resolution video from the 1980's fill a screen which had far too many pixels for the poor pop star's face.

He checked his watch, they had just over an hour before the car hire desk opened just a short walk from the hotel. He hadn't known if Tilly would want breakfast, but he knew that he needed something. He reached out to the fruit bowl and grabbed a banana before opening his phone and checking the traffic on their route. His map offered him two routes with just sixteen minutes difference between the two and with the current traffic they should make it in less than a couple of hours. He then ran a search of the footballer through all of the social media apps, The style of the posts suggested that someone managed that for him, the last thing posted was a photo of a suitcase at the airport with the message "time for a rest" and a sun emoji, nothing of any value and yet still 22k likes. There were a few more pictures of Matt and an actor that Adam recognised but he probably wouldn't have admitted to watching anything that she had been in. Their feet and the sea, on a boat just offshore and, sitting by a fire, all carefully posed to show no signs of alcohol or debauchery. A couple of selfies came up taken by people who had recognised him at a restaurant or a bar. Adam recognised the 'event' bar in one picture but not from the night itself.

Adam found nothing to suggest that the 'footballer, athlete and part time DJ' as his online profile labelled him, Matt Riley was no longer in Spain. That news alone was one big relief, now all they needed to do was to find him and let them have his villa for the day tomorrow. This time it would be Adam's turn to do the talking and he hoped that the fairly weak plan he had would be enough.

The whole morning had been spent thinking about each of the possible questions he may be asked and rehearsing his answers. He needed something to keep himself busy whilst he waited for Tilly so, flicking through his phone he started preparing a playlist that he thought Tilly might enjoy on the drive.

Adam heard the door open and instinctively looked up to see Tilly stood with a towel wrapped around her head but otherwise completely naked, he looked away immediately whilst sitting up straight, he sensed her waiting then heard her voice,

"I thought we might just pick up some croissants from breakfast as we leave and get on the road, we can eat in the car or stop somewhere nice on the way, it is ok?" Now that she was directly talking to him he had no choice but to look up, telling himself - it's just a body, don't stare. But he couldn't help it, she had a beautiful body, he tried as hard as he could to keep his eyes looking at hers as he responded.

"Yes, that will be fine, the car hire place opens very soon so we can go as soon as…" he couldn't finish the sentence as she walked towards him, picking an apple from the fruit bowl, she smiled at him and turned to walk back to her room. He watched her leave, he knew that she knew that he was watching but, he would have to be a fool not to. She half paused and looked back as she almost swung around the door out of sight, he sat in awe for a few minutes before immediately looking back to his phone and added a few songs that had instantly leapt into his mind.

She reappeared a few minutes later in a T-shirt and shorts, but not looking like a tourist does in a T-shirt and shorts, she looked like she had just stepped off of one of the yachts in the marina, or out of a gym in Kensington or, anywhere else that beautiful women wore T-shirts and shorts.

"I think I'm ready" she offered, "Do I look ok?" Adam could only smile as he stood and took a final look around the room.

"I'm going to miss this place" he said as he picked up both his and Tilly's bag and headed to the exit.

Tilly had phoned reception with her breakfast request so as they arrived at reception a staff member appeared with a giant white paper bag which he went to hand to Adam before realising that his hands were full. Tilly interjected with something in Spanish and took the bag, thanking the staff for all of their services they left the hotel and headed just a few doors down to the car hire office.

The salesperson behind the desk at first appeared to be shocked by the thought that someone might want a car today but, after some negotiation from Tilly including an acceptance to pay the collection fee because someone would have to get the car from the basement car park she was offered one of just two vehicles. Either the cheapest or the most expensive in the range. Adam saw it being the perfect sales pitch, but Tilly wasn't fussed. She chose the better car which provoked a fair amount of huffing from the salesperson as he collected different pieces of paper from the printer. Eventually he could find no good reason to delay them further and he picked up the phone. After a few barked commands, he hung up and indicated that they should wait at the corner of the street and the car would arrive.

Adam picked up their bags and headed to the corner. It took three looks at Tilly's watch and a discussion about whether they should go back into the office, for the car to appear. A scruffy youth stepped out and almost grunted as he handed the keys to Tilly before immediately turning and walking away.

"Welcome to Valencia, enjoy your journey!" Tilly half called before looking back at Adam and apologising. She looked at the key fob trying to find a button to open the boot, locking the car fully before finding the button that opened the boot. The graphics that probably once indicated which of the three sections to press had appeared to have been wilfully scratched off even though the car itself looked almost brand new.

The bags fitted easily into the boot and Adam and Tilly settled into the now regular pattern of their journeys. Whilst Tilly was adjusting her seat and mirrors, Adam was typing the address into the satnav. The journey passed without any excitement except for the sight of a lorry full of goats being transferred from a vehicle that had broken down into a replacement truck. The tyres crunched into the gravel of the car park by the harbour and they slowly strolled to the cafe for a drink and, if they were both honest, to use the facilities before they tried the bold approach of knocking on Matt's door.

It felt strange to be back in the village and seeing the road to Sam's house brought a tear to Tilly's eye. She knew how difficult things had been for Sam trapped in the house just waiting for a call. If she had heard any more news, then she hadn't shared it. Tilly had so much to tell Sam that she hadn't been able to during their brief chats. The house was still under observation so there was no way that Sam could know that they were in the village. They nursed the last of their drinks, both waiting for the other to make the decision before, in a determined act of decisiveness for Adam, he spoke up with a commanding,

"Come on then, it's time." Tilly nodded before, underwhelmed by his authority, she added,

"Let me just go to the toilet again."

"Ok I'll wait by the car" was the best he could then manage.

Adam was then stuck just standing in the heat alongside the car waiting for her to return and unlock the car for him. He felt ten years old again, waiting for his mother to say goodbye to whichever ancient family member he had just had to spend hours listening to. Now though he was stood in the heat of a Mediterranean summer, looking out across the small beach alongside the dock to where children were playing and mothers were chatting. The slight breeze was enough to keep the sails full of the two yachts sailing past and beyond. On the horizon a giant container ship was carrying its load on towards Italy. He felt the car unlock before he heard Tilly approach. She apologised and, looking at how cute she looked, he couldn't help but instantly forgive her.

Chapter 26

We Can Make That Happen

The drive to Matt's villa took just a couple of minutes, their study of maps online and the photo views had shown them that there was almost a lay-by for cars outside of the garden wall. Tilly pulled into this space and parked. A look across at each other and a quick,

"Are you ready?" and they were out, ringing the bell at the intercom by the gate. An answer came quicker than he had expected, a strict Spanish voice came through the intercom. Adam spoke with his rehearsed intro,

"Good afternoon, we are here to meet with Mr Riley." The voice came back instantly,

"Mr Riley is not expecting any visitors today thank you. If you wish to make an appointment, I presume that you have his contact details." Whoever the voice was, was good, it seemed like she must at some point have been a doctor's receptionist.

"I'm sorry I don't have an appointment but I'm responding to a conversation I had with Matt a couple of days ago, I think he might want to know that I'm here." The voice paused for a second.

"Please wait for a couple of minutes, I will contact Mr Riley." The intercom clicked off and Tilly pointed at the logo at the bottom of the unit, telling him,

"It is a remote service, he could be anywhere, but this company answers the door, probably the phone too and will either let you in or, more likely, keep you out here without him even knowing. Let us hope they believe you." An awkward few minutes passed before the door opened, and Matt appeared stood wearing just a pair of loose trousers,

"Hi, how are you, I wasn't expecting a visit,"

Adam was almost shocked that here he was in the company of a celebrity again, he tried as hard as he could to just think about his prepared approach.

"Yes sorry, I know but you said when we spoke the other day that you wanted the band for a party, we can make that happen," that confused Matt,

"Wait, what? Sorry, I… oh, sorry I didn't recognise you. Come in." He opened the gate a little wider and allowed them through, shaking Tilly's hand and saying hello to her as he did. Matt guided them through to a large patio area, whilst Adam followed, trying to understand all the tattoos across the footballer's back. Glasses and bottles left on the tables and around the garden indicated that last night's party had not been finished for long enough for the tidying up to have been done.

"Please, excuse the mess, it is still early, would you like a drink?"

"Could I please just have a water thank you." Tilly responded,

"Yes, great idea" Matt agreed and before Adam could speak Matt had called out,

"Sal, could you bring us some water please? ...and some glasses?" He moved a bottle from one table to the next and pulled a chair across to sit down at the cleanest of the available tables.

"So, what are you talking about? What was that all about the other night? The police told me to forget all about it and not mention it to anyone. It sounded too weird, so I haven't said anything, I'd be in a world of trouble if anything bad came out."

"I don't know any more than you do by the sounds of it" Adam responded, "They were looking for something and had heard that someone at the event knew more than they did. I presume they got what they needed or, surely, we would have heard more."

Adam knew that his last sentence made very little sense but also knew that Matt probably wanted to know that he didn't know less than anyone else. And Matt wanted the reassurance that he had done the right thing. Adam had spent long enough sitting in meetings to learn just how many people like to just hear people speak, regardless of the value of the words that they are actually saying. Tilly had encouraged Adam to try to bond with Matt but, beyond their shared experience as hostages Adam really couldn't imagine having much in common and they had agreed that to probably wasn't a good idea to dwell on a subject that could only bring about more suspicion. Adam needed to get the conversation back on track.

"I didn't say the other night because I didn't know what was happening but, I am with the band" he offered,

"Wow cool" was Matt's immediate response. Adam had guessed that meeting a man who knew someone would not be unusual for him so why wouldn't he be with the band? He carried on,

"Look, you know the band are brand new? Well, they have hit the ground running and things are progressing far quicker than we would have expected. We want to take advantage of the summery sounds of their songs and get a single released as soon as possible."

Matt had been nodding throughout, he was liking being an insider which was exactly what Adam had been banking on. "We thought whilst we were out here, we should try to film something for a video. We don't have long, getting a permit to film in public here in Spain is a nightmare of paperwork and so we need to find a private property."

Matt was still nodding in agreement. He supposed it would be difficult to get approval, he didn't know. The drinks had arrived carried by Matt's famous girlfriend and, for once, Adam had to agree that she was absolutely gorgeous. Far better in real life, with possibly no make-up on, than she appeared whenever he had previously seen her in the papers or on TV.

"Thank you" they all said almost together.

"So, you want to film here?" Matt had played it perfectly, Adam was quick to keep talking,

"Well, I know you wanted a band to play at your party and, well, we'd need to arrange things properly but, if you'd let us film here then we will get the band to play at your party." Adam could see Matt was smiling, why not, it's a win win he thought,

"Yes, absolutely, when do you want to film?" Adam picked up his glass and offered it for a cheers which was returned, Tilly rolled her eyes a little thinking that Adam might have been over-egging it a bit there but, he had played his part excellently and so she raised her glass to clink too.

"You know we don't have long, we have engaged a local director and film crew, we would like to film towards the end of next week if that's ok but, obviously we would need to have a rough plan of where we could put cameras and stuff, because of the timings it will only be a fairly simple shoot, we want to let the environment provide the story so there won't be a mass of people.

"We will use the natural light and might just bring a few lights for any night scenes if the director wants it, they have agreed whatever the theme, there should be no more than six actors, that way, we keep your house clean and we don't need extra paperwork for the filming, again, so much here is based on admin!"

Tilly was trying to get Adam's attention, to tell him to slow down, not talk quite so much and to breathe. His last overload had almost come out in one breath. Adam had told her that there was a recognised technique that, if you say enough quickly, people are more likely just to agree because they won't want it known that they hadn't followed something. Matt simply looked like he was being told that he had just scored a hat trick in the world cup final. Adam continued,

"But the director would really like to see the property tomorrow if he could? It won't take long. He will just need to look around at what you have here to work with I mean, this lawn looks perfect with the backdrop of the pool."

Matt was nodding along, before he added,

"Well, there is also the dock if you want." Adam knew that it was exactly what he needed to see but he was desperately trying not to let his face show how happy he was.

"Yes, come on, I'll show you." Matt was already enthusiastically out of his seat and heading across the lawn. Tilly and Adam shared a smile before following him. The far side of the lawn had a glass partition, similar to the one at Sam's house preventing people getting too close to the cliff edge. It opened at the far end onto a platform where stairs went down but Matt was stood with his hand outstretched indicating what looked like the kind of gantry that would be used to change the bulbs in streetlights.

"I've just got this fitted, I'm afraid it will only carry two people at a time but if you want to get in. You just have to keep your hand on this button and it will go down." Matt ushered them in and, leaping towards the stairs called out,

"I'll see you at the bottom." Matt raced down the stairs beating them by just a few seconds and was hardly out of breath.

"I reckon that would make a great scene for the video, the guitarist on the lift you know like that 'rain' video in front of the church, the drums could be on the deck here." Matt's boyish enthusiasm was infectious, Adam bit his lip fiercely knowing how he would feel if he knew the truth.

"That certainly seems like a good idea, would you be happy with us using the lift?"

"Yes, of course, I mean, I don't know if you'd want it, but I have got a friend with a yacht. We are lucky, the bay here is quite deep so we can get boats right in here." Adam couldn't believe his luck. The villa was exactly what Hafidi needed, and Adam was sure that the plan was going to be a success. Smiling at Matt confirmed the situation.

"This is all looking perfect, are you sure you wouldn't mind having the band and a crew around?"

"No sure, and look, I hear what you are saying about paperwork, if you need any extras, well I'm sure I could find a few people that would do it just for the blast and, well I know you didn't really recognise me but you must know Sal, I'm sure she'd play a part if you needed it."

Matt was almost begging them to use his place, if anything it was all going too well. Adam was wary that his enthusiasm could be a problem if he got too close to Hafidi. They were walking back towards the villa, Adam was impressed and could see why the plan was such a good idea, the house was perfectly set up as a party house in a delightful location. He needed to tie things together.

"OK well look, if you are sure we can use it, the director, as I said wants to see the place before he decides on the theme, I'm afraid his English isn't great so Tilly here will give him the tour if that's ok? He doesn't like having too many people around him unless he is working and has control of the whole event. She will though make sure that he sees your ideas and I'm sure that he will be delighted to know that you and Sal would be willing to appear."

"Yes, that would be amazing, look, would you like another drink?"

"That's very kind but I'm really sorry, we have a load of stuff to get organised. Things are moving so quickly at the moment. Can Tilly take your number and we will confirm what time that he will appear?"

"Absolutely, no problem" Matt gave his number fluidly, Adam finished by saying,

"Please don't worry about anything to do with the house, you can leave it just as it is. We will get people in before and after to make sure everything is exactly as the director wants it and we'll make sure that it is left tidier than we find it. Look, I'm sorry that we met the way we did but, it would be great to turn it into something positive."

Adam slid into the car and settled heavily into the soft leather upholstery. Tilly efficiently started the car and drove off rapidly. They made it just around the corner before she slammed the brakes on and just let out the biggest scream of relief as the brakes squealed. Adam started laughing and she drove on. She got about a mile down the road before she pulled over again. They looked at each other and simply giggled with relief. Tilly almost burst as she admitted that she didn't know where she was going. Adam just leant back and looked up at the sky. They had expected this part to be the most difficult and yet everything had gone to plan. They now just had time to spare.

"Ok, so we need to find somewhere to stay tonight. We should stay away from the town here, but I don't think we should go too far, do you have any ideas?"

Adam looked at her, almost in disbelief, he really hadn't thought at all about the rest of the day but, of course, they now had a whole afternoon, evening and potentially half of tomorrow to pass. He knew they were waiting for the phone call from Hafidi. He tried to imagine the ideal place for that call to take place, his mind went again to his usual point of reference and asked himself,

"What would Bond do?" He then realised, as Tilly laughed, that he'd actually said it out loud. He imagined scenes of the hero at the casino or the ballet, but Bond always happened to be in the most amazing places, Adam had been impressed by the local area, but he suspected that the world of high-end luxury and casinos were perhaps still a little outside of his reach.

"I don't know. Are there any interesting towns or villages? We could check into a hotel and just take a walk exploring before dinner?" Tilly seemed happy with his response. She took out her phone and opened up the maps,

"Are we sticking to the coast, or would you like to head inland a bit?" She asked, Adam thought, he had always suspected that the attraction of Spain was the coast but that was probably only because of the stories about 'Brits abroad'.

"Can we head inland?" Adam asked. Tilly smiled, responding cheerfully,

"Of course," before typing a new destination into the satnav.

"I have an idea, are your legs strong?" She challenged,

"I can walk" was his only response.

"Good" she laughed, "Allez les bleus!"

Adam looked out of the window at the rugged countryside now flowing past him. They were heading towards the mountains, he worried that she had got the idea to do a mountain bike trail or some ridiculous activity that he wouldn't be prepared for. He chose not to ask any further questions, he just wanted to enjoy the afternoon. The scenery developed as they left the coast behind, the greenery became more pastel hue looking out on rocky fields alongside the river valley. The mountains rose in the distance. Not knowing where they were headed gave a thrill to every road sign, every name on every sign sounding exotic and full of adventure, but good adventure, rather than the fear that had filled his recent days.

Soon the horizon became dominated by one clear hill rising majestically from the surrounding flatter lands. He could see the castle walls following the ridge above the town a long way below. Adam was searching for a better word than wow - he knew that he had a tendency to use that word too often and so perhaps it did not show just how impressed he was. He had been a member of English Heritage when he was younger. Cooler than the National Trust and, by cooler, what he had meant was that they had more castles. Yes, his friends all claimed that they were just piles of stones. Places where people once lived in the cold. And yes, that was true, but amongst those cold stones, the world he knew had been created. It was amongst that rubble that battles were fought. Not only to decide who ran the country but on a more local level. Deciding who would get to farm on that field and who should be able to build a house there.

The basis of the society he lived in was created amongst walls like those throughout England and, as he thought about it, he presumed amongst countries like Spain too. He knew they had had a civil war more recently and that had probably got rid of a lot of that feudal stuff, but, he suspected that there was still a certain amount of power held by the owners of buildings like this. Spain still had a King didn't it? He was trying to work out if asking the question would sound too ignorant when Tilly spoke up,

"Have you seen the castle?"

"Yes, it's impressive." He knew his response sounded weak, but it was all he could manage.

"That's where we are going. I hope you aren't scared of ghosts because we are staying there, and it's over a thousand years old. There must be a couple of ghosts don't you think?"

He wished she hadn't focused on the ghost bit. He had never been a believer in the supernatural but at the same time he had never wanted to not believe either, just in case. When he thought about it, if there was such a thing, then there's a good chance that a building like the one on the hill would have them but, he had always wanted to focus on the life in a building than the death. How many people had celebrated events there? How many parties? How many important decisions?

"We're staying there?" He could not hide his excitement.

"Yep, well, just beneath the castle, it's a very old hotel but I have heard that the gardens are very pretty and it's a special place." Once again, Adam sat back into the leather seat of the car and thought again of how much his life had changed in the last four days.

"You are amazing" was all he could find to say as he looked across at her. She glimpsed quickly across at him, and smiled as she looked back to the road and gunned the accelerator to overtake a lorry full of chorizo.

Chapter 27

Like An Aggressive Rant

Adam had known he was smiling for the whole of the rest of the journey, and his smile had only grown wider as they had entered the town. The typical concrete buildings narrowed and towered over them as they approached the centre before they began the climb onto the side of the hill. The rocky sides of the mountain merged into the edge of the castle wall. A tower stood protecting the corner of the wall looking just like the image from the front page of the very first book of castles he had read as a child. A couple of hairpin bends later and the road had already brought them above the height of the rooftops. A stream now running alongside the road with a beautifully ornate bridge crossing the babbling brook allowing pedestrian access to the castle gardens. The structure of the rocky outcrops had been softened with flowerbeds filled with colour and pristine lawns winding between the roadside and the next layer of the cliffs. Adam was busy still looking high above him to where the castle stood, powerfully studying the surrounding countryside, as if there was an imminent threat and that it might need to hold out a siege for the next one thousand years.

Tilly turned off the road, a narrow gateway brought them into an even more beautiful garden. A wall of almost perfectly white stone topped by a black painted wrought iron fence separated the gardens from the road. As they drove further into the property, the garden became even more verdant, and the foliage surrounded the road. Prize specimens that looked like they had been planted hundreds of years ago had been accompanied by a softer growth of shrubs and herbs around their bases. The narrow drive built the suspense of what they might find. Adam wouldn't have been surprised to turn the corner and find a dinosaur standing in the middle of the road. Eventually the drive opened to show a grand old building nestled amongst the trees on three sides. A gloriously huge and obviously ridiculously expensive iron sign stood with the name of the hotel inscribed through it. Tilly parked on the far side of the car park, under an old wooden roof designed to keep the searing heat of the sun off of the parked vehicles.

As Tilly activated the handbrake, the phone rang. They both jumped as the phone rang through the car speakers. She bit her lower lip as she looked at the screen, confirming her suspicion. It was Per. She looked across at Adam who was already reaching for the notepad. Tilly waited for the start of the third ring before answering very calmly with a crisp "Mr Hafidi."

Hafidi didn't appear to take a breath before going straight into what sounded to Adam like an aggressive rant. Adam watched Tilly for clues, but she kept her calm, professional face throughout. Allowing Hafidi to speak before quickly giving her responses. It wasn't long before she pointed to Matt's address written on the pad and took the pad to read it to Hafidi. She gave him the address and repeated it three times. The meeting was on. Tomorrow at 14:14. He told her he didn't like round numbers and repeated numbers were lucky so 14:14 it would be exactly. Before she hung up there was one more topic that she wanted to cover.

"We have not discussed the price yet. I trust that you will not have any concerns about our charges."

Adam could see by the look on her face that the conversation had reached this point, this was the most delicate part of the negotiation, neither Adam nor Tilly had any idea as to when this would normally be discussed or indeed how much would be an appropriate figure. It had to be enough to justify the risks they were undertaking but not so much that Hafidi thought that they were pushing their luck. And more importantly than that, they needed to get Jada back.

Hafidi's voice appeared to change in tone a little,

"I think you know enough about me. I have a reputation for being very good to my friends, you will be happy with our arrangements."

"I don't want to waste your time and I don't want you to waste mine. You also know that others will know already that I have spoken with you." This was a line Tilly had rehearsed, it sounded straight from a film, but they knew that Hafidi would not expect them to have contacts and therefore he probably thought that he held all the cards. They wanted to make Hafidi think that he shouldn't mess them around.

"I can assure you that I am not wasting your time, I have a need in that area and, if you can provide what you promise we will both be happy. My offer is two thousand Euros per landing. If your dock is not as good, it will be less. If it is better, I can give you more."

Tilly breathed out, this was exactly what they had wanted, now they had a figure to work with.

"That is reasonable, but I have a better option for both of us." They heard Per take a puff on his cigarette before she continued. "A 50% discount for the first three months so that you know you can trust us, and we can learn how you work. If we don't agree then the deal will be over, and you will walk away." Tilly paused, "And to show us that you trust us, you will bring the girl Jada tomorrow and give her to us."

The line went quiet for a while,

"What do want from her?" They now knew that he had the upper hand, Tilly paused herself before answering,

"Her, nothing else. We have a few legitimate investments in her businesses. It is not good for us to have anyone sniffing around." She could feel Hafidi pondering, looking across at Adam who was quietly perspiring into a puddle on the seat. Unable to understand the conversation, and unable to help in any way. He offered a smile. He didn't know what else to do. That made Tilly smile. Amongst all this tension, she was glad he was there. The fact that he was completely unable to do anything right now didn't matter. She was just glad that he was there.

Hafidi's voice cut back in,

"And if I say no?"

"Unless I don't know something, you have no other use for the girl but, if you want to keep her, that's fine, but our price will go up and there is a greater risk to you because the money will link to her." This was the risk, he could walk away, then Jada could be in even more trouble, but, he needed that mooring point. If he was willing to kidnap her then surely, he wouldn't refuse this gift.

Again, Hafidi was quiet. Tilly had reached out and was squeezing Adam's hand waiting for the response.

"OK, I'll bring the girl. If the place is as you promise you can have her as a deposit. But I will keep her until I have seen the place." Tilly nodded, then realised that Hafidi would not have seen it.

"OK. Bring her. We will meet you at 14:14. I trust you will not be late."

Hafidi laughed,

"I am never late."

She trusted that,

"Tomorrow then, don't be late."

Tilly hung up, sat back then looked at Adam and laughed again in nervous relief,

"14:14 tomorrow and exactly that time. Please call Matt immediately." Adam sat back for a second, so far everything they had planned had happened. Could their luck hold? As soon as he thought that, he tried to clear his mind. OK, focus he told himself as he dialled Matt's number. Matt's voice answered the phone almost immediately,

"Adam, hi, how are you? I'm on the boat with Terry right now, he would love to be involved, how are you getting on with the director?" Adam's relief was clear, Matt was so excited by the project.

"Wow, that's great, I have literally just spoken with him, he would like to come tomorrow at 14:14."

"14:14? Could he be a bit less exact?" Matt laughed,

"Yes, I told you he likes to control everything - time as well. I hope that's ok with you, he has asked though if it is just he and Tilly that walk around the premises, apparently I talk too much for him to concentrate! I hope that's OK?"

They could almost hear the disappointment in the air, but he responded quickly,

"Yeah OK, that's fine, I've met a few actors who are funny like that."

Adam laughed, "Yep, tell me about it. If it's OK, Tilly and I will get there a bit early just so Tilly can be sure where everything is and check that you are ok with everything?" The response was prompt,

"Yes, it'll be great, I'm looking forward to it."

They said their farewells before hanging up like they had been best friends for years. Tilly turned the car on,

"Where are we going?" Adam asked in surprise.

"He deserves a gift, if this was real surely a record company would give him something for his time? It's an investment." There was of course sense in her thinking. Adam immediately had the fear he always had when approaching Christmas or birthdays.

"What can we give a professional footballer? He won't want a box of chocolates." It was Tilly's turn to laugh now,

"Didn't you see his house when we visited? What do you think, a crate of wine or a selection of spirits in a hamper? There will be a good wine shop in the town, I was going to suggest we walked down before dinner, but I wouldn't want to carry that much back up the hill."

Chapter 28

Pick A Name

Jo was sat in the middle of the bus at a table with Jack and Jim. She had been working with the band on what Shy called 'media training'. Jo had laughed when he had first told her that he wanted her to train all of the bands. She had no background in the media, and she had never thought of herself as a teacher. She took every one of her roles seriously and so, she had studied hours of interviews to see how the best journalistic interrogators worked to get the answers they wanted. She could also now tell if a band had been given any guidance when she read their interviews or saw them, even a two-minute clip online could ruin a career these days, so it made sense. Most bands didn't understand the need, so she had evolved different ways to try to engage them.

Today though she was just carrying out practice interviews. Recording each interview, she would then save them in her library so that, when the time came, she could forward those videos to local media outlets. Increasingly she was also sending more to online 'influencers' who could then pretend to be interviewing the band themselves. It saved the bands so much time and it meant that she could maintain a degree of control over the messages that were sent.

"So, I'm here today with Jack and Jim from the band, actually guys, we do really need to pick a name, I know that you keep putting it off but, we only have three days left here, when we get back to London we are going to have to really get going with everything, we've got venues booked and stations primed but we are going to have to get a name out there." The interview stopped before it started,

"Out there" mused Jack, there's a name, "the out-theres".

"Outhere Brothers has been done" Leonard interrupted immediately, Jo, Jim and Jack all looked at him, "Boom, Boom, Boom" he looked almost shocked that they didn't recognise it. "Anyway, it sounds like we'd be on drugs."

"True" they all nodded, Jack looked out of the window,

"The Orange Trees?" Jim picked up his phone,

"One song on Apple Music. Just Orange?" Jim offered,

"Too many of those" was Leonard's response,

"Do we really need to find anything that has never been done before? We aren't that original and there are so many bands in this world. It would have to be really obscure for no-one else to have ever used it" Jack added.

Jo wanted to let the band choose their name but had to guide them a bit.

"It doesn't have to be completely unique but, it would really help if whatever name isn't currently on any of the streaming services or such." she advised. "If you like something that is in use, we would have to find a way to adapt it enough, to make it different."

"Orange Orchard?" Jim proposed which provoked a laugh from the others, "London Orchard" was his follow up,

"London Orchid?" Leonard let the name roll through his head before adding "that works."

Jo was just watching, she didn't want to influence the band, this had to be entirely their decision, but she liked this idea, she could see the others were considering it too. Whenever she was close to a band, she imagined the fictional announcer welcoming the band to the stage in the way that only stand-up comedians use now. From the village fete stage came, "Ladies and Gentlemen, please welcome to the stage, LONDON ORCHID!" And then the voice becomes that of the radio presenter with the chart rundown "and this week at Number One it's London Orchid with…" Yes. Jo felt it worked for both of those scenarios, she could see the rest were thinking it too,

"But what's the T-shirt?" Leonard asked.

"I like the sound, but I can't see it," Jack turned to the window of the bus and tried to write the words in the dust but it was almost invisible so he asked, "Has anyone got any paper?"

Jo went to her bag and pulled out her spare notebook, she tore out a number of sheets and handed them out to each member of the band,

"Have a scribble, see what you get! Ladies and Gentlemen, London ORCHID," she left them and went to sit next to Shy.

"How are they doing?" he asked as she sat alongside him, the road ahead stretching out across the now familiar landscape of rocky fields and orange trees.

"I think the sight of orange trees is getting to them! They wanted to call the band Orange." Shy smiled,

"My favourite colour, but, orange juice, agent orange."

"I know! What do you think of London Orchid?" It was Shy's turn to ponder,

"Sounds good but what's the visual? They aren't an orchidy type of sound! They're more like a beautiful flower with a vicious thorn - but not a rose, simpler than that." Jo hadn't expected that much of a horticultural response.

Contemplating his comments, she sat back again, letting the road carry her thoughts. This had been a heck of a trip. She still hadn't worked out how to balance that night at Manuel's with the rest of the trip. Manuel had visited the next morning to apologise and check that everyone was ok, at the time she had been very careful to ensure that the band had spoken about their feelings and that they knew that they could get proper help if they needed it but, she wasn't sure that she had looked after herself. She could still see the faces of those around her and the fear that filled the venue.

Manuel had claimed it was something to do with a drug trafficker that the police were looking for, their location so close to Africa meant that crossings were common and there were a lot of drugs in the area he explained - although Manuel was keen to inform them that his venue was probably the cleanest of the lot. He had set his business up so long ago and his family roots were deep in the area, that explained how he had avoided being taken over by one of the gangs that ruled the coast, he informed them. Jo wasn't surprised, she knew that a lot of pubs and clubs knew who the local dealers were. Either making deals with them to keep them all away, which could prove extremely expensive, or they would employ one and pass them the role of 'security' for their investment. It took something special to keep a location perfectly clean and Jo had wondered if he really could have or whether he was just too naive, believing his own ideas.

She had to admit that she hadn't seen any of the signs of drugs whilst she was there. She was particularly good at identifying them, particularly if there were famous people around. Looking back, she had had a few scary moments in her life and this week had certainly been one of them. When she thought of the night now, it was more like watching a film. She certainly didn't feel the fear as viscerally as her memory of the attack she had suffered a few years previously - walking back to her car after a gig, or even the day she was set upon on her walk back from school. She had always said that nothing would stop her doing whatever she wanted, but she had made some adaptions. She wondered what she would learn from this experience, other than the 'event' which she was sure would come back to her to deal with at some point.

From day one she had known that this band were special, Jo now realised that they were so much more than that. Shy had been great as he always was, encouraging her and just asking the right questions when he needed to. They both knew how great this band were. Each of them were going to have to step above the level that either had worked at previously. Shy had called her away from the band at dinner to explain how he felt that this was the next step. The one that would take them up to the big league. They had both been busy making lists of venues to book and timetables to follow but they also knew that, if they got the right people to join the bandwagon, they might need to accelerate their plans dramatically. Shy was already thinking of employing three new staff just to support Jo with this band. Whilst the idea of having a team around her would help, she was also unsure. She had never been a manager before. She liked to have control of everything.

She liked the way Shy gave her the freedom he did, but she wasn't sure that she could give anyone else the same level of freedom. She had spent some time genuinely telling Shy that they should employ someone with more experience to take on her role with this band. In her opinion, they deserved the best but Shy had insisted that she 'knew' what this band needed.

He had been watching everything she had done and how easily she had fitted into the group dynamic. He had told her,

"Experience doesn't always build chemistry".

Jo was now calling venues that she had only previously visited as a concert goer, and she had been just tentatively looking at the calendars of bigger venues above to see if they might have space. She checked her spreadsheet once again. First single, tentatively here, first few gigs here, second single, more gigs and radio, and, if (Big IF) if things go well… who knew where they could finish the year. There were of course, a lot of extra lines on her spreadsheet of things to do but the biggest empty line was still the name. You can't advertise a band with no name, and she couldn't even commission a designer for the logo or the first runs of merchandise.

Jo thought back to the bands she had worked with who had come to her with designs for whole ranges of T-shirts and album covers. One had even designed their own pinball machine. This band weren't like that though. If you spoke to each of them, they all had this idea that one day they could imagine being in that place but each of them would tell you that right now they had to focus on the next gig or the next song. The T-shirts and record covers and pinball machines would come when it was time. She was sure that if she told them to dress a particular way or to sound a particular way, they would follow her advice, but she wanted the band to be their band, not an image that someone else had created, there were too many bands like that already.

Jo went back to see how the band were getting on, they were engaged in what looked like a serious discussion,

"What's going on?" she asked like a worried mother as she sat in the spare seat on the opposite side of the bus. Jack was first to speak up,

"We were wondering if ethically and morally we could name the band after Leonard's links with criminality and a potentially controversial method of hunting." Jo's shock was clear to all of them which just made them all laugh. Leonard cleared things up,

"I once missed a band practice because I was on Jury Service at Snaresbrook Crown Court. They were thinking of 'The Snares.'" Jo felt the relief wash over her and giggled before her professional head took over.

"I like it on the basis of the drums but, yes, it might not be too popular with the animal welfare people." She thought for another few seconds. "But, what about 'Jury Service', you are all good people, you would do your civil duty, Rock and Roll has always encouraged the rebels, why can't we be the band for the good people?" Paul was the first to laugh,

"We? We've done it lads. Mum has joined the band!" Cheers rang out from around the table as Jack reached over and pulled her across to encompass her in a giant hug.

It took her a while to straighten her hair when she was finally released before she glanced up the bus to where Shy, Jorge and Nic were all looking to see what the fuss was about. She waved at them and sat back down, accepting a can of diet coke passed from the box in the middle of the table.

Leonard leant back,

"So, Jury Service." A moments hush fell across the table, "I like it",

Jim added,

"I'm in" and he placed his hand into the centre of the table, Paul and Leonard were next on and Jack went on top before saying,

"Come on Mum, you're in…"

Jo put her hand on the top and had genuinely never ever felt better. They each sat back, took a swig from their Diet Cokes, Lemonades or most wild of all a strange local can of blueberry fizz and looked at each other.

Jim couldn't stop nodding, Jack had a grin large enough to cover three faces, Leonard was laughing and Paul, with a huge grin that almost completely obliterated the rest of his face, had already grabbed a pencil and was writing Jury Service as if he had been given lines at school. Each time trying to use a different font. Jo was overwhelmed. She knew how this band had made her feel and the fact that they had welcomed her so fully was such an honour. She sat for a good few minutes, just enjoying the feeling, before getting up and walking to the front of the bus, a quick nod to let the band know that she would be back.

She picked up her bag from the seat behind Shy and he turned to ask what was going on,

"I'll let the band tell you" was all that she said but a huge smile across her face let him know that it was all good as she turned and walked back down the aisle to the band. Jorge had been listening too and he and Shy both stood up to follow her back. The band were all busy at their pads as Jo sat down but, one by one they looked up to see what was happening. Shy and Jorge's expectant faces were looking at them quizzically. Eventually Shy asked,

"So, what's happening?" The band all looked around unsure of who should speak, Leonard and Jack were the usual spokespeople, but it was Jim who spoke first.

"I think Mum should tell them." Jim said with a huge grin, the others all smiled and nodded, Shy and Jorge both looked at Jo,

"Mum?"

"The band with no name are no longer without a name" she waited for what she had hoped would be a dramatic enough pause,

"May I introduce… Jury Service."

Shy broke into a smile immediately, Jorge looked at Shy, speaking it out loud himself, nodding, after handshakes all around, they both then headed back to their seats talking animatedly.

"Right then boys" Jo spoke authoritatively which made them all laugh, "This is your first chance to see the inside of my magic folder!" A chorus of oohs was heard,

"I'm going to hand you out a number of sheets, each sheet is full of sample band logos designed by my favourite artists, I want you to have a look at all of them and let me know what you think of the general vibe of each page. Remember, these are professional designers, if you asked any one of them to make something look more childish, they could all use comic sans. If you wanted it to look more metal, they could all add an umlaut. Just have a look and see if any one of them seems in tune, or, if looking at these gives you any better ideas. We could commission anything!"

Handing out the sheets made her feel like a mother and despite the fact that she was only six months older than Paul, (The youngest of the band) each of the band said,

"Thanks mum" as they took the sheets from her.

"I'll leave those with you, let me know if you want anything and… be good."

As she walked the short distance back to the front of the bus, she was almost dancing, she placed her hands on the back of the headrests to Jorge and Shy's seats across the aisle and leant forward to ask,

"What do you think?" Shy was still smiling. He just looked at her like a proud father would.

"You've done a great job. Mum." She nestled herself into her seat, a thousand newspaper headlines in her head,

"The Jury's out" being the one that caused her the most concern but, she could worry about those later, she tried to close her eyes before realising that she was crying. The emotions of the last few days finally letting her know that she still had to look after herself. Another hour to Barcelona, she had time to try to sleep.

Chapter 29

Strutting Like A Peacock

By the time she awoke they were pulling up outside the venue. This gig had been in Convoke's plans for a long time. Shy had always thought that they would have more success with a European crowd and so he had invited a whole load of 'industry' people to this gig. They had debated changing the headliner but Shy had sent so much publicity about Convoke he felt his loyalty was important. That and the fact that Jury Service still had nothing recorded yet meant that he wanted to stick with the original plan, but his team had been sending messages out that it was worth people's while getting there early. He felt that those that bothered were the ones that he wanted onside the most. He was also flying out a couple of radio people from the UK who he would make sure were there to see both bands. He had visited the venue the year before and was thrilled that he was putting a band into what was a historic and a beautiful venue.

Shy had spent far more than he had originally planned to spend. The venue itself was expensive. Then he had paid for a film crew and added video screens on the stage which he had decided would be worth it as they could also use the footage in videos going forward. He had paid double the price to get Jury Service filmed too but he was more confident of getting his money back for that. With those costs and the deliberately low ticket prices and benefits he had offered, the profits they had made from the rest of the tour would disappear tonight. Along with another big bag of cash but, he hoped that the gig itself would be a huge investment going forwards.

Shy's hands were sweaty as he stepped off the bus into the even sweatier heat of the city, there was no air flowing down this side road alongside the venue except for the hot blast being blown out of their bus. He watched both bands stepping into the light and looking up at the giant sign above the door. 'From England, Pure Rock and Roll, CONVOKE and JURY SERVICE' and then in fluorescent text below what he hoped translated as 'Half Price drinks all night. Shy had worried that it might seem desperate, but Manuel had reassured him that people will see the reason and know that to appear at this venue, then it must be a quality band. Manuel had also arranged a deal with the owner of the venue and their drinks supplier that had helped cover some of their costs.

They had advertised heavily around the universities and the music stores in the city. He knew he had the product; he now just needed the audience. Both bands were impressed, he could see that and he felt a paternal pride. He laughed to himself, if Jo was Mum then, well, he might be the grandfather. Jo was already taking photos of both bands arriving, the sign, the building itself, he looked at the whole scene with pride, his memories of his father watching everyone working on the streets of Dhaka suddenly made sense. He clenched his fist then wiped his hand against his trouser leg, trying to dry it before walking up to the door of the venue itself. As he reached the top step, the door opened and he was met by a giant of a man who didn't bother with a handshake but went straight for a suffocating hug.

"Shyamal, my friend, welcome, I am Frederico Armas, Manuel has told me all about you and your bands, we are glad to have you."

Shy was encompassed in two short arms. They were not long enough to reach all around him but there was no way that Shy was getting away. Smothered with the tang of cologne, the laundry soap in the fabric of his clothes and a whiff of recently drunk coffee.

It was not until he was released that Shy was able to respond. He straightened both himself and his clothes before thanking Frederico for the opportunity. Shy was using all of his skills of flattery, telling the enthusiastic hulk just how glad they were to be here, how he had been here to see a band last year and how he had been struck by the beauty of the building and the sound that had been produced there. The giant ushered the bands forward,

"Come quick, you can collect your instruments later". Frederico held the door open for all of them, ushering them into the grand foyer which also served as the box office, a thick and heavy carpet was decorated as ornately as the marble walls. Columns rose to the vaulted ceiling and busts of notable people. Two sets of double doors led through to the theatre space. The bands were subjected to a welcoming speech before the doors were opened. The lights from the stage flooded into the foyer. Nic had travelled with most of the kit ahead of the bands and was already working through the lights with the director from the film crew. Jack was first through the door, strutting like a peacock, making sure he turned towards Jo who of course was filming them, the gladiators heading into the arena. These gladiators had no fear, they were so confident of their abilities. Shy knew that he had so much to thank Jo for. He approached her and smiled as she continued to film him. Shy reached out to take her hand,

"Come on, the film crew will film them now, take a moment to enjoy this, look around you, don't forget to live in the here and now."

The words confused her, she was living, she was loving the experience, but she let him take her by the hand as he led her to the stairs heading up to what once would have been the dress circle. The stalls seating had all been removed to leave a large dance floor in front of the stage. Jorge had seen them leaving and took control of the bands, he gave them some time to pose for their own photos and 'feel' the room before encouraging them all back to the bus to get the instruments they had left onboard and anything else they would need for a sound check.

Chapter 30

Heading For A Shower

Adam had smiled the whole afternoon, the whole evening and as far as he was aware, the whole night too. That morning, he woke up feeling his whole body smiling. He stood and looked around him, again he hadn't pulled the curtains, so the sight of the garden greeted him. There were bees and butterflies already busy around the flowers. The sound of the morning song of the garden welcomed him as he opened the door. There was a slight breeze in the trees above but not enough to be felt in the shelter of the garden. He walked out and sat himself down on the low wall alongside the three steps that led to the lower section of their private garden. He could see the small pond at the far end, still shaded by the ancient wall and the cypress tree that towered over the tranquility of the garden.

He guessed it was a type of dragonfly that was sweeping over the water and he wanted to look to see better but, he had just sat down and there was so much beauty that he didn't want to rush things. He sat there for at least ten minutes without moving, simply studying the shapes of each flower and the range of colours he found in the garden. He was lost in the serenity of the moment before becoming aware of his leg going dead and chose to try to stand. He went and fetched himself a glass of water and once again chose to sit in the garden, although this time selecting one of the cast iron chairs. He spent the next ten minutes or so believing he was a lottery winner, sitting in the garden of his own mediterranean castle, choosing whether to take his sports car for a drive to the coast for lunch or to ask his chauffeur to drive him down to the chateau. Perhaps going to see how the grapes were growing for this year's harvest.

The only thing that made him feel even more like a winner was the sight of Tilly, arriving at the doorway wearing an oversized T-shirt. She walked carefully over to him, watching to avoid the stony ground under her bare feet, giving him a gentle kiss on the forehead she asked if he would like a juice or some breakfast. All he could do was smile and shake his head, watching as she pranced back into the apartment, happier with the smooth floor under her feet.

Now he knew she was up, he wanted to get ready. They had agreed to have a wander around the castle before they drove to Matt's house, how else do you pass the time? He knew that the almost exactly six hours they had would pass slowly. He went to his room and collected his clothes before heading for a shower. When he came out, Tilly was still sat in her T-shirt, on the couch. Her legs tucked under herself with her coffee cup clenched to her chest.

"I've checked three possible routes, they are all clear, it will take us one hour to get down to Matt's. I think we aim to be there a bit early. We can then grab some lunch at the beach, I know that we might not want to eat but, we should." She was gabbling a little. The first sign of nerves that Adam had truly been able to identify. "So, do you want to go for a walk? I really don't know how I'm going to cope this morning. I keep thinking of…" Her sentence faded away, he knew exactly how she was feeling,

"Do you think there is enough up there to take our minds off of things?" he asked.

"Probably not, but what else are we going to do, nothing much happens in the morning here. We could visit the Spa?"

Adam had never visited a spa and truthfully, had no wish to now, but he could understand how it might help Tilly.

"We could" was his response,

"Really?" Tilly almost squeaked, "What would you go for, I don't think you are a spa kind of man!" She almost laughed as she said that which Adam felt was fair. He certainly had never considered himself that kind of man, but he also wasn't entirely sure of what Tilly felt about 'that kind of man'.

"Well, I've never been before but I have never shot a gun before or been kidnapped or stayed in a castle or…" He was willing and able to go on, there were so many new things he had done over the last short few days.

Her laugh told him that he didn't need to continue, she was already reaching for the brochure that had been left on the corner table.

"Ok, Massages, Body treatments, Facials, Waxing, Reflexology, Sculpting. What would you like?" The realisation that he might have to now do something was starting to hit, and it scared him. She read the blankness in his face,

"Have you ever had a proper massage?"

"No" was the very quick response.

"Oh, are you ticklish?" She kept giggling as she was talking. Adam had no choice but to laugh too,

"Oh, you are, that would be no good, perhaps we should practice first", she just left that comment dangling as he felt himself blushing more.

"OK look, it says here that they do hot rocks, all you have to do is lie still whilst they put these stones on you, you don't have to worry about being tickled but the environment is just nice and relaxing, could you manage that?" He desperately wanted to say no. He would rather do anything else but at the same time, he knew that the wait for 14:14 would kill him if he did nothing. The embarrassment factor of just walking into the spa would be enough to keep his mind off of the meeting with Hafidi. He had promised himself that he would try new things on his journey and so, he guessed this must be happening for a reason.

"Ok if I have to, what will you go for?" Tilly just smiled and refused to answer,

"Come on then she said, you should bring some clean pants but, give me a couple of minutes to pick my clothes up and I can go there in my dressing gown."

Adam was torn as they were walking across the courtyard to the spa rooms, firstly he was walking tall because alongside him was a woman who made him feel special and, he knew that she wasn't wearing much, if anything, under that gown but on the other side, there was the knowledge that they were only there because of the situation and, coming up, well, he didn't want to think about that. He wondered if any of his family had realised that he wasn't at home? He had often wondered if he had died, how long it would have taken anyone to notice, well now, here he was, quite the opposite, he was genuinely alive for the first time in many many years and, they didn't know.

It took him a minute to adjust his eyes to the darkness in the 'treatment centre', Tilly had started talking to the overly made-up matronly looking woman behind the counter. They seemed to be speaking for far too long and the woman kept looking at him in a way somewhere between disgust and pity. Eventually, Tilly was given two sheets of paper, she handed one to Adam,

"Here, you need to sign this so if they kill you or they pull one of your legs away from your body you cannot sue them, she also asked me to tell you that the girls will only do the treatments that are in the brochure so we shouldn't ask them for any more. I don't know why she said that!" Adam blushed even more than he was already doing and again, he was glad of the darkness.

The woman had reached under her desk and pulled out two paper bags handing them over, a quick conversation with Tilly and she turned and led him to a little door behind her.

"OK, in here there is a towel a dressing gown and some paper hmm what would you call them, shorts? We get changed through here and then we walk through to the spa room." She handed a bag to Adam and led him through to a space with cubicles,

"You can be numero uno, I'll be dos." She disappeared into the cubicle and Adam did the same, already disliking the memories of changing rooms. He looked into the bag, taking out the gown and the towel. Looking for the shorts he had been promised, he saw nothing there and dipping his hand in there was still nothing inside. He desperately lifted the gown and they dropped out.

Picking them from the floor he was worried that they were seriously expecting him to put them on, would it be odder if he stayed in his own shorts? He didn't feel comfortable with either option, eventually deciding that it was all in, he tried them on, choosing to make sure that he avoided looking into the mirror he then wrapped himself tightly in the robe and stepped out. Tilly was already waiting for him and took his hand before leading him into the next room. Adam literally gasped as he took in the space around him. A vaulted stone ceiling met white stone walls, with such soft lighting that it rather felt like the walls themselves were glowing. Two clinical looking blocks sat in the middle of the room maybe two metres away from each other. At the end closest to him, a couple of steps led to the scene that looked to Adam like a catafalque, well, he thought, if he died here, he guessed it could be worse.

Tilly could see his concern and tried to reassure him with a smile which, if he was honest, didn't help at all. They both climbed onto the tables, a genuine "Are you OK?" came from Tilly, "you can ask them to stop at any moment and just lie there if you'd prefer", she said this as she laid face down on the bed, turning her head to watch him, he laid himself down then tried to put his head in a position that felt vaguely right. Unable to find one he just lay uncomfortably. Looking up as he heard a door open, two younger girls walked in, both pushing a trolley in front of them. They both looked more like they were preparing to perform a service on a car than any kind of relaxing treatment.

Chapter 31

Here They Are

It wasn't until the car reached the motorway that Adam felt even nearly comfortable. For an experience that was meant to be calming and relaxing, he had never before felt so tense. He was now fluent in ways to tell people to relax in Spanish, he had heard 'Relajarse' so many times over the past two hours, but he hadn't been able to feel anything other than embarrassment and discomfort. Now they were on route, the drive was fairly quiet, with Adam and Tilly both knowing that they needed to play their parts perfectly. They arrived at the beach exactly on schedule. They bought lunch at the beachside cafe although neither of them ate more than a quarter of their food. Adam drank two bottles of water and a diet coke. Noticing the effects of dehydration on his mind as they had driven, he wanted to make sure that he would be able to act if he needed to. Both regularly checking their watches before, with a silent nod, they decided it was time to go.

This time Tilly drove the hire car straight up to the gates and rang the intercom. Within seconds the voice welcomed them by name and the gates started to slide open. They were asked to park alongside the yellow Lamborghini. That request made them both laugh. They hadn't noticed the car park on their first visit but on their drive, they had been debating what car various people they had met would drive. Tilly had been certain that Matt was a Lambo kind of person. In her words -

"A man who doesn't know cars but just wants to be noticed." She had also bet that he didn't drive it far, it would scare him too much so he probably has a smaller BMW or Mercedes that he will claim allows him anonymity but really lets him feel safe,

"Probably blue though so he can still say he's different." Before they had parked Matt was already on his way over, with a cheery

"Hey, how are you?" Handshakes were exchanged and drinks accepted. Matt was quick to acknowledge the purpose of their visit.

"You wanted a tour first?" he directed at Tilly, "I'll get my girlfriend to show you around, she is actually here more than I am and knows the important bits. She is also an actor so will understand more about what you need." His girlfriend was not in sight but, regardless he turned towards the house and shouted,

"Sal, here they are, Adam and Tilly". Adam was just opening the boot to get their gift out as Sal appeared. Tilly went straight over and rather than a handshake went straight for the more European air kiss, Adam stood rather awkwardly behind with the giant bouquet that Tilly had insisted on buying recognising that the drinks are probably more of a gift for Matt. Knowing that he couldn't get Matt's gift box whilst holding the flowers too, Adam looked at Matt awkwardly before Matt took the hint and asked if he needed a hand. Adam handed him the flowers,

"We just wanted to give you both a little gift of thanks for the time…" Matt took the flowers with a little awkwardness and a polite,

"Oh, you didn't need to" Sal, seeing the flowers immediately almost screamed in an obviously well-rehearsed dramatic display of extravagant thanks. Inwardly Adam screamed too, she wasn't his kind of girl but, it was quite clear that Tilly knew exactly how to become best friends with a girl like her. Adam turned back to the boot and lifted the box out with a look to Matt,

"And these are for you." Matt's smile almost couldn't get any wider

"Thanks that's great dude, thanks, here bring them round." He quickly led around the corner and the group headed off, Adam desperately trying to close the boot whilst carrying the box whilst still pretending to be cool.

After a reasonable amount of general chat, Sal offered to take Tilly on her tour, Adam and Matt stayed chatting on the terrace, both doing their best to avoid the obvious questions that both knew the other wanted to ask, but at the same time both hoping they didn't ask for obvious reasons. Adam was trying not to look at his phone to check the time, trusting that Tilly would be back, he was fairly certain that Hafidi would be on time. The last time he had seen Tilly and Sal they had been heading inside, Tilly was still dressed in just a T-shirt and short skirt with a little bag hanging loosely across her body. Adam had to consciously keep making sure he didn't look too much at either Tilly or Sal, dressed as she was, in just a bikini. Adam had never felt that that kind of attire could possibly be appropriate for just walking around in and now he really just didn't know how to cope. He hoped that he would get used to it, but he still felt his mother's eyes on the back of his head whilst she made a comment about how disgusting it was and how certain it was that "She'll catch a cold."

Matt had brought a glass of ice with a little bit of water in. Adam, once again, had that moment of seeing himself in a film. Wondering why on Earth he would be here, talking to someone who drove a yellow Lamborghini and who could walk into almost every single restaurant, club or bar in England and not have to pay for a drink. He sat back and closed his eyes for what he felt was only a second, but it was long enough for Matt to ask him if he was ok. Waking instantly, he responded with a quick apology,

"Yeah, sorry, it's just been quite a week."

"Sure, I guess it must be tough" Matt responded. There was a moment of quiet as they both imagined the week they had just had.

They were rescued from the awkwardness as Tilly and Sal emerged from the house. Matt instantly leapt up and offered them both a drink and then ran off to fetch them. Tilly and Sal were still chatting away in Spanish although Sal kept pausing and asking for the right word, Matt returned and explained that Sal was almost fluent now, but he still didn't really have a clue about what was being said most of the time. Adam could see Tilly looking at him. They had hoped that all of Tilly and Hafidi's conversations would be private, but they would have to be more careful.

"Do you speak any other languages?" Adam asked generally, Matt answered first,

"I barely manage English, but I can remember un, deux, trois" Tilly laughed at his attempted French accent, Sal responded,

"I can get to twelve in French, but it confuses me when you have to start adding ten" Tilly looked even more confused by the statement but she shared a look with Adam recognising his lead.

"How about you Adam, how's your Spanish?" Sal asked and now it was Adam's turn to laugh,

"Tilly has tried to teach me a few words but I'm afraid I'm not great with languages, she can speak every language so doesn't understand why others can't!"

"No, I'm not that bad," Tilly laughed, "but, I'm not as good as I should be in English." This made both Matt and Sal look shocked,

"Your English is perfect" she almost snapped, Tilly laughed again,

"I can't pronounce things like 'cousin'." It was true it had taken Adam a while to try to describe the way to form that word and Tilly hadn't quite mastered it, but her vocabulary was far greater than most people who would sit their GCSE's this year. As the group were questioning Tilly who was having to admit her ability in six languages, Matt's watch flashed enough to gain all of their attention.

"Looks like your man is here, spot on time!" Matt seemed surprised by the punctuality. He was nervously standing up, Tilly had already beaten him and almost leapt out of her chair.

"It's ok, please, I'll show him around, you guys stay here. We'll give you a shout when or if we need anything." Adam was trying his best to look relaxed but, looking at Matt, he wasn't the most nervous man here.

"So, you're a big music fan?" Adam asked, he was worried about breaching the subject in case it showed up his lack of knowledge but, he wanted to think of something other than Hafidi.

Tilly walked around the side of the house to see a convoy of vehicles flow into the car park. An electric blue Rolls Royce at the front followed by a blue Range Rover and following them a blue van. Tilly paused, wanting to see Jada but not wanting to be distracted and desperately trying to look calm. She placed her hand onto her bag, just checking that the Beretta was still there. The door of the Rolls was opening even before the car had stopped and Hafidi stepped out. He looked as ridiculous as Tilly had remembered. Once again she thought that he must have his own air conditioning unit plugged into his outfit to allow him to wear so many clothes in the heat of the day. He opened his arms as they approached each other.

"I like your house, and the gate system, very nice, of course we will have to change the provider of the monitoring. But I can arrange that." Tilly had wondered how many faults he would find which he would use for negotiations.

Tilly answered in French,

"Of course, we recognised that we should put a system in which would allow you privacy but, of course for our own security, we will want to run our systems when you are not attending." she had spotted his face register the change in language but, he responded in perfect French,

"I understand but there cannot..." he emphasised the not with a flourish of his finger, "Not be any concerns that I think you are recording my visits." Tilly recognised his flourish with a gesture of her own, mirroring his body language and exaggerating her confidence.

"We will arrange a codeword for you to use to switch the monitoring off and restart it at an agreed time afterwards. We will monitor the number of times that codeword is used." Hafidi nodded, he was impressed by her professionalism. He had only ever used property he personally owned previously but, as his operations had widened, it was getting harder to find appropriate properties available and his accountant had advised him that the properties he had been buying might start to look a little suspicious to an enquiring mind. Since his previous discussion with Tilly, he had spent more time considering this kind of approach. He didn't like involving too many people but, this system might help him. He could become much more adaptable in delivering his products and if things went bad, it was not his name linked with the property.

Tilly was leading Hafidi through the gardens keen to ensure that he didn't get the chance to head off course.

"I will take you down to the water first, I presume that is your priority. There is space at the front of the house for a helicopter, I don't know if you use them?" She didn't give him time to answer before continuing with her sales pitch.

"It has been a while, but I can show you photos of a helicopter here if you want proof." Hafidi nodded, she doubted this would be within his expectation or need but, well, who isn't impressed by a helicopter. Sal had sent her the photos from a party they had held when they first bought the property. A 'friend of a friend' had persuaded an American basketball player to stop off on route to another party. She hadn't told him that no-one else had been allowed to be outside when it landed because they wouldn't have been able to be far enough away or the fact that they had had a visit from the local police the next day because, apparently, you needed permission for that kind of thing.

She headed to the far side of the garden and turned to show Hafidi the gardens and the fact that none of the neighbouring properties looked into the garden whatsoever. She was very conscious of the fact that she had to be seen to be showing him the locations for the music video and this would be the only point she hoped at which Matt and Sal would see Hafidi. Hafidi's extravagant attire certainly fitted the image Tilly had of someone who would work in making music videos.

She made a point of waving her arms and pointing in various directions, she could see that everyone on the terrace was looking intently, even Adam, so she chose to give them a wave. They all waved back. Perhaps too much enthusiasm from Matt and Sal but she couldn't stop that, and she knew from the processions at the club that Hafidi liked to be recognised. She turned once more to talk to Hafidi who was still waving back at them. Tilly momentarily felt a tremor of fear for potentially putting Sal at risk, she knew how easily he would be able to get to her. Tilly kept Hafidi talking for a short while, making sure that it looked like she was selling the property and Sal's acting skills before leading him onwards towards the lift and the dock.

So far, Tilly was happy with her pitch. She gave a silent thank you to her father. When she was younger her father had been insistent that she should experience a few different working environments. He had arranged for her to work during each of her summer breaks from university. The one she had found the easiest was working for a property company basically just guiding groups of old men around empty offices or warehouse units whilst she did her best to appear charming with them. Making sure that she was alert enough to never get close enough for any one of them to touch her. She had been able to tell which groups needed a little more encouragement and she had finished the summer with higher sales figures for her colleague who she had meant to be shadowing than any other member of the team had managed. Apparently, her colleague had always been towards the bottom of the office leaderboard previously. She was glad that everyone knew whose success it had been, but she certainly left hoping that she would never ever have to sell herself in that way again.

She knew that today though was different. This sales pitch

was the biggest she could make. She desperately hoped that Jada was in the van, and she was desperate to ask, but she suspected that that negotiation would follow when necessary. They stood at the top deck next to the lift and Hafidi looked to the sea, he had a few questions about the approach and the size of boat it was regularly used for, Tilly had to admit that this wasn't her speciality and instead referred to the photos that Sal had sent her on her phone of a few of the boats that had come to visit. Tilly made sure the helicopter was amongst the pictures that were in the album as she showed him, he continued nodding before asking about the lift.

They entered the small carriage and Tilly nervously stepped closer to Hafidi to get in, she once again checked the gun, this was the point where she knew she was most vulnerable. They were out of sight and once the lift was on its way down, they were probably out of earshot too. Tilly had arranged with Adam that, if necessary, she would fire a warning shot. If that happened Adam was to call 112 immediately and guide Matt and Sal to the safest place and hide. She was relieved to have learnt on the tour that they actually had a safe room, but Tilly hadn't been able to tell Adam that, she hoped that Matt and Sal would be bright enough to not forget they had it if the need arose.

The journey down in the lift felt a thousand times slower than it had the first time she had used the lift but, Hafidi seemed to be enjoying the ride. When they reached the pontoon, he strutted back and forth, umming and ahhing a few times, looking up at the stairs,

"Ok. Can you be ready for a first run on Monday?" Tilly hadn't quite been ready for the question, in her world arrangements took weeks if not months.

"Are you prepared to meet your side of the bargain?" She thought quickly and answered hoping that he hadn't seen her flinch. He strode to the lift, opened the barrier and invited her in, as she stepped onto the narrow metal platform his comment was simply,

"It's a pleasure to do business with you although I am a little disappointed that you felt the need to be armed today." She looked him straight in the eye in shock,

"But, I understand, my reputation meets people before I do but please, try harder to hide it next time." Tilly had instinctively moved her hand to her bag to check that the gun was still there, although she wasn't entirely sure that she was glad that it was. There was no doubt that he was better at this game than she was but, she then thought, well at least he knows that I'm serious.

The lift up seemed to take even longer. As they reached the top, Tilly started talking, wanting to control the discussions again as they avoided Matt and Sal on the terrace,

"Let me know the times that you want access to the property and at what time you will be leaving. I will forward you the contact number and the password to disconnect our feed. Between the times you give me, you will be responsible for the site security and by that I also mean liable for any damage or losses." She had gone into her full office negotiation mode. There was many a self-proclaimed capitalist entrepreneur she had seen become scared by her glare and choice of words in that environment.

Tilly had felt that gaining a strong hand here could not be a bad idea, she was still feeling guilty that she may have put Matt and Sal in danger but, she would fix that later. She might need to pull a few favours, but she was sure that she could ensure that enough rugby names were at a party that Matt would be hosting to make the venue safe after she cancelled the booking. That was for later. She was careful to direct Hafidi away from the house as they reached the top of the lift, they waved again at those sitting blissfully unaware of the situation. She felt sorriest for Adam. She could only imagine how he had been feeling and still would be, until the whole thing was over.

As they reached the cars, Tilly stopped.

"So, we have an arrangement." She spoke firmly and once again in Spanish. She had always felt that the language had sounded more aggressive than her native French.

"We do." he responded and nodded to the beast sat in the passenger seat of the Range Rover. He got out of the vehicle and slowly walked to the side door of the van, opening it again with an almost pantomime slowness, he barked and a few seconds later Tilly saw Jada appear at the door, a hood over her head but, Tilly was sure it was her, she resisted the urge to run, choosing instead to look Hafidi once again in the eye.

"I presume that we will not have a reason to meet again. All necessary arrangements can be made using the number that you have. If you do not respond to any message I send or if I do not respond to yours, we may each presume that there is a reason why our agreement is over. So far as I can see there is no need for that to be for many years. I hope that I can trust you to ensure that I continue to have no reason." He almost looked genuinely upset that she might doubt him, but he simply got into the Rolls, nodded and said,

"I expect the password by 21:21 Sunday night."

The cars started rolling with choreographed synchronicity

towards the exit gates where, annoyingly for the ballet they were performing, they had to wait for a few seconds for the gate to register their presence before it opened. Tilly made sure that the gates were fully shut before turning back towards Jada, still stood with her head bowed and covered by the hood. Tilly didn't want to scare her and really didn't know what to say. Tilly stood, hearing the birds singing and, in the distance, the sounds from the harbour and then she became aware of her own breathing, she tried to speak,

"Jada" but the sound didn't come. Seeing her friend, such a strong person, just stood there, looking so helpless. She took a few steps towards her before trying again,

"Jada" it sounded weak and questioning but Jada heard it, she half turned towards the sound,

"Jada, it's Tilly, remember me?"

Chapter 32

That's Amazing

Tilly heard a cry, the like of which she had never heard before as Jada dropped to her knees. She rushed over, dropping to her knees and scrabbling to get the hood off of Jada's head. Jada flinched from the sunlight, desperately trying to adjust to the bright afternoon sunshine. They hugged, both of them crying. Tilly soon pulled herself away, lifting Jada to her feet,

"Come, get into this car, I'll be back in two minutes." Jada grabbed her,

"Please don't leave me..." Tilly was ripped by the emotion in her words but knew she had to get Adam.

"Please, Jada, it's ok, a friend has helped us, let me get him and we will be away, and we are only a few minutes from home." At the mention of home, Jada collapsed into more tears,

"Where is Sam, is she OK?" Tilly reassured her that she would be home and safe soon, but she had to get Adam. She opened the passenger door of the car and ushered her in, leaving the door open, conscious for Jada not to feel trapped. She ran back towards the corner of the house, she had to pause, wipe her eyes and brush her knees, controlling her breathing before heading back to the group who were sat waiting at the table exactly where she had left them.

"He loves it." She exclaimed, trying to sound victorious and waited for the cheer to subside, "He has pictured a simple summer party, lots of pretty people enjoying the sunshine with the band playing in the garden. He liked your idea of the guitar on the lift and wants to film a few extra scenes, he wants drums on the pontoon and the singer might need to use the bedroom, she rolled her eyes which made the others laugh, but… he loves it!" She paused for a minute letting the message hit and wondered if she should have tried a career as an actor herself. The excitement in both Matt and Sal's eyes was clear.

"We need to work on dates, but you know we need this quickly. He has another project starting in two weeks so we need to get it really soon, are there any dates that we can't do?"

For the first time, she saw the concern in Adam's face.

"We have been asked to attend a sponsors event in New York on Monday, I can get out of it if we have to, but it is a big thing" Matt had started answering the question leaving Tilly trying to reassure Adam with a look. Matt had been looking at Sal throughout, Tilly could see her disappointment when Matt said that they could miss it and knew immediately that Sal did not want to miss the New York trip.

"That's absolutely fine, go to New York, I know a restaurant there that you simply have to go to, we will pay for your evening, when would you be back?"

"The event is on the Monday night, its theatre and then a gala afterwards, if we were going, we would look to fly back maybe early Tuesday?'

Tilly pitied Matt as he was talking, she could see his enthusiasm, guessing that for someone who seems to have so much, he is obviously still just a little boy who has seen something that he really wants.

"It's ok, if we look for next Thursday, would that be ok?" Both Matt and Sal were beaming and nodding as Tilly spoke. "Great, ok, let's say Thursday unless you hear otherwise, and would it be ok if we kept Friday in reserve in case he needs a bit more time?" Sal answered "Of course, thank you." Sal reached over and rested her hand on Matt's, she could see how much Matt was enjoying the idea too. Tilly started to stand,

"That's amazing, I'm really sorry but you know we have a lot to organise, we really should get started! I'll send you a message with the restaurant details, I'll book Sunday night but let me know if you would prefer any other time." Tilly knew that she was being forward about the restaurant but as soon as they had mentioned New York her mind had gone to a memory from what now seemed like a previous life. Booking the place would be easy and it all would help Matt and Sal believe in the story. They were all on their feet, hugs were exchanged and hands shaken, Tilly told them,

"Please, you don't need to see us out, stay here, have a drink, open one of the bottles we brought."

Adam was amazed at her calmness and the way that she had them obeying her every word. Matt thanked her again, seemingly not wanting to let go of her hand before Adam gave him a tap on the shoulder and he released his grip, a few more words and Adam and Tilly were away, as they turned the corner, she broke into a run, Adam followed her, he had presumed that everything was ok but he really did not know what to expect now. As he came around the corner, he was relieved to see Jada in the car, he almost burst out laughing. Tilly was already opening the driver's door and calling out that he would have to jump in the back. He was more than happy to jump in the back and was in tears before the gates had opened.

Chapter 33

Chattering In Spanish

Tilly was watching her mirrors, still not sure that it could have gone so easily. She barely saw the truck fly out from the side road. Adam's world was filled with black and white. He felt the car flying and waited for the impact of landing, his legs kicked against the seat in front of him as the car rolled onto its roof and he felt his wrist snap as it cracked against the door frame. He desperately tried to hold his head away from the roof which was now sliding along the ground, a lighter thud and the car came to a stop against a garden wall. He couldn't see anything ahead of him, the airbags coating the windows, a distinct metal tang in the car, the smell and taste of metal and heat filling the spaces. Just complete silence. He sat still for a second, trying to come to terms with why the world was now upside down. Realising what must have happened and reawakening that there were others in the car, he tried to speak,

"Tilly, Jada, are you OK?" He felt that his voice was weak, but in the silence, it sounded to him like he was shouting. He was relieved to hear affirmative sounds from both of them,

"Ok just stay still, I'll try to get out, wait there." He was desperately reaching for his seatbelt to release, as it did he felt the impact as his shoulder crashed into the roof and he felt the pain like a lightning bolt shoot down his arm, he half rolled, restricted by the fact he was a slightly larger than average adult in the back seat of a family car. He reached the door and tried to open it, unsurprisingly it failed to move, he scrambled to rotate his body to try the other side.

The window lay in a million pieces all around the car and the road outside. He contemplated trying to slide through the window before deciding that it perhaps wasn't his best idea, at least not until he had tried the door. It swung open exactly as it should displaying the best of German engineering. He crawled out, dragging his arm behind him then used the side of the car to support himself as he struggled to stand. Looking around him, the truck was stopped maybe fifteen metres away. Steam rising from the radiator. Two elderly men were coming down the road towards him, both trying to make to look like they were running, whilst one was holding onto his waistband as if his trousers were falling down and the other was holding his hat.

Adam reached down with the one arm he could move and tried the door handle in front of him, again it swung open cleanly and Adam bent to try to release Tilly's seat belt, he felt the warmth as much as the wetness as he realised there was blood coming from somewhere. He looked and saw a clean red stripe across her leg. The wound looked superficial, he could treat that later, he needed to get her to safety first. Telling her he was about to release the seatbelt and that she should try to hold herself up as best as she could. He released the belt and she fell to the floor, crashing into him as she fell, causing him to almost scream in pain, as it was, holding in the scream only caused a worse gurgling sound. She cried but managed to crawl herself clear of the vehicle. Adam scrambled to the other side and performed the same action with Jada, as they both lolloped away from the wreckage, the first man reached Tilly and reached into his pocket for a handkerchief to press against her wound.

Adam tried to talk to Jada, asking if she had any pain but all he could focus on was the amount of pain he felt running through his arm, his brain had assessed discomfort elsewhere too, his hip, his other arm, his ankle and on the side of his head but that was all being overwhelmed by his "bloomin' arm". He swore as he tried to move it to adjust his shirt that had wrapped around him. Leaving Jada with the second bystander, he tried to walk towards the truck. His brain was already asking if perhaps this was not an accident. Not knowing what to expect, he looked at the other vehicle but saw no sight of the driver. He limped to the side door then, looking through the window, remembered he was in Spain seeing the steering wheel on the other side of the cab. But no one was inside. He walked around the truck and opened the driver's door. The key had been removed and there was no sign that the vehicle had been driven. The pain overtook him and he sat on the kerb.

More people were appearing from their homes, a woman appeared in front of him chattering away in Spanish. All Adam could do was focus on her teeth slapping up and down like one of those wind-up sets of dentures that would whizz across a child's table and her arms frantically waving, Adam laughed at the sight in his mind before bowing his head and closing his eyes. When he reopened his eyes, he blinked five times, trying to register the connections that were occurring in his head. He saw the camera, the plain white T-shirt, the tanned legs and then the concerned face framed by perfect blonde hair, too perfect. He shook his head, as if the recognition of who she was and how she fitted into the story was the ball bearing on one of those annoying puzzle toys and if his head moved in a particular pattern, it would fall clear. When that failed, he rubbed his eyes again as if that might clear the view, he opened them again and she was still there,

"Adam, are you ok?"

Her voice was so soft and gentle, Tilly had said that the Spanish accent was fierce, and he had agreed with her at the time but, he had never heard anyone sound like this before.

"You don't remember me, do you?" Her eyes were searching straight into his soul, yes, he recognised her, yes, he knew that he had seen her before, but he could not place her.

"I am Becky, I was in the car with Lieutenant-Colonel Bally and Sargento Ortiz when you asked for directions. I didn't know who you were at the time, but I've been trying to follow you since, it hasn't been easy." His head hurt but, yes, he understood. Not why she had been following her but how he had seen her before, she reached out a hand, "Come on, we should get away from here."

He took her hand, surprised by her strength as she dragged him from the kerb, Jada and Tilly were sat hugging each other, the bloodied handkerchief still held over her thigh, but it seemed that the flow of blood had stopped. The two men had been joined by a small crowd of locals who were all animatedly discussing what they felt must have happened. Becky offered her hand to Tilly and, although speaking in Spanish this time, seemed to give her the same instruction, Jada and Tilly helped each other to stand whilst Becky barked some instructions at the crowd. She led them to another car, ushering them in. This time Tilly and Jada took the back seat leaving the passenger seat for Adam.

Becky had got in the car first and was busy brushing a collection of snack wrappers, a banana skin, an orange peel, a comb and a few other bits and pieces off of the passenger seat.

"I'm sorry, I've been in here on my own for too long," Adam had managed to sit into the seat but was now trying to reach the seatbelt without causing his arm too much pain,

"Can you manage?" She asked before half reaching across him and then deciding that she probably couldn't reach, "it's OK, I'll drive carefully. Can we go to the house?" She had turned to look at Jada as she spoke, Jada had been staring wide eyed seemingly unaware of anything that was going on but, she managed a nod. The car eased away and as she drove, she spoke,

"OK, I'm sure that you all have so many questions, I'll try to answer them all in time. Firstly, I am Becky Lourdes. I work for the British Government. My mother was Spanish, but I grew up in England which might explain my awful accent. We have been working with the Guardia Civil for some time looking at Hafidi's connections. I am sorry that we couldn't prevent your kidnapping Jada and, I'm afraid that the Guardia would not let us take further action to release you, but we are close to shutting down Hafidi and his numerous businesses. You might have given us the perfect opportunity."

They were already on the road leading to the house. Becky had been driving smoothly but at a speed that suggested either an intimate knowledge of the road or a rally driver's disdain for the risk of oncoming traffic.

"Will Sam be at home?" She asked. At the mention of her name, Jada visibly shook,

"Is she OK?" She asked. Tilly nodded both to Becky and Jada,

"She's strong, you know she is but, you both need each other." Becky drove up to the garage door, winding the window down to activate the intercom but before she could press the button, a voice crackled from the machine,

"Who are you?" Sam sounded aggressive and almost broken. Becky, Tilly and Jada all started speaking at the same time,

"What? Who are you?" Was the response from Sam sounding increasingly frantic, Adam raised his hand to quiet them all.

"Sam, it's Adam, please let us in and come down." They heard her almost crying,

"Adam?" and the door started to open. As soon as she could Becky drove on through, Sam was already running down the stairs, she ran first to Adam's door before seeing there were people in the back, the howling scream was unexpected, and the tears were instantaneous. It took Adam some time before he managed to open the door, reaching across himself with his 'good' arm before shuffling his legs out and trying to stand. Tilly wandered over, looking at his arm sympathetically before asking him,

"What have you done to that?" As if he had been to blame. Becky had stepped away from the group for a second and was tapping a message into her phone.

It was some time before they found their way upstairs and Becky was able to start explaining her side of the story. She explained that Hafidi had been active in France and Spain for many years but was now planning on expanding his operations to the United Kingdom. They had been monitoring his interactions with a known trafficker based in Southampton and had been trying to work with the Guardia to cut the supply at the source. It had not been easy. Hafidi knew a lot of people and it was suspected that his payroll went a long way through both the police and the local politicians, which was why he had been able to succeed for so long and which probably helped him to feel invincible.

The interest from the UK though had meant that his allies in the Guardia had not been able to stop every investigation. All they needed now was to actually intercept a load on route. Tilly looked sharply at Adam.

"Do you know something?" Becky asked. Adam looked at Tilly before speaking.

"He is bringing a load to land at the house we were at earlier." Becky looked surprised,

"When?"

"Monday, I don't know what time, we were arranging his use of the house in return for Jada."

As if for the first time, Adam realised just what he had done and what he had got himself involved in, he, as far as the law would see it, had planned to go into business with a criminal. Not only that but had fraudulently misled a famously nice man and put that football legend and his family at risk. He dropped his head once again and tried to lift his hand to his face but was reminded of the pain. Once again he felt the emotions of the last week hit him, and tears grew in his eyes, but he caught himself. Part of this journey was to stop him from crying. He raised his head and looked straight at Becky,

"Look, we found out that Hafidi had taken Jada to force her and Sam to let him use this place. He wasn't going to just let her go so we thought that if we found an alternative he would release her, most of this happened by luck but, we found a link with Matt Riley and his house would be perfect. We found Hafidi and offered the house. We were going to take each step at a time, we couldn't inform the police until we had Jada safe."

Adam was expecting her to put him in handcuffs immediately and he wondered how much pain that would cause in his shoulder. Instead, she smiled.

"Well, you've done a good job, but it's not over yet." Becky stretched her feet out and smiled, Adam sat back,

"No sorry, it is time for the professionals to take over. We don't know what we're doing, we've just been very lucky." Becky nodded and looked down at her glass of water.

"You haven't been lucky, you saw a chance and took it, you have saved Jada and that was your aim but, whatever you think of drugs, they cost lives, and they ruin millions of others. For every man like Hafidi we put out of business we prevent hundreds of new people being exposed to that evil." Becky was speaking with a passion that no one had expected.

"And then if you think that addiction is fine and that drug addicts need their fix and deserve the suffering they have to undertake, what about his other trade? What about the girls he takes from their families and sells? Getting them addicted to his products first and then putting them to work to satisfy the needs of any of his customers. If you help us, just until Monday we can stop this completely." It was Becky's turn to look straight at Adam. He in turn looked to Tilly, and Sam, and Jada, they were all looking at him but, he could tell by their eyes that his adventure was not over yet.

A couple of hours had passed since they had got back to the house, Tilly had been down to the shop and bought some painkillers for him, she had tried to get him to go to the hospital as she was sure that something must be broken, it had taken him a long time to take his T-shirt off and had needed Tilly's help. When she saw the colours his skin had turned to she had gasped. He had expected the bruising and could feel the swelling, but it was obviously worse than she had expected. He had taken the full dose of painkillers and then an extra tablet and chosen his largest shirt to try to put back over that arm. He assured her that if it didn't feel better tomorrow, he would have a look at it.

He had no wish to go to hospital, he hadn't actually considered medical insurance and since Brexit he wasn't sure what arrangements were in place. He decided that he would have to think about that. When they walked back out into the garden, Sam and Jada were both curled up like nesting squirrels on the corner sofa whilst Becky was stood at the edge of the cliff, keeping watch on the maritime traffic like a motherly lighthouse.

They all visibly flinched as the electronic sound let them know that someone was approaching the house, Adam was the last to get inside to where the CCTV was showing three cars waiting in the street.

"Is it your people?" Sam asked Becky, who nodded,

"I'll fetch them and bring them up." The others looked around at each other before Jada asked,

"Should we sit here, there should be room for everyone?" She had headed towards the sofas.

Sam nodded and started walking to the windows,

"If we open these up, we could bring chairs from the terrace too."

They shifted over to the seating area, Adam noted Tilly bagging the most powerful spot. Lieutenant-Colonel Bally appeared at the top of the stairs, alongside him a man impeccably dressed in the uniform of a stereotypical diplomat, a loose, creased linen jacket sat on top of a smart shirt and a perfectly knotted red tie, loose blue trousers and shoes that looked like they had spent many hours walking around the edges of marquees and perhaps more than a few cafes and bars.

Behind them there was Mercedes and three other men all fairly similarly dressed in dark suits. Each person walked in and almost instinctively knew which chairs to sit in. Mr linen suit first asked if he may sit here, pointing to the yellow velvet armchair by the window. The suits all took seats in a less prominent position, Becky had noticeably waited until L-C Bally had chosen his spot before making a move for the seat directly opposite. Sam played host and offered the tray of drinks. Once everyone had settled, Becky spoke,

"Hi, just because I know most people in the room let me start the introductions, I'm Becky, Military Intelligence currently attached to the British Consulate in Alicante, I've been working with Lieutenant-Colonel Bally and others on the case of Per Hafidi for the past two months." She had been looking at the suits as she spoke. Adam was surprised by the Military Intelligence part of her speech, that's MI5 he thought, or 6? He could never remember which was which, not that it really mattered, it just meant that she was even cooler than he had first thought.

Bally took up the mantle next, looking mostly at Sam he explained his role, the diplomat looking fellow turned out to be exactly that, James Perry-Lloyd and the suits were from various departments of the Spanish police from what Adam could understand. Once everyone had been introduced, Perry-Lloyd took control,

"So, it appears that we have all wanted to get this Hafidi out of circulation for some time and until our mutual operation began when young Rebecca here came over - we hadn't been getting close. Rebecca has done some sterling work building a portfolio of evidence that in my opinion should be enough for any judge to lock him up and throw away the key. I have however been regularly informed that your lot requires more physical evidence." He had been looking straight at Bally for most of the time but spread his glance around the rest of the suits at the end. A couple shifted a little uncomfortably, but they held his gaze. He continued,

"Our Scooby-Doo friends here have taken a more proactive approach and have met with Hafidi and arranged a location where, if we play our cards right, we can make everyone happy but, we don't have long. The meeting is arranged for Monday, so we need to ensure that everything is set and ready to go. The British Government are willing to offer whichever resources are necessary to make sure that this character is dealt with appropriately."

Bally took over.

"Yes, we are very grateful that and of course, as this is a Spanish national on Spanish soil, we will be dealing with him appropriately."

The tension between the two groups was obvious and Adam felt he could see both sides although he also knew that, if his life was at risk, he knew who he would prefer were on his side.

"Quite so," Perry-Lloyd resumed, "We have our criminal planning to land a shipment of what we are as yet unsure, at a premises less than a mile across the bay there. He believes that there is a business arrangement to use the property which, I understand has not actually yet been organised with the owner of the property."

At this he turned to look at Tilly,

"Not exactly." she answered.

"It's fine, I am sure that we can get the necessary access to the property without any bother, what we need is for you chaps to be able to keep quiet enough not to make Hafidi suspicious and then for you to have the necessary resources to take the fellow cleanly. We already have an agreement with your government to assist in criminal matters if we have resources in the neighbourhood which I have confirmed with Mr Calvinho there," eyes turned to one of the suits who nodded. "We currently have HMS Tottenham in dock at Gibraltar and although she might be a little bit too noticeable to park on the bay here. She does however also have with her a rather impressive collection of fast response boats that can be filled with marines and left waiting just around a corner somewhere."

Bally took on the conversation,

"I have discussed the matter with my colleagues here but, of course you recognise that this is a very limited time frame for organising a complex operation."

Perry-Lloyd was quick to interject,

"Oh, come, come, old boy,"

Adam was trying not to laugh at how stereotypical this whole conversation was.

"We all know that you chaps should be doing missions like this every week, it must be in one of your training manuals, it's not a difficult approach road, it's not a difficult site, of course I will give you all of the credit and your chaps here can even take the credit if our boys work on the water. All you have to do is pick the bloody man up."

Perry-Lloyd was managing to say all of this whilst maintaining the air of a vicar at a tea party discussing the simplest of run outs in the cricket.

"Look we need to know when we can gain access, it is reasonable to suspect that the house is being watched right now so it is not quite as simple as you would make everyone believe. But, we have agreed that we shall do our best to take Señor Hafidi and so, we shall work to create a successful mission." Bally responded sharply

It was clear that they weren't all exactly on the same side, if Bally really wanted Hafidi out of the way, Adam suspected that it could have been done sooner but the pressure from Perry-Lloyd seemed to be the driving force. Adam wasn't certain that Bally would be working all out to make sure that they got him. Perry-Lloyd seemed determined and also seemed like the kind of chap who would keep working to make things happen.

"So we need to get access to the house, I understand that the chap is a British footballer, is that right?" Perry-Lloyd had taken control of the room again. As he was talking now, he was looking straight at Adam who nodded.

"So, tell us, how did you get the house?" Adam looked to Tilly, she understood the message and took over,

"Well, it is a little complicated. We discovered that Hafidi had Jada because he wanted her house, we had coincidentally bumped into Matt after the concert and found out that he had the house that Hafidi needed. We knew he had loved the band and so used that. We asked him if the band could borrow the house to film a video. We were going to solve that problem later. For Hafidi, letting Jada free was our price."

It all sounded so easy Adam thought as he watched Tilly describing their work. Seeing that Tilly had finished, Perry-Lloyd spoke up again.

"So, it is simple, Hafidi knows when he needs to be there and he expects the house to be empty, Mr Riley then expects and apparently wants the band to be at his house to shoot a video. We just have to make sure that both of those things happen to allow us to get to Hafidi."

Tilly jumped in again,

"We know that Matt and his girlfriend Sal both are heading to New York so will not be there on Monday, but I don't know when they are leaving."

That got everyone's attention, Perry-Lloyd spoke first,

"Can we find out who they are flying with? Perhaps we could arrange a more convenient flight time."

Tilly liked Perry-Lloyd, he was obviously someone who quickly saw solutions rather than problems, Bally looked straight to one of the suits who shook his head,

'We will find out.' Bally said as he ushered the suit away to do just that.

"Do we know who provides the security for the house?" Was Perry-Lloyd's next question. This time one of the suits answered,

"Yes, it is a very sophisticated system with remote access and monitoring. We have an arrangement with the company so we can redirect the number that the system contacts so we can allow anyone to access the premises, once Mr Riley is away of course."

"Good, Good," Perry-Loyd stood up and walked to the window before turning back to face Bally. "So, we find out when Mr Riley is flying, if we can, we will arrange an earlier flight, with an upgrade if he isn't already flying first of course and, as soon as he leaves we can put some people inside to wait for Hafidi. Yes?"

"Well, we will have someone put some cameras in so that we can monitor the movements, but we cannot have people just sitting waiting for so long." He was looking angrily at Perry-Lloyd.

"It's not long. Less than 24 hours, Hafidi will have his own people in the area already watching. If the criminals can spare people, then surely the Guardia Civil can spare someone. I remember you having my people sit waiting for three days for someone you wanted. We need people in there quickly. Besides, if you had told us about your nonsense at the club..."

Bally bristled, first at the comment of the previous mission. It was a similar case except the criminal had been a British National and it was very much more advantageous politically for Bally to have that individual out of his area. It was true, Perry-Lloyd had done all the work on that one too. Bally had been made to approach Perry-Lloyd by his commander at the time against Bally's own wishes for a reason that Bally never found out. Perry-Lloyd had taken everything under his wing. It had seemed to Bally that Perry-Lloyd found these kind of operations more exciting than his usual job role. Although to be fair he didn't really have any idea of what he did day to day except that whenever there was a great party, Perry-Lloyd would be there, and it seemed that everyone liked him.

Bally looked at another of the suits, "How many people would you want to send? Do you have a team in mind?" The suit looked nervous,

"As yet, I don't know. We don't know what he is bringing whether it is drugs or people, Or how many people he will have on the boats and how many he will bring to the house. We can guess by the size of the pontoon that the boat he lands can be a maximum of 24 metres that is a big boat but, he might moor any kind of boat offshore and ferry people in. I would want not less than ten Guardia inside the house. We will need two vans of armoured vehicles that drive in as the operation begins and we would want support on the water to intercept the boat if it runs."

"Goodness gracious dear boy" Perry-Lloyd burst out, "It's a drugs bust not the Nazi invasion of Poland we are planning!"

Bally immediately stood up, "May I remind you Mr Perry-Lloyd that this is an operation carried out by our men." He paused "and ladies." he added that whilst looking straight at Becky, "We shall assess the risks and it is our decision as to which resources are required. We will not put people at risk due to haste."

Perry-Lloyd laughed, "Well there is no chance of that happening is there. Look we have this opportunity, we will not get a better chance, my men can come in and do the whole lot, but you want Hafidi for your own reasons. So let us not miss this chance. I have a dinner tonight at nine so let us have a call at eight. You can tell me what you have decided you want my help with, and I will get that all arranged. For anything else, you can contact Becky here and she will liaise with my friends here". He gestured to Adam, Tilly, Sam and Jada with a flourish. Bally looked at his lap and started gathering up his papers, after making a dramatic waft to collect the pages together he stood and spoke,

"Very well. We have a lot to do. Ladies and gentleman" he was now addressing Tilly mainly, "I thank you for your hospitality. We will allow you some time to yourselves."

At that the suits all stood to leave, Perry-Lloyd stood too but acted like it was his house and helped to direct the others out.

Chapter 34

Getting Your Hands Dirty

Once Bally and his entourage had departed, Perry-Lloyd sat himself down and addressed the group,

"So, I apologise for describing you all as Scooby-Doo characters but in my mind that is exactly what you are, people who were conscious enough to see something wrong and took it upon yourselves to find a solution. The fact that we are here today is evidence that not only have you achieved your aims but, you have also created a situation whereby an enemy of society and, to be quite blunt, a horrible little man, is on the brink of having their evil extinguished. You have done that without any of the resources available to Lieutenant-Colonel Bally and the Spanish Government so, first of all, on my behalf and on the behalf of the Great British public may I say thank you."

Jada and Sam shared a hug. It was that kind of speech. Tilly and Adam shared an embarrassed look, Perry-Lloyd continued, "Please, tell me more about you all." They all looked at each other, it felt like that moment at school where a teacher asks a question that seems so obvious that everyone knows the answer but is afraid of being wrong. Eventually Perry-Lloyd gave his choice,

"Jada, I believe that this is your wonderful house so, please tell me about you." She looked embarrassed and set her eyes on Sam,

"Well, I became lucky, I had a great teacher at university who guided me in my studies. Just at the time when the internet was growing rapidly. At 19 I started my first business. The professor helped me and it grew. My parents had invested for me and so, when I was 21, I was able to access that money and put that into the business. I made enough money that I could start investing in people and companies that I could associate with and, thankfully, many of those businesses have done very well. I just try to work hard and, well, that's me."

She looked up for the first time, unsure if she had said too much or too little. Perry-Lloyd broke the silence,

"And did your business or investment sense not make you think of doing a deal with Hafidi, a lot of money could be made without you getting your hands dirty?"

Jada looked physically hurt, "No. I would never invest in anything that I could not support, and I have no interest at all in supporting people like him." The reason wasn't clear but the passion certainly was. Perry-Lloyd started clapping,

"Congratulations my girl, you have achieved so much, and your morals are still maintained, if only the world had more people like you. Sam, tell me about you." It was Sam's turn to have everyone look at her,

"Well," she started, looking just at Tilly, "I met Tilly when she transferred schools at 15, we connected and have been friends ever since. Without Tilly, I would never have been able to go to university and, I would never have met Jada. I still cannot believe that God gave me two such kind people to be my friends. I am truly blessed. When we finished university, Sam went to London to work, Jada and I moved to Madrid. Jada working on her business and I took a few jobs in different places, we bought this house seven years ago. It was a wreck and we have rebuilt it as it is now."

Another round of applause followed from Perry-Lloyd, "Now" he exclaimed with an undeniable authority, "Tilly or Adam?" They both looked at each other, Adam nodded to Tilly, she spoke up.

"My father was a sportsman and quite successful. I grew up amongst people who did not believe that women belonged in certain places, knowing certain things, so, I have always sought to educate those people. I went into business and would listen to people who had had bad experiences with certain companies and I would set up a business either to compete directly or I'd target that business and set up a company to work with them and in working with them I would try to promote a more diverse way of thinking. My friends here have helped me throughout.'

Perry-Lloyd spoke again, he was clearly enjoying himself, "That is so honourable, congratulations, I can assure you there are many, many businesses who need minds like yours. So, Adam, tell me about you."

Everyone seemed to sit up a little more, Tilly had learnt a little bit about him over the days but really didn't know much and the others knew almost nothing. Adam looked around the room before speaking quietly.

"I guess I don't really have much to say, I have tried a few different jobs but haven't really got the drive to make things happen so I just kind of carried on. Well, I gave that up six days ago today and went looking for an adventure. I guess I went on the equivalent of those mythical 'gap year' trips to 'find myself'. Well, I met Tilly on the plane and the rest has led me to here."

Adam looked around the room, he realised that he hadn't achieved anything like the others around the room, but they were all just looking at him with an intensity he hadn't expected. Perry-Lloyd applauded but this time the others joined in too. Perry-Lloyd spoke before the applause died down,

"Adam, that is a very honourable tale, we don't all have the same privileges or opportunities or even just luck but, we can all try to be good and honest. I am thankful to you for being that and I hope that you see the reward enough in being a good person. I know that far too often in this world there is too little reward and sadly all too often there is the exact opposite given to those who deserve our thanks. Please forever hold your head high and recognise your worth and honour. I can assure you that there are very few who would have made the decisions you have made this week for the good of someone you didn't know." He been looking at Jada as he spoke, and she then looked directly at Adam as she spoke with a strength Adam hadn't yet heard,

"Adam, I am still coming to terms with what has happened over the last few days. I am sure that we will never know everything that has happened to each other, but I am so thankful to have the friends I have and Adam, you truly are forever my friend." The way that she looked at him made him feel strange already and within a few seconds he knew that he would be crying soon. He tried swallowing, tried shifting in his seat but as she reached those last words, he just let the tears come.

Tilly immediately put her arm around him, but he already had his hands to his face. He had wrapped himself up to isolate himself. He sensed Jada walk across the room and kneel in front of him, but he couldn't open his eyes or look up yet, the pain of his whole life seemed to be coming out. Adam had no idea how long he stayed like that for but as he felt himself coming back under control he heard Perry-Lloyd's authoritative voice break the awkwardness.

"I haven't yet told you all about my story, would you like to know?"

Adam felt the room's attention lift from him, Tilly's arm was still around his shoulder and Jada still had a hand on his knee but, he sensed that Perry-Lloyd was rescuing him, he wiped his eyes and tried to look up at Perry-Lloyd.

"I was born in Hong Kong, but we had moved four times before I first went to school and we continued to move after I started so, I completely understand your need for good friends at a new school Sam. My father worked for the government and although he never told me anything about any of the projects he worked on, I have since found out which department it was, and things now make more sense. As a child I could never understand why we had to keep moving and neither could the few friends I was able to make.

"Obviously I was regularly bullied at school, and, we didn't have the same approach to bullying in those days as we do now. For whatever reason, my father chose not to teach me how to deal with those situations but left it to me to learn alone. I think it took me too long but, I learnt.

"When I finished school, I expected to be sent to university because that was what my family had always done," He had looked straight at Adam as he was speaking before carrying on. "But I was taken to dinner with my father and another man who I had never seen before and have never seen since.

"I was asked if I wanted to travel and see the world from a different viewpoint or if I wanted to live a normal life." He paused to take a drink. "I chose to travel, at which point I was introduced more formally to the other man who had been introduced as a simple Mr Smith. He went on to take me into his department and I have worked with them ever since.

"If I'm honest, most of my job is spent being nice to people and attending parties and events. Telling people how nice Britain is and how nice we British people are but, every now and again, I am allowed to get involved in some really unpleasant businesses.

"I have a few things that I'd like to stop. Alas it is not entirely in my gift to be able to do that but, I make it my place to certainly do what I can. I have a few bandwagons that I jump on but more often I like to start my own. I came to Spain about six years ago now with a mission to cut down the amount of 'illicit products' that reach the UK. Originally that was merely the drug trade, but it has increasingly become weapons too. And more recently that has been the terrible trade in people. I'd like to think the lesser reliance on drugs is due to our success in taking out some very big players however, there will always be another who thinks that they can do better."

He had stood and was now parading around the room, obviously enjoying his subject and ensuring that he was getting eye contact from each of his audience.

"I am always looking for people on my side and, I like to think that you are all my friends in this mission. I really want to say thank you for all of your help, but, once I have Hafidi there are others on my list. As Adam is the only British National here, he is the only one to whom I am able to offer a formal offer to join our team however, as you may have learnt, I am a man who trusts my instincts and prefers to find a way to say "yes we can" than weasel a way to say no. I would be delighted if all of you would like to join me, of course I know that most of you already have very busy and very successful careers but, I can assure you that you can all be very useful."

Perry-Lloyd let his words hang for a minute before continuing.

"Obviously I cannot say too much about our work right now. And I wouldn't want you to make a judgement when you are all in the middle of a hugely emotional time but, I felt that this might be the only chance I got to speak to you all together. I wanted you all to know that the offer is there for all of you. I would of course be very happy for you all to speak openly and honestly together. I know that Becky here has a few questions for you, just things for our current mission. Please feel free to ask her any questions that you might have - absolutely anything. Becky will give you my contact details.

"That is what I really wanted to say, I mean it. Thank you so much for what you have done, and I hope that we can work together again. I know that Jada has already admitted that Adam will always be her friend. I would be honoured to be able to call you all my friends as well.

"Regardless of your decisions, I would really appreciate you all being my guest at an event in the not too distant future. I thank you all for being the people that you are, and I really mean that sincerely.

"I wish you all the greatest success and I shall wish you a goodnight." He stood immediately and paused whilst he looked around him to see where he had left his hat. Sam had risen first and actually gave him a hug, the others proceeded to do the same, a strong handshake for Adam and a respectful kiss on the cheek for Becky and he was gone. Before they all sat down again, Adam spoke,

"Would anyone mind if I had a beer?"

Chapter 35

A Shindig Somewhere

In Barcelona, Jury Service were in the middle of the soundcheck for their final night of the tour, with Jo and Shy watching from the balcony. Jo had never seen the band from this height before and she was much more aware of the amount the band moved onstage. She had her trusty notebook on her lap and Shy was casting his eye over the shortlist of logos that the band's preferred designer had just sent through. The piano riff blared from her phone informing her of an incoming call. The number was not one she recognised so she simply refused the call. It rang again and she shut it down once more. On the third call, Shy encouraged her to answer.

"Hello, I'm so sorry to disturb you, I know that you have a concert tonight and you must be terribly busy but, my name is Julian Perry-Lloyd and I have an offer and an opportunity for you. I wonder if you could spare a few minutes for me to explain." Something about the tone of his voice had captured Jo's attention. She looked at Shy, shrugged her shoulders and stood heading for the exit at the back of the balcony. When she reached the relative quiet of the staircase, she asked him to speak again, apologising for not hearing him clearly.

"Yes, of course, I am Julian Perry-Lloyd I represent His Majesty's Government of the United Kingdom in Spain and we have heard exceptionally good things about your band 'Jury Service'. Seeing as you are in the country at the present moment, we would really appreciate it if you would do us the honour of playing a short set at a very special event.

"In return we shall offer, not only a very handsome fee, but also all of the rights regarding any recording you wish to carry out at our location. In addition to that there will be further exciting opportunities upon your return to London." The nature of the voice intrigued her as much as the words. He sounded like a friendly uncle, but one who knew that you wouldn't refuse him because he also had those sweets in his pocket and making him happy brought everyone joy. He'd be the one that got people dancing at a birthday party or telling stories at a wake.

Jo had dealt with a huge variety of people who wanted various things from her and who had used a number of different techniques, but this approach was new. "I'm sorry but, what?" Was all she could manage. She immediately regretted her unprofessional response, but it was too late.

"Oh, I'm sorry dear, it is just that, well, I know it is short notice and everything but, we are arranging a superb party. There will be lots of wonderful people there. It isn't far from where you are now and, of course, we will arrange everything for you. I know that you are meant to be flying back to London on Thursday but, if you would only need to be so kind as to come and play a few tunes for us just down the coast. I will personally arrange the RAF's finest to get you all back home as soon as we can and well, in addition to that, you'd have a great story! There'll be some great footage for all of your socials and not only that, but I also know that we have a few rather high-profile events in London that could raise the awareness of a band worldwide."

Jo had a chance to regain her commercial persona, "I'm sorry but Jury Service really aren't a 'government party' kind of band." Perry-Lloyd laughed,

"No, no, of course, I'm sorry I tend to see almost everything as a party, party is perhaps the wrong word. We have these 'events' every now and again just really to remind people how great Britain is, and presenting bands like yours is part of our way of showing people the quality we have on our shores. The gathering will include a number of sports people, actors, and business people from the United Kingdom and across Europe.

"I know that you have a few guests at your concert tonight. I know many people from the music business will be coming to our party too. Some of whom those you have in Barcelona tonight, Steve and Eugene for example, and a few that I notice that you haven't people like Robert Cray and Janice Topley. Of course, I would be delighted to introduce you to all of my contacts. It really is meant to be a mutually beneficial event for everyone." Now he was even more like that uncle because now he knew exactly what buttons to press.

"Look, this all sounds amazing but," Jo was desperately trying to wrestle the reality of the situation and the plans that they had made with this now completely random but seemingly irresistible offer. She was desperately trying to think as she spoke.

"You know that we are meant to be flying in just 48 hours. I will have to speak to everyone, I can't just make the decision myself." Jo could feel her heart racing, the two names he had mentioned were exactly the kind of people she would want to get behind the band, but she would have to do loads of work to even get close to them. This seemed to be too good an opportunity. She was desperate to say yes but she knew that right now, the band trusted her, and they had accepted each of her suggestions, but they had all been involved in all of the decisions. She knew that that wouldn't last but she also knew that today wasn't the day to risk upsetting them. They could still easily decide to walk away, and she could not let that happen. She had no doubt that the band would agree but they had to be asked.

Perry-Lloyd's response was as polite as she expected it to be. "Of course, my dear, as soon as I put the phone down, I will send you a mobile number. If you have any further questions, please call and my assistant will gladly help you or I shall call you back to make the necessary arrangements. I very sincerely look forward to meeting you on Thursday. I apologise again for taking you away from your busy day and indeed for adding just a small, but I am certain a rewarding piece of work to your canon."

Jo knew she would say yes but she agreed to let him know once she had spoken to the band. After hanging up she stood for a few minutes to replay the conversation in her head. How would she explain this to Shy? How had he got her number? How had he known the band name? Had Shy been behind this? Was it his test? She had so many thoughts, she was sure that it couldn't be a test, the man played his part too perfectly it must be real, mustn't it? Her phone beeped and the text message came through, "Please contact Melissa on this number with any further questions or to find out just how magic this event will be with your involvement."

Jo walked back into the arena. Hearing the power from the stage she couldn't help but just watch for a minute before heading back to sit alongside Shy who looked at her expectantly.

"Have you ever heard of a Julian Perry-Loyd?" she asked him, looking at her notepad to confirm the name she had recorded. He looked blankly.

"He says he is from the British Government. He wants Jury Service to play at a shindig somewhere down the coast on Thursday."

"A shindig?" Was Shy's first question,

"Well, that's not exactly as he described it, but he's got something going on and the guest list is stellar, it includes, Robert Cray and Janice Topley! He knows their name. How could he know their name already?" Jo was struggling with all of her questions, Shy added,

"That's quite a shindig, how do I get an invite?" Jo didn't answer him but instead went on, "He says he will get the RAF to fly everyone back afterwards but, well, it doesn't sound real." She was looking at Shy as the band reached the end of their song. They heard Jack call through,

"It all sounds great from here. How does it sound up at the back?" Shy stood and clapped as he responded,

"You guys sound great, the acoustics in this room are so great, I love it." Jo stood too and they headed back towards the stairs, Shy spoke as they walked,

"Look I don't know where he found your number let alone found the name of the band but, I don't think you can refuse particularly the chance to play in front of those names. I know that the government sometimes does things with bands but, we have never found the 'in' before, this could be huge in so many ways, the guys have to say yes."

Leonard was talking to Nic confirming tonight's timings as Jo and Shy approached the stage, "Jo" he called, "Nic says we are on at nine tonight, is that right?"

"Yes" she replied, "Remember we have a later curfew tonight. You guys have 9.00 to 10:15 then Convoke are on at 10:40." Leonard nodded,

"Yeah OK, sorry I'd forgotten, it's been a heck of a week!" This sounded like the first time any of the band had sounded tired.

"Look, before you get back on the bus, can I just get the guys together for a quick word?" Jo knew that she sounded a little nervous.

"Yeah, of course. Guys…" He called out to the band. Jo had long ago learnt that if she was shouting it sounded bad and needy and would immediately annoy people. Having one of the band gathering people together made it feel like it was their meeting rather than hers. They had to wait a while for Jim who had wanted to fix a part of his drum-stool. Once they were all gathered Jo spoke up,

"OK Guys, I know that you don't like surprises but, I've got an option for you," She always had their attention, but she noticed that all seemed to be fully alert, almost nervous looking. Should she start with the gig, the RAF flight, the guest list? She discounted the guest list, the names wouldn't be important to them. She wasn't even sure whether to mention the government, they hadn't discussed politics yet, it was one of the things that she had on her list of subjects to discuss but, that needed the right time. "We might have a little change to our flights home on Thursday." She saw a look of disappointment from Leonard and Paul.

"How do you fancy being flown home by the RAF?" They all looked at her in shock, Jack interrupted,

"I'm not flying via Afghanistan" which caused laughter amongst the group,

"No, nothing like that" she quickly reassured, "A flight from somewhere, not that far away but a military base back to Northolt or somewhere and cars from there back home." Paul was the first to respond,

"What the hell are you talking about?" Which again caused a round of laughter,

"OK, there's a gathering on Thursday" Jo wanted them to know how big the opportunity could be, "Lots of VIP's, but fun VIP's, actors, footballers and the like and they want you to play a few tunes, it seems your reputation is growing faster than even I had expected. You'll only have to play for 45 minutes or so and we get the private plane back with all the kit and caboodle."

She paused to watch the group's reactions, Paul looked to Jack who nodded, Jo was looking at Jim and Leonard. Leonard didn't look too impressed, but Jim was smiling. She waited for a collective response, Paul spoke up,

"We can manage a few more songs, can't we?"

All nodded. Jo noticed that Leonard was the least enthusiastic but she would make sure she spoke to him later.

"That's great, look we have a couple of hours now before the gig, we have a few options, One. I can get you a guide to take you around the sights of Barcelona, La Sagrada Familia, the magic fountain and stuff, Two. You could visit Camp Nou, Three. You could get lost in La Rambla, we could just go and get some food, or we could head back to the hotel for a couple of hours, what do you fancy?"

They then had a discussion about the need for both culture and sleep. Jack and Paul chose the Sagrada Familia and Leonard and Jim headed for the hotel. Jo arranged both before dialling the number Perry-Lloyd had given her. A beautiful Spanish voice answered which surprised her, but, after a brief sentence in Spanish, the voice changed. The same person but now speaking with a very well-educated British accent.

"You are through to Scenic Solutions, Catherine speaking. How may I help you?"

"Oh, I'm sorry, I was given this number..." Jo had barely paused before the voice spoke,

"Is that Jo?" Jo was rather taken aback, whatever Perry-Jones did, it was clear to her that he was very quick. She confirmed and, within a few of what seemed to Jo to be the most politely put questions she had ever heard, she was being told the full itinerary. They were to be picked up at their hotel at 14:00 hours (The voice used the 24-hour clock which Jo felt odd, but she guessed that picking up a band at 2am is not an unusual thing so the clarity helped). There would be refreshments both on board the transport and at the venue on arrival. If there were any special requests or dietary requirements, they could let the staff know at any time. Once at the venue they would be given time to prepare and then they were free to relax in their own private area or they could circulate and enjoy the rest of the entertainment as they wished. At 17:45 they would be asked to perform. After their set, they were once again free to either relax, circulate or if they should so wish, they could be transported to their hotel from where they would be collected at 7am (with apologies given for the early start) before being transported to their plane back to London. The voice also asked for an email address so that they could send through the details of the stage set up so that if there was anything else that was needed, Jo could let them know. This was going to be the easiest gig Jo had ever organised.

Chapter 36

Too Early For Champagne?

Adam woke to find the sun shining around the edges of the blinds in his room. His first sense was the smell of the linen, then the heat, then the comfort of where he was. He half rolled over, picking up his phone to see what time it was then laid back into the safety of his pillow and tried to hold the phone in a way that allowed it to recognise his face. He opened the news app first, just to see if there was anything he should know, then his emails, the usual shops advertising their sales, a hotel company he had once stayed at and a ticket agency informing him of a host of concerts he would never go to. A game of cards against a cartoon character and then he chose a podcast, laid back and laughed at the news of the day discussed by two people who knew so little. He lay there for almost thirty minutes before getting up. When he appeared downstairs, he was welcomed by everyone accusing him of being a sleepyhead, for once he was happy to accept the accusations.

Sam appeared with an orange juice and Adam joined the group at the table on the terrace. He had missed Perry-Lloyd who had already been in to say hello and to ask them all to stay in the house for the day. Perry-Lloyd had promised that he would come and give them all a briefing at the end of the day. It was Jada who first brought up the offer of 'work' that Perry-Lloyd had offered during his last discussion, "I like him, he gets things done." She said, "I think he is the kind of man that I would be very happy to do business with. I just really wish I knew exactly what he had in mind."

"I can't help thinking of his reference to Scooby Doo" Sam added, "Do you think we could become an investigative gang like that? I'll be Daphne of we do" that drew laughs amongst all of them.

"I really don't know if I can take on any more work right now." Tilly spoke earnestly "Whenever I've opened my phone, I've got another 50 emails, and I can only put off things for a couple more days. But at the same time, I have really enjoyed being back with you guys and anything that brings us together…" she wistfully let the sentence fade before startling them all as she spoke again,

"But what do you think it is? Perhaps it's more Charlie's Angels." She held her fingers up like a gun and held her pose. 'I've always quite liked that idea, travelling the world rescuing good people, punishing the bad people." Again, there was more laughter around the table as the three girls started making poses around Adam who was told to stay still and be 'Charlie'.

"What about you Adam? You are the only one who doesn't have a pre-loaded excuse. Perry-Lloyd obviously has loads of connections, he could be your ticket anywhere. Where would you like to go?" The question had been asked amongst the laughter, but the seriousness of the content and the possibilities really hit Adam. The group continued chatting for some time. Adam still had so many questions for each of them that he was either too shy or too polite to ask. His brain kept inventing new ways to explain what had happened to this group of friends, how they had become friends, what they really did for work, of course they had all shared a certain amount of information but it hadn't really given him much of a clue and when they had been answering his questions they had each been a little coy.

The old friends all knew each other's stories and obviously didn't feel the need to brag in front of each other. He had heard more in little snippets of conversation and was trying to piece together the bigger picture. Adam looked around him, knowing how little he knew about each of his three new friends he had found around this table but also wondering how much more he had to learn.

Adam had sat there for some time before he finally found a chance to excuse himself from the group. He had asked if he could leave to have a shower and to get dressed properly. He had increasingly been feeling like an outsider, not getting the in jokes or lacking the knowledge of the people mentioned in the stories. Stepping into the full rainforest downpour setting of the shower, it took him a while to balance the temperature away from the scalding heat he first encountered before he finished with a refreshing cold blast. He dried himself and pulled on his T-shirt and shorts before laying back on his bed. Once he had settled, he found himself staring at the blank TV screen as if he was just a hardwired layabout who, seeing a screen, would simply stare at it regardless of the content. But he was seeing things on the screen. He was seeing himself and his life, the one he had lived up until last Saturday and the one that he might have in the future.

He realised that he probably would never be quite as strong, fast or clever enough to be a film star kind of secret agent but what about an international problem solver? He was convincing himself that he had always been on the side of righteousness and that he always wanted justice to be done. He had spent a few years as a child telling people that he wanted to be a soldier when he grew up, but that was before he thought about having to deal with death, and before the more common morbidity of 'normal life' had overtaken and all those career ideas that you have as a child, Sportsman, Rockstar, Doctor, Nurse, Teacher, Policeman or Firefighter were overtaken by the reality of administration, accountancy, distribution or estate agency. The jobs that he and his friends had fallen into. Only one of his friends had ended up doing the job that they had always wanted to do but that was because it was Leo, and his father had a business selling fish, and Leo had never had any ambition to do anything else.

Now though, now a new Adam had arrived, this Adam was capable of independent international travel, no more package holidays for him. He could identify which of the doors in a strange foreign restaurant was the Gents and he knew that it was perfectly acceptable to have a beer at lunchtime - as long as you were having it with a meal. He had started his working life when whole departments would disappear to the pub at lunchtime and sometimes never come back. That had not been acceptable for a long time at his workplace and, even on the odd occasion that he could convince a colleague or two to sneak over to the Lady Grey for a pint of craft ale, it usually was just a pint. A wild second if there was a very special occasion; an ashes test match being on the screen or after a very difficult morning briefing but, never a third.

Adam felt sure that Perry-Lloyd would join him for a pint. They would probably always find the best table was free waiting for them. He would have delightful stories to tell about bumping into 'Blowers after day three of the test in Nagpur or having dinner with Simon Callow after a show in the West End. He allowed his thoughts to move to the job that Perry-Lloyd did, he had said he started bandwagons and Adam wondered what they could be. He had images of a gallant knight riding on a stallion to rescue a damsel in distress, but he transposed that into the modern world by aiding an independent person to find their own solace whilst driving a white electric sports car.

Adam knew he was dreaming of an idealised world that was too much to be true so he looked towards the darker stories that Perry-Lloyd might tell. He was sure that there must be some truly horrible stuff that goes on. Adam wondered if he could cope with the less glamorous side of the job before quickly twisting the argument to convince himself that he could. He told himself how he had been close to Hafidi and although he was certain that somewhere down the line Hafidi was involved in some dark business, Hafidi didn't look strong or mean enough to do any of it himself. He had others to do that for him. If Perry-Lloyd only ever went for the heads of organisations, then surely it couldn't get too unpleasant.

Eating in restaurants or visiting clubs and casinos, Adam could see himself doing that. Someone else would deal with the basements and the warehouses and the genuinely horrible bits. He looked at his phone, it was still only 11am. It was going to be a long wait for showtime. They had collectively decided that they would sit out on the cliff edge at the mission time and see if there was anything that they could see. They had no idea what to expect but they thought they'd see something. He checked his emails one last time, noted that the shop he had bought his last coat from was having a sale but, he thought, he wouldn't need another coat if he was going to live in Spain. That was enough thinking, he rolled onto his side and decided to try to have a nap.

A clatter at the door and a large amount of giggling woke Adam up. Tilly had burst in followed by Jada and Sam who both stopped at the door,

"They thought that I should check that you were ok." Tilly laughed, "And we were all wondering if you'd got dressed yet." They all cackled at this and Adam, embarrassed, pulled the duvet around himself.

"Oh poor boy," it was Sam he could now hear, "he's wearing a shirt you have at least half your answer, come on, let him sleep." She grabbed Jada's hand and pulled her further down the corridor.

Tilly was then left, halfway between the door and his bed, she paused, threw her hand to her mouth and blurted out an apology.

"I'm sorry, oh I'm so sorry, sorry" as she rushed out of the door, almost slamming it shut behind her and Adam was left in darkness again. He rolled back and stared at the ceiling, with a whole host of new questions and of course a whole load of things that he should have said and done rather than reacting like the rabbit in the headlights that he probably had looked like.

He spent another forty-five minutes contemplating his life before he finally rolled onto his side again and closed his eyes. It was only an hour later when he was woken by a knock at the door. He groggily offered a

"Hello" before the door cracked open an inch and he heard Sam's voice,

"Would you like a little lunch before the show?" He mumbled his thanks and assured her that he'd be down in a minute. He stumbled to his feet and found the trousers he had intended to put on a couple of hours ago before realising that he probably didn't need to dress smartly, he grabbed his shorts from his bag and pulled them on before heading downstairs barefoot.

By the time Adam walked out onto the terrace the others were sat with a whole table full of bowls filled with salad, breads and a variety of snacks, they had obviously been busy whilst he was sleeping and had prepared a feast as if they were at a picnic concert. Adam checked his watch and asked if they had seen anything so far.

"A boat flew past about an hour ago at high speed, but there was no way to know if it was a goodie, a baddy or someone just wanting to fly, other than that nothing unusual." He looked across the water, there was a fishing boat about midpoint on route to the horizon and a giant tanker a good distance further out but other than that, the sky was blue, the sea blue too and everything looked normal but, as he sat down, the atmosphere was far from it. He took an apple from the table and bit into it, before instantly remembering that the apples weren't as soft as he was used to and rather than taking a nice big mouthful of juicy fruit, he instead rather grazed a scrape off the top.

Sam had asked Tilly about whether she was planning any trips in the near future which sounded like the sort of question that a hairdresser asks when they really aren't interested in an answer. It was exactly the same situation that they were in now. They were all stuck in these chairs whilst someone was carrying out a complex operation with potentially lethal weapons very close by. None of them really wanted to talk and it wasn't long until they all accepted the silence, broken only by the occasional look at a watch and someone asking what the time was. They were each scanning the horizon looking for any signs of movement and looking across the bay towards Matt's house. They couldn't actually see the house, but they studied the sky above looking for signs and hoping that something would show them that everything was going be ok. Although none of them knew what they were looking for.

Perry-Lloyd had informed them that there was no way to avoid Matt receiving a message to tell him that his alarm system had gone down for a short while but, when he called to ask, it would be one of Perry-Lloyd's people who took the call. Just as it would when Hafidi called to ensure that the system was deactivated. Perry-Lloyd had been delighted to know that Hafidi's people would indeed telephone him to let him know they were coming. He had taken care of all of the negotiations with Hafidi since he had taken over Tilly's phone number. "There are very few criminals that like telephone conversations these days, if it isn't face to face its via one of the messaging applications, they are easier to control and bizarrely enough, usually have better security regardless of what you read" Perry-Lloyd had informed them.

Jada had just got back from another visit to the bathroom, Adam wasn't sure if it was just nerves or if it were something medical. He didn't think he knew her well enough to ask but he worried that perhaps he should, maybe later, she was rather thin…. The shrill ring of Jada's phone shocked them all, she answered immediately.

"Hello Jada, Perry-Jones here, I just thought you'd like to know, I've just had the phone call, the alarm system is going off in ten minutes. Hafidi has assured the security team that it will only need to be off for thirty minutes or so. We have the boat in our sights and our teams are all in position. I'm sure that you are looking out for the show, but I hope you don't mind that we want to keep it as low-key as possible. I hope that you won't hear any sounds, but you will see his boat arrive. Once it's unloaded, I guess you might see it leave and depending on how quickly we are able to ensure that everything is 'tidy' onshore, you might see the boat's interception. We might even bring the helicopters in for the show if needed! Anyhow, I just thought you might want to know the operation will be starting soon."

The news brought even more suspense and a flurry of activity to the table. Sam offered to refill everyone's drink. Jada wondered if they would be better off sitting right at the cliff edge. Adam just started to feel rather numb. He desperately wanted justice to be done but Jada was free and that was all he'd signed up for. He was simply helping Tilly to start with, he didn't know what he was going to do tomorrow or the day after. He didn't know what else Hafidi was up to but also, that felt rather out of his business.

He wondered if that would be an advantage if he worked with Perry-Lloyd, could it be a good thing that right now he really wasn't sure if he cared what happened next? He liked Perry-Lloyd and he felt that he trusted that he was on the right side of things.

Adam sat back, contemplating his future and felt like he had been in exactly this situation before, sitting somewhere remote thinking about how different things could have been. Each time he had sat like that before though, something had taken him back to his dull old life. Now he was decided. Tilly had helped him, and he had helped Tilly, now Perry-Lloyd had helped him and he felt that he had to repay the favour. He was going to work with Perry-Lloyd. He hoped that the rest of them would too. He felt a kinship with these three girls, he knew he wasn't part of their 'gang', but he had fitted in, they had accepted him and now they did have this shared history.

He would accept Perry-Lloyd's offer, he had decided that he had been in Spain for some time so he might as well stay there for a bit longer. He hadn't thought too much about the rules about visas or anything technical, but he was pretty sure that Perry-Lloyd could fix that. He'd need to learn the language but, if Tilly, Jada and Sam were around, he was sure that they would help him. He would surely learn pretty quickly if he was using it every day. Yes, he was staying, he was about to announce that to the group when Tilly pointed out to sea.

"Look" she squealed. A boat was coming in at a fair pace, it was bigger than Adam had expected, it had obviously been hugging the coast far closer to the cliffs than looked safe. It was only in their view for about a minute. There was a man at the bow, looking like the antithesis of the figureheads that used to adorn the ships of the past. The bright white bow was crashing through the low waves, another two men stood in the cockpit, and a further three men were standing on the deck at the stern. There was no sign on the deck of their cargo and, if it wasn't for the posture of the men or the fact that it was only men, it could have been any rich boys toy just whizzing from beach to beach as they often did along this stretch of coast, searching for a peaceful bay in which to swim or drink or play.

None of the group knew how much could be stored in a boat like that, or indeed just what it was they were carrying but the men looked serious. As the boat disappeared around the headland towards Matt's house, they were all caught up in the silence. Jada got up, walked across the lawn kicking at an errant stone that had somehow found its way there on route. Reaching the edge of the garden, she stood looking as far around the corner as she could. The sounds of the waves rolling against the cliffs below them echoing faintly upwards and the birds singing in the bushes or squawking high above them in the crowns of the palm trees were all they could hear.

One by one they each stood, Sam first, walking a little quicker to stand by Jada. Tilly and Adam, both looked at each other before slowly heading towards the cliff edge As they neared, they could see that Jada was crying, Sam was trying to comfort her so they gave her a little more space and headed a little further along the garden, leaning onto the glass balustrade, Tilly turned to Adam,

"Are you going to work with Perry-Lloyd?" Adam wasn't really prepared for the direct question. He took a deep breath knowing that he had made his mind up, but he was now wary of telling her. He didn't know if she would encourage him or the opposite.

"I reckon so, I mean, I came on this trip to find something to do. Things seem to have found me." He looked at Tilly and saw the way she was looking at him which made him feel a little weird, he really wasn't used to being studied.

"You're a good man Adam" she said in possibly the softest voice he had ever heard. She was still looking at him when they heard a cry from Jada,

"Come look!"

The boat was flying at high speed straight away from the coast, there were four men all now clearly heavily armed stationed at each corner, they must have seen something. Adam felt his heartbeat rise. Now he really did care. He hoped that the cargo was all now in Perry-Lloyd's hands, and it was an empty boat racing away, but none of them were happy that it did indeed seem to be getting away. Four smaller speedboats then flew around the corner, each looking more like a dart, slicing through the waves.

The machine guns fitted on the bows sent a very clear message. Two helicopters appeared from the opposite direction. Perry-Lloyd was putting on quite the show. The chase was over in seconds. The first boat reached level with Hafidi's boat and the pilot instantly cut the engines. It was clear that the larger boat would not have a chance of outrunning these bolts of lightning buzzing around the scene and it appeared that none of Hafidi's men were prepared to die today. The group of spectators cheered when they saw the darts encircle their prey. Slowly one of the boats approached and tied up alongside what now looked like an oversized tub of a boat floundering amongst the more attractive, faster and, perhaps more pertinently, heavier armed craft.

The boarding party acted swiftly, presumably handcuffing each of Hafidi's men before taking them down into the craft. And then, within minutes, the procession set off, the white boat at the front leading the formation behind. The team of spectators all looked at each other before Sam initiated a group hug which lasted long enough for Adam to start to feel a little awkward, wondering how he would be able to get away. He had had to crouch a little to join the hug and his back was now hurting.

It was Tilly who eventually broke the group,

"Come on, we should have a drink to celebrate, is it too early for Champagne?" Sam had the initial response that Adam himself had also been thinking,

"We don't yet know what has happened at the house, shouldn't we wait to find out first?" The others nodded and they all headed sombrely back to the table and sat rather awkwardly in almost silence, waiting for the news.

Chapter 37

A Brightness Of Mind

To be fair to Perry-Lloyd it was probably only 15 or 20 minutes, but it had felt like a lifetime, the doorbell shocked them all. Sam ran to the screens and Tilly had run to the front door. When Sam remotely opened the gates, Tilly was already there to meet him, the others close behind. Perry-Lloyd looked serious but couldn't hide his smile as the group appeared in front of him. He ushered them to sit but they were too full of suspense so instead he just manoeuvred the group until he was in a position to rest himself on the arm of a sofa.

"Well," he began, "I usually find myself briefing Westminster before talking to anyone else, but I have someone else dealing with them right now, it is also unusual for me to be able to report a mission has gone quite so perfectly to plan."

He really should be on the stage Adam thought, all of his stories had perfect timing. The group had cheered with the news, he continued to report that they now had ten men in custody here and two of his men were with Lieutenant Bally and a detachment of the Guardia-civil. The Guardia-Civil had just taken Hafidi and a number of henchmen into custody. Another cheer erupted,

"Yes, all good news" he continued, "And we were also able to ensure that his 'cargo' were all safely recovered." His tone had changed and there was a gravity to his voice. "Yes, we had a few bags of drugs. Enough for him to spend a long time thinking about his profits, but, more importantly to me, we now have 12 women or girls, I only spoke to them briefly and I am afraid that not all of them were able to understand me. I am sure that it will be some time before we find out exactly what horrors they have seen. I am not the best judge but I suspect the youngest cannot be older than eight, I'm afraid it was not a pleasant experience to find them but I can assure you, we will work with the very best healthcare teams to ensure that they are given all the support that we can to help them. I won't say recover because you don't recover from their trauma but, we will do all we can to help them live." At the end of that sentence, his whole body slumped, the silence held them all. Sam fetched him a drink from the bar, and they all stood together in silence for a few minutes.

"Still, we have a party to arrange." Perry-Lloyd shocked them as he swapped characters. He burst into life almost leaping to his feet, "Jury Service are booked, Matt's House is the venue. He is bringing some guests. I'm afraid that I have a few people who will have to attend but I would like your assistance to ensure that the event is a complete success. And I hope that you shall do me the honour of being the guests of honour." He looked at each of them, seeming to enjoy the smiles facing him. As he studied each of them, they had all looked to each other for affirmation, he went on,

"I hope you don't mind that I have continued my research on each of you, I know that ladies, you all have built very successful careers and a network of friends and colleagues, please, if you would like to invite any of your contacts, let me know. I also understand if you would like to keep this as a more private event for yourselves. I will give you some time to consider if you want anyone to come, but I really should ask each of you if you have considered my earlier proposal to work together in the future.

"I accept that this might all appear rather bizarre but, honestly, as I guess you have worked out by now, I have the fortune to work with some of the very best. When I am planning events or working on a project there is often a need for those plans to be put into place very rapidly. The simplest plans can be communicated quickly and, looking at the quality of the team around this table, I am in awe. Sam, you have a brightness of mind. You are fluent in three languages. I hope that you don't mind me saying that I know that you had a difficult childhood but, seeing your demeanour in everything you do, no one would be surprised if you told them that you had been educated, from birth, at the finest of schools. You have only yourself to credit for that and your hard work and commitment in each of the business endeavours has been clear to everyone.

"Jada, I heard you claim that your successes have come simply from the advantages that your education gave you but, look around at your empire. There are plenty of people in this world who have failed and yet, you have not only achieved a great business success but you have chosen to do it ethically and, with a care, that the businesses you operate but also each of those that you invest in take positive approaches to the causes that you hold dear.

"Tilly, again your fluency and abilities show your skills in negotiation and rapidity of thought, your plans in this project have all worked fantastically and then we have Adam. Adam, you are rather a mystery, of course I have spoken with your old employers and others that know you. They have all admitted that you are hardworking and dedicated. Your modesty is perhaps your downfall. Your dedication has been evident in all of your endeavours, and, I don't know if your friends have told you this, I have had separate conversations with each of the people around this table. I hope that they won't mind me saying that they have each praised your attitude and the brightness that you bring to each of them. I am genuinely pleased that you have all helped me so much over the last couple of days.

"Individually and collectively, you are all capable of doing so much. You know that I would like you all on my side, but I completely understand if you choose that you have enough commitments of your own or, if you simply do not wish to get involved." Perry-Lloyd paused and allowed his comments to sink in before it became clear that he was waiting for a response from someone. He looked around the table to find that everyone else was either doing the same and looking to others to speak first or were simply avoiding his gaze.

Adam chose to break with his tradition and spoke first.

"I think, firstly, we all would like to thank you sir. Yes we started our part of this, but I am sure that the conclusion wouldn't have been quite this tidy without your involvement. Secondly, as you know I have nowhere near the same level of intellect, ability or business awareness as my friends around this table but, I also don't have anything else to occupy my time now so it really would seem, that, well, I guess, if you have something for me to do, I think I'm available."

Perry-Lloyd stood and reached across to shake Adam's hand,

"Thank you dear boy, but, just one word, please don't ever underestimate your achievements or your abilities. Success in this world should never be measured in commercial gain although sadly it all too often is, if we had more people like you the world would be a much better place." Adam stood back, relieved as much as anything else, he instantly felt taller and let out a huge sigh.

It was Tilly's turn to speak,

"Mr Perry-Loyd, as you know, my business keeps me fully entertained and, bar a few days here and there, I have been at work every day for the past I don't know how many years. These last seven days have taught me that my business can survive without my constant supervision. I cannot offer all of my time but, I would be delighted if you would consider my involvement in any projects for which I could be of assistance, whether that be short term projects or maybe just fitting things in alongside the work that I am not yet able to fully release myself from."

Jada looked at Sam who spoke up on behalf of both of them. "That goes for us too, we are both deeply honoured that you have offered us the opportunity and we both know that we would thoroughly enjoy working with you. Like Tilly though, we are already fully committed to a number of projects which we personally care about deeply, but we acknowledge the help that you have afforded us, and we would also like to work with you in the way that Tilly described. We all had a chat last night, after Adam had gone to bed, and obviously, we still don't know exactly what nature your projects take but, we would be delighted to be considered for temporary members of your Scooby-doo gang."

Perry-Lloyd sat back smiling.

"I know that people close to me generally find it annoying when I predict their answers in advance but, I don't think that it would surprise any of you if I were to say that your responses were exactly what I expected and to be honest, I hoped for. As much as I would have loved to have the gang all together full time, I am not sure that His Majesty's Government would afford me the resources to cope with all four of you wanting to fix the world!

"Adam, if you are ready for a new mission in life, I can give you that and, with the support of these others in the room, I am sure that the world will be a much better place. Are we all agreed?" He looked around the room, Adam hadn't noticed that Jada had already left the group and was now appearing with two bottles of Champagne,

"You know I love arranging parties don't you Mr Perry-Lloyd or, is there some other title that we should now call you?"

By the time Perry-Lloyd left for the night they each had a list of things to arrange for the party. Adam had also received a transfer into his account together with an emailed shopping list of things that he would need. Perry-Lloyd had been quite insistent that he took at least one of the others with him when he went shopping. Adam had found that a little insulting but, as Perry-Lloyd had explained, he thought that Adam was more likely to buy things that he was familiar and comfortable with rather that things that would suit the new persona that his friends had seen. Having someone with him "should at least make him consider alternatives." It made sense to Adam. He had never enjoyed shopping and, seeing as the shopping list wasn't just confined to clothes and shoes but included an allocated budget for a very nice car, to be bought with cash, he was glad that he would have someone to accompany him for that at least.

Adam laid on his bed looking at the ceiling and once again checked the balance of his account. Opening the app, he was still shocked by the figure looking back at him. His account had never had that many numbers in it before. He still wasn't certain that it was real. He had accepted a new job but all he knew about the role was that he would be working for Perry-Lloyd or James as he had asked them to call him. He had even said that they could call him Jimmy as his friends did, but that hadn't felt right and even after explaining that, and after he had left, they had all continued using his surname.

Adam still wasn't clear who exactly who he was working for.

Perry-Lloyd had said he would officially be working for the British people although he hadn't clearly described how that was. Was it a separate company, the government, the military, there were still a few points he had to clear up. He was sure that he would know more after he had spoken to Kelly who James had said would call him tomorrow to introduce herself. His head was still spinning, a thousand what-ifs whizzing through his brain but, the only thing that he was certain of was that he had made the right decision and for once, he was glad that it was his decision alone.

Chapter 38
Anything Else That We Need?

The next two days disappeared into a whirlwind of shopping, party organising, and journeys to and from Matt's house. They were all enjoying the distraction from the pressure that they had all been under. Matt was back from his trip to New York, and they were all maintaining the story that the gig was for the video. Adam couldn't believe quite how much was being laid on. He had been given the job of liaising with Matt and Sal and so he had been on site to deal with the deliveries and the building of the stage and various tents and awnings. By the time the day arrived, Adam was sure that he was on a film set, the only concerns he had were that this all looked to be far too high a budget for a small band but Perry-Lloyd had insisted that Matt wouldn't care for that. They would find a way to explain that if necessary. So far, Matt had just been impressed with the multitude of florists, artists and creative types who really had made his house look fantastic. He must have taken at least a thousand selfies. Adam kept thinking that he'd have to have a look online one day to see, although so far he had managed to avoid both Matt and Sal's requests to be in a picture. He was sure that some of his old schoolmates or work colleagues would surely see at least one of these pictures and wonder how on Earth Adam had got there - he must be so cool these days but, Adam felt that famous photo's might not be the best thing for his future career.

Tilly, Jada and Sam had decided that they should each buy an outfit for Adam, having found it hilarious that he didn't like shopping. They had then demanded a fashion show to vote for the outfit that he would wear to the party. Their choice seemed a success, he had received compliments from so many people about his outfit. That was something that had absolutely never ever happened before. Perry-Lloyd had asked them if they could get a cab rather than fill up the valet car parking that had been arranged. Most of the guests' cars were being moved to a warehouse just out of town by a team of drivers to keep the house clear. The group had decided to take the short walk down, they would get a cab back. When they arrived the team of serving staff were being briefed on the lawn, a crew of tech guys in multi-pocketed shorts were crouching in various corners of the stage, and more people in shorts with not quite as many pockets were setting up camera positions around the site. Perry-Lloyd had set up his 'office' at a small cast iron table and chair set in the far corner of the garden, he summoned them over with an elaborate flourish.

"Come, come, join the melee!" He cried. Perry-Lloyd was obviously in his element. He was reaching around and gesturing for more chairs which were brought rapidly by a flurry of attendants who appeared from almost nowhere,

"Do you like what we have done with the place?" He was just like a proud uncle at a birthday party for a much loved niece, "I have so much to thank you all for, I've got the itinerary here, everything is almost finished ready for our first guests to arrive at seventeen thirty and, don't worry, I have arranged that a good number will be here spot on time. Sam has arranged for a number of entertainers to be busily keeping the guests amused so there shouldn't be any awkward moments.

"Food and drinks will be being served by our waiting staff or, people can head directly to the bar if they would prefer. We have a couple of guests from His Majesty's Government who I'd like you to meet, and they do like to be made a bit of a fuss of. We will have a formal welcome at eighteen thirty. Don't worry, one of the bods from the embassy is in charge of that kind of thing, I prefer to keep out of the way of cameras as much as I can but some people like that kind of attention so, I'll let them have their thirty seconds. We then have a comedian guy onstage who I've been assured is very good and then we will be straight into the band, coming onstage at nineteen ten. They have ninety minutes and then we have our big fireworks finish that Jada has taken care of. Our circulating entertainers and food service will reappear, and Tilly's DJ will take over the stage until the local police tell us that we have exceeded the very proper terms of agreement that I have made with the local powers here. If any of you happen to be approached at that time, please direct them to me and I will buy us however much extra time it feels like we need.

"Are you all happy with that? Do you think there is anything else that we need?" Adam looked at his friends, they all were smiling, Jada and Sam in almost matching outfits with the sun glinting off of a ring that Adam had spotted for the first time on her ring finger. Tilly was looking even more stunning than usual in a trouser suit with her hair cut a little shorter than it had been previously and Adam, well, by the time the night was over, the morning mist was rising on the sea, the brightness of the day reclaiming the shadows. He kicked off his shoes and looked once again at his bright yellow socks. Adam smiled.

Postscript

Thank you for reaching this page,
please let me know what you thought of the book,
I hope that you found something in the story.

MS 2024

info@marksayersbooks.com
www.marksayersbooks.com

About the Author

Kayak Coach, Canoe Coach, Magazine Advertising, First Aid Trainer, Cricket Coach, Writer, Guide Dog Fosterer, just some of the full time or voluntary roles that have brought Mark Sayers to the start of this book.

Living just outside London, his travels through the UK, Europe, North America and Northern Africa have influenced his writing. Looking for Somewhere is his first novel.

For more information, please visit
www.marksayersbooks.com